The Woodland Tombs Of Eliantar

by

Gary Gaugler Jr

The Woodland Tombs of Eliantar

Copyright © 2015 by Gary Gaugler Jr.

Gaugler-Libby LLC

Allentown, PA

For sales, permissions, and all other inquiries, contact:

http://eliantarbooks.wix.com/eliantar

ISBN 978-0-9962820-0-0

Allentown, Pennsylvania

First Edition

Acknowledgments

Thank you to my wonderful family who has not only always been understanding, but also incredibly encouraging. I love you all. Thanks to Dan Mare for his amazing cover design that perfectly reflects my vision. Special thanks also to Scott Cormack for giving Dan a hand! Martene Fay Bruder for her ability to adapt her artistic abilities into cartography. Amber Moschini and Elizabeth K. Rosen for copy editing. Catherine M. Wilson for formatting. Liz Bradbury and Patricia Sullivan for being my first beta readers and a wealth of support during the creative process. A special thanks to all of my other beta readers: Kristen Cremeens, Casey Gaugler, Lenora Dannelke, Nancy Benner, William Benner, Aida Cruz, Pamela Gaugler, and Gary Gaugler Sr. You've helped both me and this story grow. None of this would have been possible without the love, support, and persistence of Stephen Libby. Thank you for pushing me to not leave this story sitting on a dusty shelf and thank you for giving my life so many smiles. I love you.

This book is dedicated to Stephen Libby. I've long dreamt of other worlds, filled with magic and fantasy. Our life together has served to inspire me even further. Thank you for adding some magic and fantasy to this world.

Mount Pyrall

Errandomn

Fornar

Ivory Towers

Woodland Tombs

Tacia

G

Eliantar

ALL

CHRONOMETER
CATHEDRAL

Steedo

Quale

WATER
CITADEL

KEY

🌲 = forest   ⋀⋀ = mountains
❋ = sand   ⌄ = sink holes

Prologue

Once Upon a Time there was no Happily Ever After. You see, not all stories from worlds other than ours are glowing tales of princes rescuing princesses from evil dragons and witches and living happily ever after. Not all worlds are beautiful sprawling domains with grassy hills, sparkling streams, and enchanted creatures. Many worlds are black voids where very little life can even exist, and the life that is there is as black and insidious as the realm itself. In worlds like that there can be no happy ending because there was never hope to be found in the beginning.

There are also worlds, however, that are beautiful fairy-tale worlds of splendor that become dark realms of evil over time. These worlds with tales of crumbling majesty are rarely spoken of in nursery rhymes or bed time stories.

Eliantar was one such world, although to have seen it in its glory, one would never suspect the imminent downfall that awaited the celebrated land. What proceeds is the story of Eliantar in its final years. The sad irony was that the waning years for Eliantar, the last decade before its demise, were the best years in the lands long history. However, it is terribly disheartening to begin a story at the end and although Eliantar did not have a Happily Ever After, it of course did have a Once Upon a Time that generations of the world's inhabitants told to their children.

Once upon a time in a universe far away from any known before, a group of elemental gods came together to create a new world. They all agreed that it should be a paradise, one that would outshine all the other worlds that they had created. And so, summoning all of their strength the group of gods created an enormous flat plain in the black void of space.

They realized at once they had made this planet far too large as their intention had been for a small paradise. It was their belief and their experience that when they tried to make a beautiful thing too large, it didn't stay beautiful but rather, ate itself from the inside out.

And so in a fluid movement, most of the planet was consumed with raging waters, leaving a still quite large island in the middle. The edges of the new world were ridged with mountains for containment.

Following this, they all agreed that they would each take a day for themselves to bring to this world what they envisioned as paradise.

Thus, the gods and goddesses had successfully created another beautiful world. Most of the gods had chosen a section of land along the perimeter of the world to represent the element they controlled, but there was still something missing. All throughout the middle of the land there was nothing but empty fields. The gods often found newly created worlds that didn't include humans, lacked a certain luster. And so, on that ninth day, humans were brought to rule over the land of Eliantar.

Galaxies away, a much older world was dying. The gods, in their graciousness, took the humans from that world that were good and just and sent them to Eliantar. The people called themselves Elites and brought all of the wonderful things to the world that humans do. Towns were built with libraries and schools, old laws were written again for the new world, and a monarchy was created to uphold the laws, oversee protection from possible threats, and keep the world unified. Arktur the Courageous became the first King of Eliantar and the people rallied behind him as he had bravely settled and established the new domain.

The gods also worked together to pack the lands with lesser creatures. They filled the forests, the lakes, and deserts. There were even rare species that were willing to live on the highest mountains or in the hottest environments. The world was almost finished and they could sense it. Eliantar was nearing the perfect harmony that they had envisioned days ago. The gods were very pleased with themselves until they noticed one small problem.

Eliantar was a very small world. But, then again this is what they had wanted. It seems that gods, especially these gods, were terribly indecisive. And why shouldn't they be? After all, humans were modeled after the gods and they were terribly indecisive creatures. In any case, no matter who was to blame, Eliantar (though a paradise) was far too small.

To add to that fact the realms that the gods had created were, for the most part uninhabitable for humans, which left them even less space. They knew they'd have to figure out a way to make this new planet exist without overpopulating it in a few decades. After hours of discussion they only had one clear alternative.

Homosexuality was a naturally occurring phenomenon in the human race. Even when the gods had tried to find ways around it on other planets, after a few hundred years homosexuals would emerge in the human race at about a one to ten ratio. So, to control the population the gods increased the homosexual demographic and in mere moments, nine out of ten people on Eliantar were homosexual and it would stay this way until the end of the planet's time. Not all of the higher powers were huge supporters of this proposal, but it seemed their hands were tied.

There was one final change made to the Elites of Eliantar. The gods were so thrilled with how well they had done. They had never put so much of themselves into a world before that they held this planet above all others in their minds. To illustrate this, they granted the humans special powers. It was nothing, of course, that could ever compare them with gods, but powers of survival and strength that would aid them along with their superior intelligence. Surely this land would flourish and all would be virtuous. It seemed infallible.

The factor that the gods always managed to forget is that no land is completely good. Something can be made beautiful and superb, but that does not make it invincible to darkness. Sooner or later good and evil must both exist in the same space and then the fight begins to bring balance between the two. As long as both good and evil exist, one cannot survive without the other. Even though worlds that rule with goodness may seem better, it can be rest assured that they also are tinged with hints of evil. If a world has no evil, than there is no cause to be good. Therefore the ones that would be good are corrupted by evil themselves and thus a new group must use the light to stop them. It's a terribly depressing point but an unavoidable one. It was a point that the gods had once again forgotten, for evil did eventually find its way to Eliantar.

It came in the form of Skarsend, the god of death and destruction. Though his role was necessary to maintain the balance of all things, Skarsend was hungry for more than just balance. It was in his nature to crave chaos and he was furious over the beauty that his brothers and sisters had created. Transforming into a scaly, winged monster, he flew across the land terrorizing all and killing whatever he could. The gods rallied as did the Elites under King Arktur. The beast, severely weakened, attempted to return home. He found, however, that he was no longer welcome, for the others had finally grown tired of his maliciousness. He was stripped of what powers they could take and cast back to Eliantar for the Elites to judge as they saw fit.

The monster that was Skarsend was locked away and doomed to spend all of eternity in a place that only few knew of. He swore to return and bring more onslaught than before, but he was paid no mind and left to rot and be forgotten.

The only remnant of Skarsend's memory came in the form of King Arktur's advisor who, with her gift of foresight, was able to see that Skarsend would not remain bound forever. She ranted and warned of the apocalypse he would bring with him when he broke his seal.

There is a light at the end of every tunnel of darkness. You see, as dark and unsettling as it is to read about heroes dying, picturesque lands being ravaged, and evil triumphing one must always remember that this, too, is not forever. Bad things may happen and heroes may fall, but eventually one day, in one way, death finds everyone. The wicked are not immune to deaths cold grip. It is easy to forget that fact…as bad things start to happen.

Towards the end of her life, she asked her friend, the King, to construct a great monument that would serve as a reminder of her warnings. Before the massive cathedral, the seer gave her last prophecy. She told of a great hero who would one day come and challenge Skarsend for the fate of Eliantar. Her words were inscribed on a pedestal, before the cathedral. They served as a beacon of hope for the next 2,000 years.

> *When the people have lost all hope and the world turns to black,*
> *A hero will appear from out of the gloom to bring Eliantar back.*
> *He will travel across the land through desert, water, and fire*
> *And crush the Tyrant's plan; destroying his funeral pyre.*
> *He will unite the lords of realms, for only through them will there be*
> *A way to stop the coming doom and set their peoples free.*
> *When this hero is set to come, no one knows what the future brings.*
> *The spell is this: Eyes on the clock, for when the pendulum swings.*

And so…the beginning of the end. Once Upon a Time the land of Eliantar existed quite happily for over two thousand years until the Good Queen died…and there was no happily ever after.

Chapter 1

His rugged muscles tensed up as he crouched low behind the boulder. With his left arm, he gripped the wooden bow, the sinews in his arm, tight with anticipation. His right arm bulged with muscle as he pulled the string back slowly, very slowly. His eyes never flinched from their target.

He was average height for a man but had an exceptional build from his time living off the land. He had lost his hair at a young age but it worked in his favor. His smooth head only added to his rugged exterior. In fact, at first glance one may have taken him for a menacing individual, if not for his eyes. His eyes were the bluest blue, and they were kind. One glance into the hunter's eyes was like looking into the calm, crystal waters of a lake.

Ara Tataman was beautiful, and yet he maintained his solitude always. It was never the case that Ara had to be alone in the world. Every village he went to, several eligible young men expressed their interest in him. There was even the occasional woman from time to time who would make a pass at receiving attention. No, it was by Ara's choice that he was alone. To him, it was self-preservation to not be hurt and experience loss as he had in the past. To others however, this was a complete waste of good looks.

Such was his attitude, that love and dependence on another person was not only a danger, but also a distraction. He worked hard, harder than most people he came across and he was proud of that. Ara was most proud of himself when he was exhausted from a job well-done. Luckily for him, money was no priority since a job well-done for a hunter usually didn't grant great fortune. A true hunter of Eliantar learned to take what the land offered and use the little money they had for necessities that the gods didn't provide themselves. Most nights he slept under the stars in a clearing or if the weather was bad, would find a big tree to rest under. Occasionally a kind villager would offer him a place to stay, but he rarely accepted. He did not care about having money or supplies to build a permanent residence as he felt more fulfilled roaming the countryside. Some of the animals he caught kept his stomach full. The little clothing that he owned was sewn from dried hides that he had skinned. Though, this was obvious just by looking at him.

Today he wore a sleeveless, form-fitting red vest that he had tanned himself. All the young men had ogled him as he'd passed through their small town that morning with his bow and arrows on his back, watching his powerful chest challenge the confines of its crimson prison. His pants and boots were also hand-made, albeit in brown and were just as tight. The fit of his clothing was less for fashion and more for function. While in the woods of Tacia, the forest realm, Ara could leap through the snarls of trees without getting snagged much easier without looser clothes.

Ara found that the little bit of money he did make from selling meat and pelts, he donated back to the towns that purchased them in the first place. A recent wide-spread epidemic had ravaged Eliantar in the last ten years. The cure for the virus had been discovered but the smaller towns and villages that he'd passed through were too poor to bounce back quickly from their losses. He felt it was of more importance to show generosity and self-sacrifice, than have money. He never told the townspeople the reason why he took an interest in helping to counteract the virus's destruction. That was personal.

Despite the fact that he kept to himself, he did try to put other Elites and creatures ahead of himself. And though this time pained him as much as it had every other time he hunted in the past ten years, he narrowed his gaze and released the arrow from his bowstring.

The dilla fell, dead, and Ara made his way over to it, tossing his bow over his shoulder. The weapon was light, made of the durable silver-neqmi tree found in Tacia. Ara had carved it out himself years ago. The arrows he fired were of the same wood and tipped with molten silver. Silver was a commodity in Eliantar, but Ara had yet to find another way to make his arrows puncture without it. He continued to rub the bow that crossed his chest as he strode to the carcass. Though he abhorred weaponry and violence, his silver bow was the one thing he cherished above all others.

He bent over the dilla and whispered in his deep, gentle voice, "May your death not be in vain. May the gods take your eternal soul and reward you for your nobility. May you know that at the price of your death, so many others shall live on because of your gifts."

Ara was kind. Dillas were not highly regarded or noble. Nor were they recognized as being anything other than slow-moving and stupid.

They were native to the desert realm of Errandomn and killed what little vegetation it had. They were fat and low to the ground, weighing a solid 200 pounds which was remarkable considering they were only three feet long. Their meat was worthless as it was tough and gritty. The only value in a dilla was the armored skin that it had. Though not exorbitant, Ara could earn a few coins off the hide and a pelt shop could fashion some cheap body armor.

Taking care not to look in the beady eyes of the creature that rested above its trunk-like nose Ara set in to the deed. When he was done, he clawed at the orange sand around him, digging a shallow, yet respectable, grave. Setting the remains inside, he filled the hole back in and offered a moment of silence in honor of the dilla who had lost his life. Excessive to some, but an important sign nonetheless to Ara Tataman as the sands whirled around him.

Sand. That one word easily summed up the geography of the realm of Errandomn. It was endless amounts of sand. Ara guessed that it was beautiful to Elites who were seeing it for the first time. It was a bold orange, shiny and soft. But to Ara, it reminded him of death. The two suns seemed to show more spite to this realm than to most of the others. They heated the sand to the point of scalding. Even with shoes or boots on, the locals could sense the wrath of this place. When there was a breeze it was a burning wind that seared the land. It was debatable that the night was worse than the scorching days. When the suns had set, a frigid gale pierced the desert. It seemed as though death came in either extreme, so unlike the green fields of Eliantar Proper.

Ara made it a point to stay on the outskirts of the outlying realms that he visited. He did not want to intrude on the various tribes' land. He also knew that the deeper he invaded, the more difficult it was to get out. Though he had never been very deep into Errandomn, he'd heard stories that there was more to this world than orange sand, even though that was all he could see now. Enormous, gaping sinkholes were rumored to litter the ground further out and magnificent, jagged mountains touched the sky with their tan fingers. The sand gave way to hard, cracked ground where no water ever touched. Ara shuddered.

Perhaps, he thought, the real thing that terrified him about this part of the world was the inhospitable nature of the indigenous species, more so than the environment. Tamalus looked a lot like Elites until

8

you took a second look. They were at least a foot taller and far broader than the average human. They lacked any hair, any speed, and any emotion. They lumbered through their desert world, slowly and silently. Their skin was a deep gray, oily and sinister. Dressed simply in brown sacks and carrying long spears, most Elites dared not approach them. They may have looked like civilized man, but they were far from human. They preferred a life of isolation and the Elites knew that if you were smart you would respect that desire.

Still, he knew he couldn't judge any creature that preferred a life of isolation. After all, it was a life that he himself had chosen. Perhaps that was why this desert realm spooked him, he thought to himself. In a way it actually echoed the man that he had become. How he had changed in the last ten years. He had always taken great pleasure in the simple beauties of the world, until his mother died.

That had been the saddest day of Ara's life and it had changed him forever. He had recently turned 20 and was running through the cobblestone streets of his small town. It was a beautiful, quaint, river settlement near the ocean. Dainty homes lined the roads and there were tiny shops on every corner. No one that lived there was rich, but everyone seemed happy. Children played in the streets with the cheap handmade toys they'd bought from the store. Each alley had a different, wonderful smell. One smelled of freshly baked bread. The next smelled of fish that had been newly cooked. Another would smell of sweets and cakes. It was the only town he'd ever known and the only one he'd ever cared to know. The people would sing and dance and the clock tower in the center of town had a chime that sounded like the call of a million song birds. It may not have been the wealthiest or most polished city in Eliantar, but it was charming nonetheless. He had been so excited that he found a new home of his own to live in within the village and he ran to tell his mother. When he had burst through the door, he found her in bed, the color of a ghost.

The Elites called it the Iniquitous Virus and it had struck once again. The virus had ravaged the land for some time and like all of its previous victims; it attacked with little warning and killed in a matter of months. Like so many other small towns, the potion-cure for the virus was too expensive for the members of Ara's fishing village. His mother, gods bless her, was too proud to ever admit that she wasn't well. She likely ignored the symptoms of listlessness and the aching body pains. She never liked to worry Ara.

And so on that dreadful day, a beautiful woman with a beautiful soul was lost and suddenly Ara became disenchanted with the world of beauty he'd once known. He felt his own soul slip away from him on that, the loneliest of days.

He decided that moment that he couldn't stay, as he had planned, in the small town. It would only remind him of his mother. He selected only the basic necessities and traveled abroad from town to town. He never told a soul that he was leaving. He thought of all of all his friends and neighbors. He couldn't face them now. They had once filled him with joy, but now he only thought of them as shadows of a former life; a life that was not his.

His once-glowing personality darkened even more over the next few months as he realized he possessed no skills to earn money for food. Raised as a fisherman, he found that he was utterly useless once he moved inland. The Elites, for the most part, were far from sympathetic. Since he had nothing to offer, he was quickly cast out of the towns that he passed through. Even villages that were financially stable rejected his presence. No one was generous to someone they viewed as a lazy beggar. On the verge of starving, and not being welcome in towns where money was king, Ara began his training on the art of survival. He began spending most of his time in the forest realm of Tacia to the far west. Here, he had shelter from the elements under the enormous trees and as long as he stayed in the outer edges of the forest, he didn't become something else's prey. Here he bonded with the indigenous tribe of Tacia, the Arbestees, a shy bird-like humanoid species, who were experts at surviving the forests.

He hid in the trees and watched children come and go, picking plants and berries. From his observance he discovered what was safe to eat. It didn't take long, however, before he desired more. He knew he lacked the skill to work as a woodsman. And so he began to quietly follow adults that would come, deeper into the woods to see how they hunted game. Some were quite skilled, but most were clumsy. Though meat was highly sought after, those that lived in smaller towns couldn't afford the luxury prices of butchers. Therefore, most of the hunters he watched were just farmers who were hoping to catch something on their own. The rich and proud families did not hunt, or at least did not speak of it, but Ara was not too proud. His real luck came when he could view a real hunter, often an employee of a town's butcher shop. But, he had an extra leg up on even these experts. His months living in the woods had taught Ara more than some of these so-called hunters.

Seeing the strengths and weaknesses of the different bows that the hunters used, Ara knew the best tree to craft his frame from and the most flexible leaves to make his strings from. In no time at all, Ara was eating better than he ever had. He was selling meats and pelts of a higher quality to towns then their own hunters did. And though he was now welcomed with open arms and begged to stay, he continued to travel on and never stayed in one place for long. He couldn't bear the thought of ever experiencing loss again. To never care for another Elite meant to never hurt again the way he once had. After seeing how he had been treated when he was down on his luck, he was motivated even more so to never associate with others more than necessary. Elites were self-serving and he would learn to be no different. And so, ten years passed with Ara existing as a vagabond. He was neither happy nor unhappy. He was existing and giving back where he could, which to him, was more than most could say for themselves.

As he approached the small desert village, he looked in the distance and could just make out the green, rolling hills of Eliantar Proper. They looked inviting, much more so than the thatched huts he was walking past. Pulling a blanket aside from one of them, he walked through the entryway of the pelt shop. He ignored the insects that filled the squalid air as he approached the gap-toothed man at the counter, tossing the plated pelt in front of him.

The man didn't respond, or even make eye contact but placed some coins on the counter next to the hide. It was a small amount of money, less than Ara had hoped, but not enough to have a discussion over. He grabbed the small coins and turned back towards the exit.

"Off on the next adventure?" came a knowing voice to his right as he pulled the carpet aside. "I would think that even for you, this kind of life would grow tiresome. Aren't you tired of running, Ara?"

The hair on the back of his neck stood on end. He had not been called by his given name in years. He avoided introducing himself whenever possible. Ara glared through the shadows and haze but could not make out more than the outline of the man who had spoken.

"Who are you?" Ara hissed. How is it that you know my name?"

The man stepped out into the light. His advanced age put Ara at ease, if only slightly so. He was a tall man but very thin and his age made him look terribly feeble. His mussy hair was completely white as snow and his eyes were the same color. He wore long-flowing, regal, golden robes to cover his sad little body. He chuckled and raised his arms to show he was harmless.

"Where are my manners? My name is Forr Suosor. I mean you no harm. I'm merely passing through town and stopped in here for a bit of shopping. I'm afraid I don't get out to Errandomn very often."

The man's voice had a hint of mischief and Ara doubted that he was merely here to purchase some second-rate pelts. The golden fabric that he wore made it obvious that dilla skin was not in his wardrobe.

"You still haven't told me how you knew my name."

"I have the gift of foresight," Forr scoffed in reply as though Ara should have known.

"But, you're blind," Ara laughed in return.

"Foresight is the ability to see in one's mind the world around oneself as well as the future," Forr said ignoring Ara's rudeness. "Many, upon first meeting me, assume that I am blind. However, this is far from true. My eyes lost their pallor when my power emerged as a child. For instance, I can plainly see right now that you're looking at me with a degree of superiority because you think that I am so frail that I may collapse. Once again, you are mistaken. I have never felt better. I may have lived a long 80 years, but it is the things that I have seen that have ravaged my physical form and taken the light from my eyes."

"Well it was a pleasure meeting you," Ara struggled to be polite as he turned and stepped outside. Older Elites had a tendency to strike up conversation with strangers and Ara never understood why and it made him uncomfortable. Even more so was the fact that this stranger knew he'd run into him. Was he psychic as well? Ara walked faster feeling that, if the man was psychic, putting a bit of distance between them would prevent him from having his thoughts read.

"No need to run from me, dear man. I am not reading your mind or stealing your thoughts. My powers do not allow me into other people's heads. I'm merely trying to make you an offer. Grim is coming you know," Forr said, after catching up to a very surprised Ara. "It'd be a shame for you to have to weather such a harsh month out in the wilderness with nowhere to call home."

Grim was the 3rd month of the year and a dangerous time for Elites. Unlike Seed, which was mild for planting or Reap which was warm for harvesting, Grim destroyed life. All of the crops and foods procured through the rest of the year had to be collected and the people had to plan on sealing themselves in their homes for the 25 days. To not do so was foolish. Temperatures dropped far below freezing and snow was relentless and merciless. Even those who had properly planned could be subject to death if their home wasn't properly prepared for the disastrous time. All were thankful that Grim took up such a small time of the year.

"Grim has little effect in Errandomn, old man," Ara snapped. "It does not get much colder here than it is now and I resent you imposing on me."

Forr responded, oblivious to Ara's rudeness, "It would still be best if you found a more permanent home to pass that time. I, myself, am on my way home to weather the storm. You know I live in the capital, in Ivory Towers itself. I am Royal Advisor to the Queen, er...or should I say to the throne."

"How nice for you but why are you following me?"

Forr sighed, "I'm afraid I was here on some rather unfortunate business. As I was on my way back to Ivory Towers and my carriage was going through this...rustic town, I felt the sudden desire to stop and visit the local pelt shop. My gift works that way, you see. I don't always know why I'm compelled to do certain things, but there's always a reason. No sooner had I started to browse and you came through. I could sense you being quite important as you put that hide on the counter and that was when it dawned on me. We're in need of a hunter! I was hoping that I could make you a job offering right now and you would accompany me to Ivory Towers. I know it's sudden, but I'm never wrong about these kinds of things. My carriage is just outside of this small village."

Ara was annoyed. Obviously this man was speaking the truth about living in the castle. He was presumptuous and bordering on arrogance.

"Your foresight is so sensitive that you felt the need to stop your carriage and step into a poor, dangerous town just because your Queen needs a new hunter? That *is* an impressive gift."

For a moment Forr looked as though he may cry. He let out a slight gasp and began nervously playing with his hands. He swayed from side to side and seemed to be at a loss for words.

"Ara," he whispered. "You must know that Queen Jenneka is deceased."

"I'm afraid I didn't," he replied without emotion. "I stay off the city paths and away from larger towns. The life and styles of the royal family do not carry much meaning for me and my lifestyle."

"Well, regardless of that, she has indeed passed. It's that terrible news that brought me to Errandomn to visit the Ambassador. A coronation is being held tomorrow for Queen Jenneka's son, the Prince. He may be young and inexperienced at ruling a kingdom, but he is next in line. Either way, I repeat my offer that you please accompany me back."

"Perhaps you didn't hear me," Ara said slowly, careful not to be too terribly rude. It was obvious that Forr had been close with the Queen and even though Ara was not interested in the offer, he wasn't so cruel as to intentionally hurt others' feelings. "I stay away from larger towns. I prefer solitude. In 30 years, I've never even been to visit one of the larger cities in Eliantar. This has not been by coincidence. I've been a drifter and will always be a drifter. I don't think a move to Castle Village would be in my best interest."

"What exactly do you have against Castle Village or any other large town for that matter? You know, Ara, most Elites would kill at the chance to live within Castle Village."

"I suppose I'm not like most Elites."

They stood there staring at each other for a moment in silence. The sand burned their feet, even through their shoes. A breeze had picked up and was whipping wisps of sand through the air around them. Ara, finally having had enough, turned to walk away.

"You can't resent those that have made out better in this world than you have, Ara. Bitterness will not make you a better person."

"Neither will wealth!" Ara barked. "My mother died for no better reason other than that she didn't have money! I resent your offer and I resent that people jump at the chance to leave their humble backgrounds for fame and fortune."

Forr sighed and shook his head, staring at the sand beneath him. Ara felt bad for a moment. All he wanted was to be left alone and he had conveyed that, at the cost of the old man's feelings.

"Well that's fine then, Ara." he grumbled as he turned away. "I had foreseen you coming with me, which is why I was being so persistent. But, I suppose I could've been mistaken. I'm sorry if I wasted your time. Good luck to you in your travels."

"Shouldn't you have seen that I would say no? And shouldn't you have seen that your Queen was going to die?"

He had asked this as delicately as he could. The point, he thought, was to prove that Forr legitimately could've been mistaken about Ara traveling with him. But, in spite of how nicely he had said it, the look on Forr's face made him regret it.

"I...may not see things as clearly now as I did in my youth.

Ara watched the man's gold robes whip around him as he crossed through the town. For as old as he was, he certainly could move quickly when he wanted to. Then he looked beyond Forr and saw the carriage that awaited him. Even from this distance he could see the intricate white frame with golden accents. The wheels glittered their silver and gold in the hot sun. The door to the carriage was a peaceful blue, the color of a clean, cool lake.

Ara looked from the carriage to the desert village that surrounded him. It may as well have been a mirage. The desert looked dry and dead. The carriage looked like an escape into a cool paradise. It was true he had always rejected a more comfortable life, but one had never slapped him in the face like this before. Would it be so wrong to attempt to live a different life?

Flanked on either side of the door was a member of the Royal Guard, the Queen's army. They were handsome and imposing, both menacing and enticing at the same time. Their silver chest armor matched the wealth of the carriage they escorted. Their bare arms were like tree trunks, flexed and ready. Ara found himself slowly approaching the transport. The guards leered at him and whispered crude things to each other. Though Ara couldn't hear what they were saying, their eyes gave them away.

Ara ignored them and called out, "Forr, wait!" Forr turned from the door slowly and looked the young man in the eyes. "I'll give it a try. If you'll still have me, I'll give city life a try."

Chapter 2

The ride was awkward to be sure and Ara was sorry that he agreed to go on this adventure. He was thrilled that the carriage was being pulled by stallops rather than regular horses. The ride would be hours rather than days. He had admired their beauty when he'd boarded. They were so like horses, yet bigger and far more muscular, bred for extreme speed.

He sat in the back of the carriage, facing forwards. To his right sat a guard who had not introduced himself yet with every bump they hit, managed to rub Ara's thigh with his hand. Across from them sat Forr, who somehow was oblivious to the guard's daring grabs, constantly brushing sand off of himself. Next to Forr sat the remaining guard whose eyes never left Ara's and looked to be thinking about more than just the job that he was currently being paid to do. Ara tried to ignore the guards and concentrate on what Forr was saying, but that was just another kind of uncomfortable flattery that he was not interested in.

"I saw the skin that you slapped on that man's counter, Ara. The castle will be just thrilled to have you. You don't just get lucky with a shot like that, you need to have skill. Skill seems to be a rare commodity these days. That's why when I have the notion I absolutely must heed my ability's suggestions.

"And you'll be paid very well to work for Ivory Towers. The amount of money that you'll earn will make you wonder why you ever wasted your time in small villages like that one. Honestly, it should be outlawed to offer so little for the hard work that you did."

"It's all a small town like that can afford," Ara grunted, looking out the carriage window. The sand was gone and now endless green grasses whipped past him, as the carriage rolled at top speed. Forr was kind, Ara decided. He meant well but he didn't seem to grasp that small towns weren't poor out of choice. They could survive. They just couldn't thrive like Castle Village or other larger cities could. Still, he hoped that his remark would make Forr uncomfortable enough to cease speaking. His hopes were dashed.

"Ah back to Eliantar Proper! Thank goodness," he sighed with relief. "I daresay it will be good to feel the cool breeze again. Although, I suppose you became accustomed to the heat and sand."

"I suppose so," he answered, finally deciding to give in to conversation. "That's not where I hail from originally, though. I hunted in Tacia for several years and just slowly made my way North. Eventually the forest gave way to the desert, but I kept going. No reason not to press on since Errandomn is where all of the textile smiths are. I assumed I could sell more hides there although, the game was more plentiful in the forest."

"Oh, so where are you from then?" Forr asked, his eyes lighting up and Ara knew he had said too much.

"What brought you to Errandomn?" Ara ignored the question. Forr smiled back, wise to Ara's hesitation, but respectful of it nonetheless.

"Well, as I said, Queen Jenneka has unfortunately passed on. I sent heralds out to the other Ambassadors and came to Errandomn personally. The Ambassadors will want to be there for her son's coronation."

"And the Ambassadors are the Queen's enforcers, correct?"

"Hardly! Ambassadors serve as governors of the five outlying realms. Eleetha II the Solemn created the posts in the year 286 after solidifying treaties with the outlying realms' tribes. At the time, and of course many times since, there have been conflicts between the Elites who work in the realms and the tribes. Thankfully now, we seem to cohabitate peacefully. The Ambassadors are there to maintain the peace more than anything. They make sure that the tribes are treated fairly. However, due to their existence, it's rare that a person like me, from the castle, travels to the outlying realms.

"Unlike you my friend, I am not much of a wanderer or explorer. In particular I find the sands and heat of Errandomn to be overwhelming, but times being what they are..." he trailed off.

"I rather like visiting new places. There are always new people to meet."

"Strange, I didn't take you for one who craved to meet a wide variety of Elites." The look on Ara's face told Forr that it was time to change the subject. "Do you know the story of how Errandomn came to be?"

"Came to be? I'm not sure what you mean."

"Ara, really!" Forr gasped in disbelief. "I'm talking about the legend of when the gods first came to Eliantar and formed it from nothing."

"I'm not a religious man," he replied, simply.

"Religious or not, it's a story that all Elites should know. Most children know the tale by heart!"

"Fine!" Ara was exasperated. "It's not like we'll be out of this carriage anytime soon and you have the need to speak for whatever reason, so *please* go on."

Forr remained seemingly unaware of Ara's rudeness. This only caused the hunter more annoyance.

"I don't think that I'd mentioned earlier that aside from my duties as Royal Advisor, I am also the Royal Historian. It's really quite an honor. Most rulers had these positions filled by two different Elites, but Queen Jenneka always held me in high regard, gods rest her soul."

"And what does a Royal Historian do?" Ara asked, looking out the window, uninterested.

"Well they keep historical documents and texts and relay them to whoever in the castle asks for them. They write the history that happens around them during their lifetimes so that future generations may study them as well. Lastly, they tell stories like the one you are about to *thoroughly* enjoy."

Forr was incorrigible and despite Ara's best attempts, he liked it. His years of tough living made him appreciate any Elite or intelligent creature that wasn't able to be swayed. He may not have appreciated conversation much, but he was enjoying this banter. He decided that he may not want to hear a history lesson, but that he'd put Forr through enough.

"Let's hear it then, this story of yours. Let us hear of gods and magic and all things coming from no things," he smiled, but not in a cruel way.

Forr mumbled softly about not having time to tell the whole creation tale and young people having no respect for elders. But, after that he launched into his story and barely stopped for a breath. Clearly, he was in his element. The guards, looking as though they had heard this story before, leaned their heads back and nodded off to sleep.

"Shortly after our world was created the gods and goddesses each decided to make their own personal mark on Eliantar. When Duna arrived, the goddess of land and rocks, she appeared as a radiant maiden with golden hair. She surveyed the land and knew right away what the world needed.

"Closing her eyes, the goddess balled up her hands into tight fists and bending forward punched the ground as hard as she could. The entire planet rippled at first and then suddenly hills burst forth from the ground. The grassy plains became uneven in a splendid way. At certain points on the planet, the goddess conjured enormous mountains to rise out of nothingness.

"Turning to the Northwest corner of the world, bordering right above where the forests of Tacia ended, she concentrated all of her strength on what kind of world was her vision of perfection.

"She brushed at the soft skin of her arms and golden flakes flew off by the millions, filling the entire region of the world with golden deserts. She then plunged her arms through the air as if punching it. Massive, dark caves and enormous subterranean sinkholes scattered her realm. When she balled her fists, mounds of boulders fell from the sky, littering all of her land.

"She was thrilled with what she had done thinking to herself that surely this was flawlessness. She called her kingdom Errandomn and filled it with mass quantities of dillas. Their armored skin would serve to protect them from their harsh environment as well as from predators that the other gods might think up.

"She gazed upon her land and realized it looked sad and a bit lonely. It wasn't just the sorrow that the desert creates. Something was missing. Such a dead place needed more life than the armored dillas.

"Though it was unusual for one god alone to create a new sentient species, she knew she couldn't wait for her siblings' permission to help her create an intelligent desert species that could thrive in this harsh environment.

"Humans were one of the gods' favorite creations. They were fashioned after the gods themselves, but with significantly less power and slightly less intelligence. More than anything the gods viewed the humans as highly entertaining because unlike the gods who had mastered how to live in a state of utopia, humans seemed to feel the need to create doom for themselves and those around them wherever they went. This may have been due to receiving less intelligence than that of the gods. But, whatever the reason, humans became a favorite on most of the new worlds that were created. In this setting though, it was unlikely that humans would flourish.

"It was only a short while later that she prepared to ascend back to the heavens and she smiled at the clan of Tamalus she had created. She had opted to create a new species that shared certain human characteristics.

"The Tamalus were exceptionally human-like. Standing upright at an impressive height exceeding that of a human by a foot or two, at first glance one could mistake a Tamalu for a human. The most obvious difference was that the Tamalus had a very inhuman skin color. To get close to a Tamalu one could see a dark gray pallor with black eyes. To further distinguish the two species, the goddess made the Tamalus nocturnal scavengers as opposed to the daylight hunters that humans were. She made them fiercely independent and created them to be loners from other species. To present them with a more regal look she presented each one with a long staff that they should carry with them wherever they went. As she rose through the sky she looked to see the slow-moving Tamalus making their way to respective caves, waiting to emerge when the day had completely ended.

"And so, that's how that sandy bane came to be!" snapped Forr brushing sand out of his hair and off of his robes. "It may have been paradise to Duna, but it's a nightmare to me."

Ara looked out the window and saw endless, rolling fields of emerald grass. He could understand why so many preferred this kind of view versus the dry sand or dark forests. Off in the distance he could see fields of vegetables. No, they weren't vegetables. Even from this far away he could make out their long, thin stalks and their radiant, yellow heads.

"Sunflowers!" Forr exclaimed. "How exciting, we're almost home! Queen Wonjj the Elder planted hundreds of fields around Castle Village during her reign. She wasn't geographically-inclined and always wanted to know when she was close to returning home. They were her favorite flower."

"They were my mother's favorite too."

"I'm sorry. Did you say something?" Forr asked.

Ara didn't answer. His mind had already taken him back ten years. He could still see the plain wooden table in the center of their first floor room. In the middle was a small blue urn that would reflect beams of sapphire light when the suns would shine through the windows. There were always fresh sunflowers poking out the top of that sky-colored vase. His mother worked so hard at the local market each day, but always found the time to stop on her walk home and pick fresh sunflowers.

When she'd passed away, Ara went out to the small garden behind their house and ripped the yellow heads from the ground for hours, tears stinging his eyes. When he'd picked every single one in his mother's patch and his hands were red and raw, he brought them in and arranged them on the bed around her. She looked so peaceful lying there in her simple white dress, surrounded by sunshine. He couldn't be sure if he'd stood there for moments or hours, but that image of her was his last and most powerful.

To see them in excess ten years later, Ara could not decide if this vision was peaceful to him or haunting. Either way he couldn't tear his eyes away and didn't even notice as the carriage began to slow.

"Well, we've arrived," Forr was positively beaming. "You may exit the carriage once we've stopped, Ara. Welcome to Castle Village!"

"I thought you were taking me to Ivory Towers."

"We're having Prince Vale's coronation today. Security will be intense and to be honest, I am late for arrival. I won't have the time to get you through. This should give you some time to get your bearings together. You may attend the coronation with the other citizens who have come today or you can wander the village and get acclimated to where you'll be working.

"Close the drawbridge!" he bellowed out the window.

At once Ara heard the heavy clanking of metal chains being cranked through gears. Craning his head out the window he could see an enormous wooden drawbridge being lifted against white stone walls.

"We do normally leave it open at all hours, but no one is paying a visit to Castle Village today as all the businesses are closed and anyone who was coming for the coronation would be where they're supposed to be already. All citizens who have come in are within the castle courtyard. History is being written today, my friend. I don't envy the Royal Guard today, they no doubt have their hands filled inspecting every citizen who shows up for this but, I digress.

"When you step out of the carriage, you'll of course be in Castle Village. If you head North, through town, you'll come to a bridge. Cross over that bridge if you so desire. The gate there will be open and you'll be in Ivory Tower's courtyard. Please take your time and look around and feel free to join the Elites at the coronation, if you'd like. I think I already said that. Forgive me, I'm flustered. I do hate being late. I'll be back for you once everything has settled down, later today."

Ara stepped out of the carriage and before he could turn back the door slammed shut behind him and the carriage took off through the town.

Turning back toward the charming village market Ara was surprised to see it completely barren of life. Every single building's doors were barricaded shut with heavy metal locks.

The castle village was grand indeed, just as the stories had led him to believe, and yet there was not a soul to be found. He began to walk forward on the pebbled streets, passing several abandoned vendors' carts filled to their brims with fabrics, fruits, vegetables, and grains of every variety. Even the stores that lined the streets had their windows and doors shut. Ara had often heard tales of ghost villages and he imagined that this is exactly what one would look like.

The citizens' houses also looked deserted, but magnificent. They were all made of different rich stone and had solid sloped roofs on them. Though fairly simple in style, they were grand in size and none seemed to be in any stage of disrepair or neglect. He could have fit four of his old shack in one of these homes.

Beyond the Elites' homes he could see some more shops on the next street. All the buildings in Castle Village must be grand, he thought. They were noticeably larger and cleaner looking than they were in every other town he'd been in. This caused a conflict within him, for as soothing as it was on the eyes, his conscience told him it was wrong to stay here.

Off in the distance he could make out the sounds of a great commotion. It sounded like a grand party. That would be the Prince's coronation. He turned away from the market and decided he'd best head North down the cobblestone streets.

As he did so, he saw the grandest thing that he'd ever laid eyes upon. A gigantic white castle rose just ahead up into the sky. It seemed nearly as high as the clouds but, of course, that was ridiculous. It had pallid steeples and towers by the dozens and hundreds of ornate windows covering every inch. It was truly beautiful, Ara decided. And yet, it was another testament to the ostentation and perhaps greed that seemed to plague the Elites. It must be nice that some people were born with more money than others. Maybe if his mother had been born to wealth, she'd still be alive today. Ara was willing to bet that no one in Ivory Towers succumbed to the Iniquitous Virus.

Crossing through the large town as quickly as he could, he noticed the quaint bridge ahead that Forr had told him about. The buildings became sparse on either side of him as he began to ascend the path. Another great white wall loomed before him that must've wrapped around the entire castle courtyard, cutting it off from the rest of Castle Village. An open iron gate at the end of the bridge was his only point of entry. Four guards stood poised at the entrance eyeing him up as he approached.

"Name, please," stated the one nearest him.

"Ara Tataman."

"Weaponry is not permitted beyond this gate, sir. I'll need you to leave your bow and arrows with us."

"I'm not going to hurt anyone. I'm a hunter."

"It does not matter, sir. Weapons of any kind are not allowed in the castle's courtyard."

"Do you actually expect that any Elite would hurt the Prince in the middle of an enormous gathering?"

"Sir, I am merely following the law. Queen Jenneka may have been quite popular but assassination attempts in our lands history are not unheard of. I've been lucky enough to have not lived through any of the wars in Eliantar's past and I'd like to keep it that way. Now, please hand over your weapons."

Not amused, but not wanting to cause a fight with four armed guards, Ara quickly handed over his weapons and continued on. He stepped into the sprawling, green courtyard that was filled with thousands and thousands of Elites. All had their heads tilted upwards to a large balcony. Ara didn't have to ask to know that the crowd was waiting for the Prince to step out onto the balcony in a grand entrance of pretension and make his speech.

It upset Ara that such a large castle was necessary for anyone to live in. Here he was feeling that he made a statement about minimal possessions and before him laid the epitome of money ill spent. Ara had already decided that he wouldn't like the Prince and wasn't interested in what he had to say. He still wasn't even sure that he was interested in the job offer that he'd accepted, but it was too late to leave at least for the moment, so Ara looked onward with the rest of the crowd waiting for the Prince to emerge.

He found a spot along the courtyard wall and looked up as the Prince stepped onto the giant balcony five stories up. He was handsome, Ara thought, very handsome. He was slightly younger than him; from here he appeared to be about 25. He looked exactly as a young prince of a world should look. He was tall and athletic looking with straight, shoulder length black hair and deep, serious blue eyes. Ara chuckled to himself at what the young Prince was wearing but also recognized that the Prince probably wasn't thrilled to be wearing it either, as he was standing there very rigidly. It looked terribly ridiculous. He wore a long white shirt and white pants. A long sleeveless powder blue robe was put over top. It was completely open in the front but touched the ground at his back. A high collar came up in the back, higher than the Prince's slim, silver crown that he wore. It looked like he was wearing a gown. Tradition was tawdry! Though, he still looked very handsome. But, handsome or not, it annoyed Ara to see an outfit that cost more than some peoples' homes.

"When my mother was alive," began Prince Vale. "She loved nothing more than being a gentle, fair ruler. It is my goal to accomplish this same deed."

The crowd went wild. Ara surveyed the fact that they seemed much taken with the dead Queen and were looking forward to the same rule of her son. Staring back up, Ara noticed Forr in his golden robes standing near the prince. He also looked thrilled to be working for someone so benevolent. The man standing to his right however did not look thrilled. Ara assumed this to be the Prince's bodyguard, judging by his clothes. The wild-haired man in his ridiculous, silver suit of armor was rapidly eyeing the crowd, his eyes darting as fast as they could. To notice this from so far below, he must be worried about something Ara surmised.

"Much like my mother," continued Vale, "I want to give back to the citizens of Eliantar. I want to be able to provide work, money, shelter, and food to those who cannot provide it for themselves. But, I don't want it to end there. Charity and respect are not just for those of us that are Elites. I want to stretch my hand out to the others who are in an impoverished condition, the Arbestees of Tacia, Vintens of Steedo, Fonnes of Quale, Tamalus of Errandomn, and the Lexerros of Fornar."

The crowd went silent and this infuriated Ara. The problem with Elites was that being human; they thought themselves better than other creatures, even if these creatures were just as intelligent as they. He was thrilled that a monarch, one who had life handed to him on a wretched silver platter, would care so much about the "lesser" beings.

Elites had always had a tense relationship with the outlying realms' tribes of indigenous species. Though they were civilized and able to thrive on their own and it was the Elites who depended on them for their resources, the land had bloody history of bad interactions between the two. Multiple treaties had been passed over the years granting the tribes equal rights, but Ara knew that many Elites still looked down at any being that wasn't human.

It was at this moment that Ara decided that perhaps not every wealthy person was a complete waste. Maybe there were some who did not let their money blind them to true important issues.

Or was it just that Ara was trying to explain away how handsome he found the Prince? Aside from his physical attractiveness, Vale appeared mature and kind-hearted. Then again, this was a political speech. Who was to say how much truth was behind it. Either way, despite his best efforts, Ara found he was anxious to hear more.

Vale pushed on, "We will not repeat old mistakes and rekindle old wars with the tribes that we share this world with. Protecting other forms of life may not be the most popular choice to many Elites, but we must remember also that they are the keepers of our forests, our lakes, and our mines. Without them we cannot survive and it would be unjust and unfit of me to allow them to try and survive without us."

At this the crowd began whooping and screaming once more. Ara was impressed that the Prince was smart enough to find a way to make this crowd realize the importance of helping others. He couldn't stop the grin that was spreading across his face.

"And so it is with great pride," Vale hollered with a hint of sadness in his voice, "that I accept the title of Crown Prince of Eliantar."

The crowd cheered louder and louder as Vale looked down gesturing and smiling. Ara was lost in the trance of the exciting event and of the handsome Prince. The Prince looked from left to right waving and waving to the crowd. It was like Ara was living in slow motion. He watched the scene go on for some time. He watched the Prince smile and laugh with his advisor. He watched the advisor guide the Prince over to the right side of the balcony and the bodyguard start to follow. He watched as the streak of an arrow shot through the sky striking the balcony and everyone screamed.

From the ground, Ara could hear shouts of "He's dead!", "Someone help us, he's dead!" First he saw Forr and then Prince Vale. The arrow had struck the bodyguard, in the spot that Vale had been standing mere moments before.

Chapter 3

The crowd of Elites turned to chaos. People ran in all directions and screamed for their lives. Ara watched as the Prince and his advisor knelt down to examine the man. Glancing around quickly, he gazed up high at where the arrow could have come from. He scanned through the petrified crowd, trying to see a pinnacle high enough, that the assassin could have had a clear shot of the balcony, which wasn't easy as the terrified people were everywhere.

Weapons weren't being allowed in the courtyard so how could someone have snuck something in? When he had entered, it appeared that the bridge was the only point of entry and it seemed highly unlikely someone could have snuck by four armed guards.

All he saw, as he stayed leaning against the wall, was the giant wall itself, which wrapped around the castle, separating it from the rest of the village. It, like the castle, was painted a magnificent white and was six or seven stories high. Surely, the assassin couldn't have been up on the top of the wall. It stood to reason that perches like that would only allow guards access and certainly one of the dozens of them would've spotted someone who didn't belong a mile away, right?

Ara's questions were answered as the wall behind him launched him forward and to his knees. Turning back, he saw he had been against a heavy wooden door that had swung open. It must be a door that barred the staircase leading to the top of the wall, Ara thought as he could clearly see the staircase behind the man that rushed through.

"What are you doing? You cannot launch into a frenzied mob like that. You could've killed someone with that door."

The man seemed disconcerted with Ara's anger and spat on him before turning and running towards the village. Now Ara was furious. Without a second thought he had lifted himself to his feet and pushed hard, trying to make his way through the hundreds of people. In thirty years, he had never been subjected to such disrespect and he wasn't about to start accepting that now. He would correct the man's poor behavior.

That man had definitely not been a member of the Royal Guard. He was a short man, for one thing and he looked completely emaciated even with his dark, baggy, shreds of clothing on. The man's white hair and green tattered clothing blew behind him as he scurried away from the castle and through the village, turning down an alley and away from the masses. When Ara finally had made it through droves of people, he took off running as fast as he could to catch up to the man. It didn't take long seeing as Ara was in phenomenal shape and this frail man looked like he'd have a better chance letting the wind pick him up and carry him than he would running. As Ara got closer he yelled to the man.

"You there, stop!"

The man stopped in his tracks and turned around quickly. Ara stopped as well. The man was terrifying to gaze upon. Up close Ara could see that the man's eyes were the color of glass, making it look as though he had no eyes at all. And he wasn't thin at all. Rather, he looked like a skeleton that had been given a thin layer of flesh to wear. His hair was white and terribly patchy. Whoever he was, he had clearly led a very rough life. He stood in place shaking all over in fear as Ara took a few steps closer.

"Who are you? Have you no manners?" Ara yelled.

The ghastly man didn't respond save for a toothless smile. He took a few steps back under a shopkeeper's veranda. Ara took several steps towards him. This man couldn't be more than forty, he suddenly realized. Although his frame and face were that of a worn man, the way in which he moved wasn't decrepit at all.

"I am appalled by your behavior, but even more so by your lack of sympathy or regret. Is this what living in a city does to a person? I demand an apology for your rudeness.

The man let out a low hiss in response and pulling his arms from within his rags, revealed he had crossbows strapped to each of his hands. He pointed them at Ara and balled his hands to fists, which released their arrows.

Ara leapt backwards narrowly avoiding the sharp arrow that sailed right by him. Before he even had time to react, there was a gigantic bang and the veranda began to collapse around him. The second arrow must have been aimed at one of the rope supports.

Ara curled himself up and tumbled out from the crumbling debris just as it completely crushed to the ground. He looked up to see the man running in the opposite direction, towards the exit of the village. He couldn't think normally anymore. He was completely consumed by rage. Then it occurred to him and he wondered how he could be so stupid. This ragged-looking man who was frantically trying to get away must be the assassin. He was so filled with anger he hadn't given the crossbows a second thought. Not that it mattered. Regardless of what he had done prior, this man had tried to kill him. It had quickly become a personal vendetta.

Ara followed him out through the village. The drawbridge was now open due to the screaming hordes trying to escape the city. Hurrying along the shimmering perimeter to the village, Ara watched the assassin come across a wooden pen of horses. Grasping onto one of the horses manes, he easily hoisted his frail body atop and with a slight kick to the black horse's side the assassin began to ride off through the grassy fields to the North and away from the sprawling castle village.

Ara, still staying a safe distance behind, ran to the pen of horses and looked to see the killer off in the distance riding at an incredibly fast pace. Pulling himself onto another horse, Ara bent low towards the horse's ear and stroked the chestnut-colored mane soothingly.

"Follow your brother," he whispered. And the horse immediately galloped off in the same direction as the assassin's horse. This was no surprise as horses of Eliantar were much smarter than horses from other realms. Though not able to speak or be considered on the same intelligence level as humans, the horses of Eliantar were highly respected.

"Don't get too close," Ara told his new companion. "We don't want them to know we're behind them."

Not even an hour later the sky was a burning orange and then quickly faded to a fiery red as the second sun set for the day. Ara began to worry. Though his horse clearly had great eyesight and a terrific sense of smell to keep up the trail of the other horse, he worried about if they became lost in the night.

It turned out that Ara did not have to worry about this, for as soon as darkness found the fields of Eliantar he could see a small fire off in the distance and he pulled his handsome chestnut colored horse to a standstill. He stared hard for a moment before his heart leapt with relief in his chest.

Realizing that he must be camping for the night, Ara smiled. The man was truly arrogant to assume no one would follow him. Then again, with their commander dead, it was likely he thought the rest of the Royal Guard were inept now, for a time.

In fact this man had every right to be as confident as he was. No one was coming. In fact, it appeared he was the only one who had seen the assassin leave the scene of the crime. The Royal Guard, at this moment was probably interrogating every citizen that they caught up with that hadn't already escaped the city. And now here he was having a small fire and basking in the freedom of the night that he surely didn't deserve.

Ara began to walk down the sloping hill towards the fire, eager to again confront the one who had tried to kill him. However, Ara didn't get very far before he realized the error in his plan and came to a dead stop.

He probably wasn't working alone. It was rare indeed when an assassination attempt took place by a lone individual. And the fact that it was in such a public location could only imply that this was a well thought out plan, and not the work of one impassioned man. Ara was usually levelheaded and it annoyed him that he hadn't come to this conclusion before. If he caught up to, not only this man, but more assassins, he could have several murderers put to justice. Though he was still furious over what had happened to him and wanted immediate justice, he knew his true duty was to be patient for now.

Making his way back to his horse, Ara laid his head on a particularly thick patch of grass. He was exhausted from the long, stressful day but didn't dare sleep. He would wait for the man to move and continue his pursuit. He would follow the killer to the end of the planet. The gentle nudge of his horse's nose against his arm finally eased his anger that he'd felt since he was attacked. As with so many other times in his life, he relaxed with the soft grass beneath him and the blazing stars above him.

When Ara opened his eyes he swore it was only moments later. However, the first sun hung high in the sky and cursing loudly, Ara knew that hours and hours must've gone by. Running back to the top of the hill, he looked out to where the assassin's fire had been the night before. There was no longer any trace of him.

"How could I have fallen asleep?" he roared aloud. "He must've left hours ago!"

Ara was sore from the previous day and of course the stressful night's sleep. He staggered over to his friendly horse, which was wide-eyed and ready for what lie ahead. Ara mounted the horse once more and holding firmly to its mane, commanded it to follow the scent of its fellow stallion.

The horse ran off as fast as lightning and Ara felt a little better knowing that they were at least back on the right track even if they were a bit behind. They rode for hours in the hot sunlight through endless fields of tall grass and colorful flowers. They occasionally came to a stream or brook and both stopped for a drink or to feverishly eat some fresh berries that grew along the water.

At one point, Ara noticed a group of farmers working to harvest crops in the fields. He pulled the horse over in their direction.

"Excuse me sirs," he yelled from his steed. "Have you seen another rider come through these parts?"

The suspicious men with their glistening, bare torsos looked from one to the other until the biggest, dirtiest looking of them stepped forward.

"That all depends," he said with a toothless smile. "What do you want with him?"

Ara responded, "I have reason to believe that he attempted to assassinate the Queen's son. He also tried to kill me when I followed him."

The men looked furious. The audacity that any Elite would try to kill the child of their beloved Queen was beyond words.

"He headed north about an hour ago," the dirty man bellowed. "He stopped to ask us if he was heading in the right direction of Fornar and we told him that he was. Don't know why he'd want to go there anyway. It's an invitation for death. It's all ash and fire."

"Fornar?" Ara said astonished. "Thank you all so much for your help. You've done a wonderful thing."

Fornar? Why would he be heading there? Of all the realms in Eliantar, Fornar was the least hospitable and certainly the one with the least Elites living in it. It was terribly hot from what Ara had been told in his travels. Also, there was the threat of streams and lakes of lava that littered the realm.

But then again, Ara thought, it couldn't be a more perfect place for someone who was wanted by the law to hide. It was also a perfect place to meet with others, who had the same dark and tyrannical thoughts that this man did.

Pushing on for miles and miles more, Ara saw no trace of the assassin but as night fell once more, he knew he couldn't push the tired horse any longer. Under a cluster of fruit trees, the man and his horse had a light meal and rested as the stars began to sprinkle across the sky.

The next morning, Ara woke early. It had now been two days since he had changed his clothes or had a proper washing and the affects were starting to show. Not that this was anything new to him. A life of constant movement meant not knowing when you could clean yourself or your clothing. He held a dirty hand to his face and felt the rough stubble from a lack of shaving. He crinkled his nose in revulsion.

What was that smell? He hadn't smelled that on himself last night before he lied down. And then he realized that the bitter smell wasn't coming from him. It was the smell of brimstone and sulfur.

"I'm almost there," Ara breathed excitedly at the prospect that this chase may soon be over.

He had raced as fast as he could and now he was finally getting close to Fornar. Jumping on his horse as quickly as he could, he raced onwards happier than he'd been in two days.

As he dashed on Ara could not help but notice the drastically increasing temperature. As he looked around he saw less and less vegetation. There were far fewer bushes, trees, and flowers here and the grass was turning from a bright green, to a dried brown.

It wasn't long before the grass completely gave way to a hard black earth. Molten lava that had burst forth from Mount Pyrall, thousands of years ago, had helped form the harsh ground of this realm.

Looking up Ara could see the great volcano in the background. Thick, gray smoke poured from its top. Although he knew the mountain hadn't erupted since the world was born, Ara still felt uneasy in the presence of something so deadly. It was impossible not to stare at...breathtakingly deadly. When his horse suddenly came to a halt, Ara was nearly jolted right off it's back.

Glancing towards where the horse's eyes were focused he saw the assassin's steed tied to a large rock. He was here! After all this time, Ara had found his would-be killer. Dismounting quickly, he cautiously made his way to the large boulder. Pressing his back firmly against the rough surface, he began to inch around trying to catch a glimpse of where the man may have gone.

Finally after what seemed like hours, Ara had a clear view of the other side of the stone and his eyes widened in surprise. He was on the edge of a drop off into a large molten lake. The fiery crimson and orange of the lake sharply contrasted with the black ground surrounding it. On the other side of the lake was a poorly built planked bridge, leading to a small chunk of molten rock that had dried in the middle of the lake. And there in the middle of the small island, stood the skeletal man.

He was looking around frantically, along the entire perimeter of the lake and way off into the distance as well. Looking terribly upset, he fell to his knees and screamed up to the sky.

"It makes no sense," he hissed with rage. "She was supposed to meet me here. I know I didn't misunderstand."

Ara inched a bit closer so he could be sure of every word that the thin man was saying.

"I've been loyal to you, have I not? Show yourself!"

A look of comprehension spread across his face, "The only reason that she would not have appeared before me is if I was followed!"

Turning around quicker than Ara could react; the man fired one of his crossbows towards the large boulder. The arrow caught his shoulder and Ara, in his pain, fell down to the rock in the middle of the lava lake.

Crawling to his hands and knees, he looked around the small island and saw…nothing. There was no trace of the man at all. Cringing in pain, he reached up and pulled the bloody arrow out of his shoulder. This blinding pain was forgotten as something hit his lower jaw and he was temporarily lifted into the air. He landed hard on his back.

Feeling the blood trickle from his mouth he tried to rise once more but felt a hard kick connect with his abdomen. Yet, there was no one there to deliver the kick. Thus, before he could receive another phantom attack, he rolled in the opposite direction from where the barrage of attacks was coming from.

He stood up and looked around. The world was swirling colors of ruby and the stench of ash. He began staggering around, trying to gain composure, not understanding where the gaunt man had gone. That was the moment he was knocked to the ground once more by the feel of a bony elbow to his forehead.

"You couldn't leave well enough alone!" he heard the man standing over him. When Ara opened his eyes, he saw nothing and that's when he realized what was going on. The assassin had the power of invisibility. It all made sense! That was how he was able to gain access to a place only permitting Royal Guards and get such a clear shot at the castle balcony. And now here he was attacking Ara who had no way to know how to defend himself.

Rolling to his hands and knees, Ara tried desperately to get away, crawling towards the bridge. He felt a hard foot crush down in the center of his back and he couldn't help but just lay there against the steaming ground.

"Why did you even care enough to follow me?" the man laughed aloud. "What was in it for you? You're certainly not a member of the Royal Guard. So, why follow me all the way out here?"

Ara didn't answer even as the frail man's body appeared once more from nothing. He sneered down at his victim and turned around laughing to himself.

"Whatever your reasoning was, I can assure you that it wasn't good enough to make such a foolish mistake. Even if you did have the power to stop me, I promise you this, the ones that I represent would have destroyed all in life that you hold dear."

At this the man turned, ready to deliver a final blow only to find that he'd stalled too long. He saw the fist coming, but it was too late and he crumbled to the ground howling in pain.

"I may not be able to make myself invisible," Ara spat. "But, I'm pretty quick and not going to stand here and let a cowardly murderer like you try to kill me."

The man cackled loudly, still clinging to his hurt face, "I've always found people like you to be so fascinating. You've gotten involved in dealings that had nothing to do with you. Your arrogance has destroyed you."

There was a whoosh of wind as the man fired from his deadly crossbow. The arrow blasted directly into Ara's right leg and he collapsed to the ground, unable to get up again. The pain he felt was unbearable. It was as if his leg was on fire but too dead to move. He knew he had reached the end and that this terrible man was about to kill him.

Ara attempted to slide his body further from the terror that was rising to its feet to stand over him. His leg was in so much pain that to move any part of his body was sheer agony. He was able to move only a few inches back and then realized he was lying right at the edge of the lake of fire.

"Nowhere left to go," hissed the skeletal man. "And now that you've reached your end don't you feel stupid for wasting your time to come after me?"

Ara turned his head. He could see the lava flowing below him. Bursts of flame shot up from the lake coming so close to his face that he could feel the scalding heat. Above him, where he had fallen, along the edge of the lake he could make out several quilled creatures, leering down at him. Lexerros, the lizard-men of Fornar, he realized. He had never before seen one and now in his final moments, he wasn't sorry about that.

They all glared at the two men through their slit eyes, hissing angrily. A few had their sharp quills fanned out. Ara could tell without thinking too hard about it that the Lexerros wouldn't be happy unless both men died on that island. Looking back up at the assassin, Ara could see that he was now also noticing the furious Lexerros.

"Get away from here you vile creatures," the man yelled. "You have no place here."

"No place here?!" one of the dark red creatures growled. "This is our home, warm blood. It is you that has no place here!"

"As a being of subhuman intelligence, I tell you again, stand down!"

Ara could see from the man's glass-colored eyes that he was terrified. His snow-white forehead was drenched in sweat and he looked from Lexerro to Lexerro anxiously.

"Subhuman intelligence?!" roared the Lexerro. "We have more knowledge of the world around us than you humans could ever imagine! We have been in this world and lived in this realm before gods ever decided to bring humans here! I'm afraid it's you who have the lack of intelligence."

"I won't ask again," hissed the ghastly man. "Leave us, animals!"

"I think not," the Lexerro responded not fazed by the threats. "This is the final time you will invade our land Scurus Subo."

"Scurus," choked Ara looking up at the man. So, that was his name.

"Don't be so surprised, Scurus, that we know your name," the creature continued. "We've been observing you and that woman meeting here for some time. The woman you call, 'Master.'"

Scurus Subo looked terrified now. Ara didn't need to be as close as he was to see it in the man's face. He stood there, frozen on the spot, shaking like a leaf. His mouth hung open slightly as he continued to look from one Lexerro to another. Ara would have felt pity for the man, had he not repeatedly tried to kill him. It was as though he were searching for one of them to jump up and defend him, which of course wasn't going to happen.

"You call us unintelligent, feeble man," the Lexerro continued mocking. "But, we do not take orders from each other like a common slave."

Scurus could take no more and raised both arms, pointing the crossbows at the reptilian creatures. The Lexerros all hissed angrily but did not back down. Scurus smiled and his glassy eyes shone triumphantly.

"Say what you will about me," he beamed. "But when my master hears about this, she will reward me greatly. You foul beings couldn't even imagine what she would do to you if she found out. But, then again, she won't have to do anything to you."

He took another step forward, directly over Ara's legs, continuing to point his weapons at the Lexerro who had dared challenge him. His arms raised, Ara could see he had a dark brand on his bicep. A gloomy turret was shown outlined with black flames.

Scurus shouted at the top of his lungs maniacally, "All of Eliantar will soon know the name of Scurus..."

But, he never finished his sentence as Ara lifted his uninjured leg as quick as he could, and was thrilled to have been able to catch Scurus off guard.

Scurus Subo screamed loudly with surprise as he flew face first over the edge of the black island and into the lake of lava.

His screaming stopped the second he hit and his body quickly disappeared under the scalding molten rock. Ara turned over and stared long and hard at the spot where Scurus's body vanished. After he had satisfied his skepticism on his enemy's death he raised his head to look up at the edge of the lake. He scanned the perimeter from end to end. The Lexerros were gone.

Chapter 4

Ara followed Forr through the dark castle. He was nervous to be here, but after everything else he'd been through lately, receiving personal thanks from the Prince wasn't the most frightening thing in the world. In spite of himself, he was actually glad to be inside since Forr had not been kidding about Grim's fast approach. The first snow had barely begun to fly and before long, large flakes freckled the entire sky for as far as the eye could see.

Ara could barely see where he was going. Though the walls all had rows of mounted candles on them, they were so cavernous that it offered little in the way of light. Forr also carried a large candle, and Ara did his best to keep up with the small, floating flicker in front of him.

He had returned to Castle Village just a short time ago and after explaining to Forr what happened, the old man rushed to Ivory Towers. He returned almost immediately and insisted that Ara follow him to receive a thank you from Prince Vale. From the moment they trudged off together, the old man had not been silent.

"Fornar! Oh gods, you are lucky to have come back alive! There are almost no Elites who dare go there, with the exception of the miners. And your leg and shoulder have almost completely healed from your injuries. How is that possible?"

"I have the gift of rapid healing," Ara answered ignoring the old man's look of incredulousness. "I don't get hurt easily and seem to heal from things much quicker than other Elites."

"Oh my. But still, Fornar is a terribly dangerous place. I assume you know the story of its creation?"

"As I told you before, religion is not very important to me. I don't believe in it and have never given it much thought."

They were crossing through the grand front doors of the castle. The foyer was massive. Doors and stairways littered the sides of the long, rectangular room. Guards paced back and forth and Ara could sense their tension. Murder was not an experience that they had had in their lifetimes as members of the Royal Guard. Ara just wanted to get in and leave quickly, but with the size of the building had a feeling they still had quite a walk and that Forr's creation story was beyond avoiding.

"It was early on the fourth day of creation that the god of fire, Migmeo, appeared. He emerged as a man of flames and took in the new world around him. He knew that having not been one of the first gods on the planet, much had already been done to the world. He surveyed what had been created and knew immediately what was needed. Focusing all of his incredible powers towards the northernmost region of the world, he made the ground open and streams of lava burst forth. The land in this area became black as the temperature was far too high for any plant life to survive. He scoffed to himself at the nerve of the plant god for putting grass everywhere. It never failed to amaze him how arrogant his siblings could be. This could not continue in his world of heat and flames."

"Are we going to the throne room?" Ara asked as Forr approached a steep staircase and began to quickly climb.

Forr answered with disgust, "No, we're not. Prince Vale is holding a meeting shortly for the Regulation Committee and wants to meet you in that chamber on the fifth floor.

"If I may continue, Migmeo observed a large mountain to the back of his terrain and he became infuriated at the mountain goddess for putting it there. They really had gone too far this time, he roared in his head. But, rather than destroy it, the angry god used it to his advantage. The new planet rumbled and roared and the mountain blew apart its peak as shots of flame and rivers of lava poured out."

"Mount Pyrall?"

"That's right. It's the most recognizable feature in Fornar and the most deadly."

After what had seemed like an endless staircase, they came out into a narrow hallway. Ara could see portraits lining the wall, but it was too dark to see of whom or what they were. Unlocking a wooden door on his right, Forr passed through and Ara followed, finding himself on another ascending staircase.

"Migmeo looked around at all of the dark earth and red fire lakes that were this inferno of a land and he was impressed with himself. He snapped his blazing fingers and reptilian-like lizards scattered all over the searing ground. They were red, barbed lizards who could change color from red to black in order to camouflage in this area and were able to walk on their hind legs. The fire god donned them the title Lexerros and observed them joyfully. The size of men but possessing the anger and raw fury of the land that they called home, the Lexerros were not a hospitable tribe by nature."

Forr shivered, "Though they were intelligent the Lexerros were not civilized. They hissed and bared their enormous fangs at the god as they stalked around him. Their slit eyes added to their overwhelmingly hostile appearance. The god shouted to the Lexerros as though he was a king, that this land of molten rock and brimstone was theirs and theirs alone to rule. He named that part of the country Fornar and said his goodbyes to his creations.

"He was quite aware that on the evolutionary chart, his Lexerros may be beneath some of his siblings' creations. However, should the species ever collide, he knew that it would be his lizards that would be well fed by days end. They were his answer to the fury he felt at the other gods' boldness."

They came out of the stairwell into another hallway. This one had many more candles and Ara could see clearly. Murals were painted along the walls displaying images of warriors and gods, animals, and beautiful landscapes. They turned a sharp corner and walked on as Forr continued to ramble.

"Right as the day came to a close and his physical body began to fade from the realm, Migmeo realized that this world was completely dark as much at night as during the day. Spreading his arms wide in a dramatic way he shot a burst of flame from each hand that soared into the sky and stayed there. Thus the world had two suns to keep it lit during the day. And that, my friend, is the tale of the fire god and the creation of Fornar."

Forr had stopped outside of a set of massive wooden doors at the end of the hallway.

"We're about to enter the chamber where the Regulation Committee meets. The Regulation Committee consists of the ruler of Eliantar, his bodyguard, the advisor, and each of the Ambassadors from the respective realms. It goes without saying, of course that Opo Scoloos, Prince Vale's bodyguard and head of the Royal Guard, has not been replaced since he was struck down mere days ago. Everyone else should have assembled by now."

"Must I go in there right now if Vale is meeting with other political heads?"

"It shall not be long and it's unlikely the meeting has started yet. The Prince merely wants to thank you and then you'll be on your way."

Ara sighed as Forr turned and opened the doors and glided into the chamber. He looked all around the colossal, circular room taking in the ridiculously high arched ceiling, than the gurgling fountains that lined the walls, and finally the pillars that wrapped around the eight chairs placed in a circle in the center of the chamber. This single room must have been the same price as a village of houses. Seven of the chairs were splendid mahogany high backs with padded cushions, but the throne was divine. It was an ornately detailed and magnificent crystal, as regal as a throne should be. Forr took a chair to the right of the throne and immediately reached into his robes, pulling out a quill and parchment to take notes of the meeting. Ara stood next to him, careful to avoid all of the eyes that were on him.

"Welcome to my home," Vale greeted Ara from his throne and Ara raised his eyes to look at the Prince. "I owe you an enormous debt of gratitude. It is not every citizen of Eliantar that would seek out one who has wronged their ruler. Would you please do me the honor of taking a seat?"

Vale gestured at the empty chair of his deceased bodyguard and the others in the room let out gasps.

"If it pleases you, Your Highness, I accept your thanks but wish to depart. I have no place here."

"It would please me if you'd stay, Ara," Vale smiled. "This is an informal gathering of the Regulation Committee. We are trying to learn as much as we can about what transpired over the last few days and I daresay your presence is imperative."

The simple hunter found himself blushing as he took the chair next to Vale. This was outrageous. He didn't belong here.

Vale was glancing over at the handsome, unwilling hero, dressed in very simple sand-colored pants and a loose fitting shirt. How different he looked from Vale who was again wearing ridiculous clothing.

The white puffy suit looked itchy and the blue cape was a bit over the top. The silver crown atop his head was the only thing keeping his long, black hair intact or, Ara guessed, with all the stress it would be standing out in all directions.

"I call this meeting of the Regulation Committee to order," Vale stated loudly. "As you are all familiar, I ask that you please acknowledge your presence when I announce your name before we delve into the obvious business at hand.

"Prince Prode of the Royal House of Procer, Ambassador to Tacia the land of forests and protector of the Arbestees."

"And might I add the most handsome one in the room," Prode responded with a smirk and giggle. "Of course I'm here. It's not like I have anywhere better to be."

Ara couldn't believe he hadn't noticed Prode when he'd sat down. Clearly, this man was Vale's twin brother. They shared the same face and physique and Prode even had the same straight, black hair that hung just past his shoulders. The only differences were that Prode was dressed in flowing, regal robes of emerald green and that he couldn't contain the silliness on his face. Where Vale was maintaining order with this meeting, it was obvious Prode couldn't quite contain himself. The Prince seemed used to this as he ignored his brother and continued on.

"Plucid Duru, Ambassador to Errandomn the land of sands and caves and protector of the Tamalus."

Almost inaudibly, the man to Prode's right whispered without even looking up from the marble floors, "Here."

The dark-skinned, portly man didn't want to be here, Ara surmised quickly. The man was hardly dressed like a noble at all. His pants and shirt were very shabby, shabbier than Ara's. They were a patchwork of dirty orange and brown fabrics, crudely stitched together. Vale had continued on as Ara continued eyeing Plucid, who kept his eyes on the ground as if waiting for it to tell him what to say or do.

"Iradt Furich, Ambassador to Fornar the land of fire and lava and protector of the Lexerros."

"I am here!" snapped the chubby, tanned woman to the right of Plucid. She certainly gave off the air that she was far too important to even be part of such a meeting as she looked furiously at the timepiece on her wrist.

Her plump frame was shrouded in a lavish ruby gown with a plunging neckline, which upon closer inspection had several burn holes scattered over it. Her red, tightly curled, shoulder-length hair bounced upon her head as she turned it from side to side, angrily surveying the other members of the meeting. She was simply oozing venom from her eyes, though just figuratively, thank goodness.

Ara couldn't help but chuckle as he stared at Iradt's monstrous bosoms hanging out from her low-cut dress or the long slit that went up either side of her gown. A dress made for a beautiful young woman was being stretched to capacity by a woman clearly past her prime, who was obviously out to prove she still had a shred of her youth left. Though what she was trying to prove with all of those burn holes and that scowl, he couldn't be sure.

"Volaticas Temed, Ambassador to Steedo the land of winds and mountains and protector of the Vintens."

Smooth as silk, the man with the long blonde hair aside Iradt said, "Here, Your Highness, and if I may say you are looking rather tense given your recent set of circumstances. That makes me feel absolutely terrible for you. I do hope that your recent troubles haven't put you on edge especially with all of the new responsibilities you have."

"You may not say. Not as long as I have the floor, Volaticas. I want all of you to know now that I am fine and I will not tolerate outbursts while I am speaking. I would like to continue and ask to not hear any uncalled for pieces of advice until asked," Vale responded quickly.

Vale was obviously familiar with the phoniness that was Volaticas. Of all the Committee members so far, none had given Ara the impression of arrogance and repulsion more than Volaticas Temed. He appeared to be in his mid-30s and looked exceptionally wealthy. His straight, blonde hair fell half way down his back and was smoothed into a long ponytail. He wore flowing robes, the color of gold which accentuated his bold blue eyes and the dozen rings on his fingers. His teeth were whiter than the snow that fell outside and he beamed with them as often as possible. It was a fine line between rich and tacky and it certainly looked as though Volaticas was straddling that line.

Vale continued on and Ara listened intently. The Prince's voice was beautiful and filled with confidence. What had come over him? He never paid attention to anyone's voice before.

"Lenta Benigg, Ambassador to Quale the land of lakes and streams and protector of the Fonnes."

"Present, Your Highness," came the response from one of the most beautiful women that Ara had ever seen. "I am pleased to be here and pleased to see that you are safe from harm."

Lenta had the face and body of a 25-year-old goddess. She dressed in a billowing, blue-sequined dress and had her long curly brown hair flowing from a thin tiara she wore. Unlike the others, Lenta carried herself and spoke with pure kindness and the utmost respect. This said a lot because with the exception of Vale and Prode, she was the only member of the Committee to be in her 20's. She seemed to make up for her lack of age with sweetness and maturity.

"Forr Suosor," Vale went on. "The Royal Advisor to the Throne, Eye to the Future, and Royal Historian."

The ancient man merely nodded his head and Ara could see the thick lines on his face. The last few days must've weighed very heavily on the old man.

"It is with great regret that I tell you all what you already know," Vale sighed. "Opo Scoloos was murdered last week in an attempt on my life. His death has been avenged by a hero that happened to witness what happened from the crowd. Ara Tataman is the man I speak of and has kindly agreed to share in this meeting of the Regulation Committee, much to my delight and great honor as Crown Prince.

"Now I am aware, in light of recent events that you'd all like to have your say about how we should approach the situation, but I must insist that we maintain order and decorum as we always do."

At this the five ambassadors had an outburst all speaking at once. Clearly they had no interest in maintaining dignity during such a tumultuous time. Ara couldn't help but agree with them.

"Enough!" Vale bellowed in an exhausted voice. "We'll hear what you all have to say but I do insist that we do this one at a time. Ara, we need to discover who would do such a thing. You've recounted that the assassins name was Scurus Subo and that he was working for an unnamed woman. Can you tell us anything else at all about him or what he said that could lead us to other rogues?"

"I've told Forr all I know. He didn't offer too much as far as why he would commit such an act. There was nothing remarkable about his appearance or clothing that would tell me his intents. Although, I just remembered that he had a brand on his arm."

"What kind of brand?" Forr leaned forward, his eyes narrowing.

"It was nothing significant. It was a black tower, outlined in black flames."

The officials exchanged looks and Ara wondered what importance he had overlooked.

"Ara that is the symbol for the Skars Shadows," Forr responded kindly. "When magic was outlawed by Queen Ramira the Bloody in the year 101, those that continued to practice called themselves the Skars Shadows, after a fallen god of old. They've been believed to be extinct for a hundred years and their group has been outlawed for over a thousand years. It seems strange that they would make a move now."

"Can this all be about magic, Forr?" Vale asked. "Tradition says that magic belongs to the gods. It is not my law. Would they truly attempt to kill me and assume that would change their fate? What can we do? How can we counter an attack like this from a group we thought was vanquished?"

Forr Suosor immediately stood up and the others fell silent. He was more nervous than Ara had seen him.

"I shall spend Grim meditating on this to see if the Skars Shadows have truly returned. At the thaw we can send the Royal Guard out. You should know however, I see nothing but darkness for the future of Eliantar. Ever since Opo's death, every time I look to the future all I see is blackness and destruction. I fear for the safety of all, both in this room and outside of this castle. The days ahead are bleak."

"Please sit down," hissed Volaticas whipping his long blonde hair around. "If the version of the story that I heard is correct, Opo warned Vale not to go out on that balcony. You were the one who saw that no harm would come to our Crown Prince and two minutes later he was shot at. Now you're claiming doom? It may be time for you to admit that since the Queen died, your power hasn't been up to par. Just say it already. Confession, after all, is good for the soul."

Prode stood up with a sheepish grin, "It only seems fit to me that we all predict Forr's future, like for instance say that no harm will ever come to him. Tell him he's as safe as safe could possibly be. Then, when he least expects it, we set him on fire."

With that Prode threw his head back and started giggling uncontrollably. It was several seconds before he realized that he was the only one laughing and that all were staring at him coldly. He sat back down in silence. Leaning over to the passive Plucid, he whispered, "Well I thought it was funny."

It became clear to Ara at that moment that the biggest difference between the twins was that Prode clearly viewed himself as a jester. He certainly had an odd, dark sense of humor. He thought of what it would be like if Prode were Crown Prince and could only envision Eliantar falling shortly thereafter. A frightening thought indeed.

"Thank you Prode," Vale rolled his eyes. Ambassador Duru, would you kindly stand and address the Committee with your thoughts on the assassination attempt."

Plucid Duru looked as though he'd been shot when he heard his name. He rose very slowly from his seat and adjusted his shabby, patchwork clothes, and spoke without looking up from the ground.

"Well, that is to say….it's very unfortunate and…maybe someone should suggest a way to…I think we should consider ways to keep us all safe….I fear for my safety too," he trailed off.

Before Ara could stop himself he mumbled loud enough for all to hear, "Sit down and let's hear from someone who has more concern for their Prince and country than they do for themselves."

Plucid sat back down quickly as the others chuckled. Ara remembering his manners looked over red-faced at Vale who glanced back with a slight smile on his face before gesturing Iradt Furich to stand up.

Iradt leapt from her chair, ashes falling from her dress and a look of fury on her face that made Ara instantly annoyed with her boldness.

"I believe that I can better illustrate what Plucid was trying to say," snapped the stout woman. "It seems to me that if the Crown is in jeopardy than the ambassadors are in peril as well. I propose extra protection for both the Prince as well as the Ambassadors. It may even be time to start using some of our lower class Elites as decoys to stand in our place for the time being."

Ara began to stand up but Vale had already reached his hand over, placing it on Ara's leg, pushing him back down. Ara felt a flutter in his chest at the touch of the young, handsome prince. His face was glowing red and he hoped no one else had noticed this.

"Thank you, Iradt. Volaticas, what do you have to say about all of this? I've no doubt that you have an opinion."

Volaticas Temed responded by smiling as broadly as he could and sweeping his golden robes to the side as he stood.

"Unlike my last two colleagues, I do not know that we need or warrant having extra protection." Iradt harrumphed and Temed pushed on. "Vale, your mother was one of the most loved and respected rulers of the past 2,000 years and in one day of being Crown Prince someone attempts to assassinate you. What will happen in three months if the Committee agrees to make you King?"

The officials in the room again began yelling at once. Volaticas looked around the room at the squabbling delegates with the same conceited smile on his face before Vale silenced them with a wave of his hand and waved Temed to finish.

"I suggest, Your Highness, that maybe it would be in your best interest to step down and let someone with more experience lead the people. I think we all want a smooth transition of power here."

"You monster," spat Forr, his white eyes glaring. "The Procer family has ruled this land since the gods first brought Elites here. It is detestable for you to even suggest that Vale step aside."

Forr was so infuriated that he clearly could have gone on forever, but Volaticas had already sat down and was clearly paying no heed to the old man. Lenta Benigg gracefully stood up to address the group, if for no other reason than to calm down the boiling old man.

"I've always felt that, in my seat, I have a great advantage in that I can listen to the others' ideas before suggesting my own. While Prode's answer was far from serious, I agree with his sense of humor and feel that at least on the outside we should appear jovial and not terribly upset with this chain of events. It will only give the enemy the upper hand if we seem flustered."

Prode looked proud of himself as Lenta continued on. "Plucid suggested keeping all of us safe and I agree. I think that perhaps it would be in our best interest to lessen our exposure for a time. Perhaps make fewer appearances."

Plucid smiled meekly while Volaticas let out a grumble. Every person in the room knew that he thrived on his social networking and parties. It was yet another chance for him to be noticed.

"I like the idea of hired protection that Iradt proposed. I hardly think that any of the Ambassadors are targets, however. I propose a new bodyguard be assigned to Prince Vale immediately. And lastly, Volaticas had the, borderline treasonous, idea to replace Vale. I couldn't challenge that idea more. That being said though, I don't think it would hurt to replace our "glamorous" idea of what the King is with a more aggressive version."

"What did you have in mind exactly?" Forr questioned.

"I believe that Vale should be trained as we would train one of the palace guards. He should be able to defend himself or lead an army into battle if he had to. No more poufy clothes or elaborate crowns. It will conjure an even greater respect and admiration from all of the people of Eliantar and I don't think any of us can doubt that."

"And who would be conducting such training, his new bodyguard I assume?" Forr chuckled. "I can't think of a single member of the Royal Guard who would take the post. Don't misunderstand me. They're all wonderful soldiers, but after what happened to Opo, they certainly seem more reserved than they ever were before. And where else would we find someone that has the skill and dedication for such a job?"

"We already have found one so willing," Lenta smiled. "He's sitting right before us all. If no member of the Royal Guard will stand up and accept the position than Ara Tataman is the man for the job. His adventure in Fornar proves that."

All eyes turned to Ara who immediately turned three shades of red. "I couldn't possibly. I don't know a thing about fighting or protecting royalty. I could never protect Prince Vale like one of the Royal Guardsmen could. You'll need to reconsider, I'm afraid."

"I disagree," Vale interjected quickly. "You fought Scurus Subo in one of the most inhospitable places in Eliantar (Iradt scowled at this) and came out the victor. You succeeded completely in protecting me.

You have done what no other member of the Royal Guard was able to do. You are more than just the average hunter."

"If I may ask," Volaticas chimed in. "How did you manage to defeat Scurus? According to all accounts of your story, he beat you severely and you have no mark or broken bones to show for it? He shot you in the leg with an arrow for gods' sake and yet somehow you're completely unscathed. How is that possible?"

Forr jumped in, "Ara is a healer. Nothing can hurt him for a lasting period of time. An attack that would kill one of us may not even leave a scratch on him. Opo had super strength and we thought that was so amazing but a bodyguard that can't be hurt…"

Prode let out a sexy growl at Ara, causing the room to roll their eyes. There was no denying that Prode just could not be serious.

"I am not completely invulnerable," Ara chimed in. "To be honest, I have no idea what the extent of my abilities are and I'd rather not find out. I healed after a few minutes from being shot in the leg, but that's not to say that had I been shot in the head, I would've lived."

"Still, it is a powerful gift," Vale smiled. "We may not know the extent of what you can do, but the level that we do know is still amazing and a skill that the rest of us do not possess and could only dream of. I certainly think that it's a phenomenal gift for a bodyguard to have.

"Don't sell yourself short, Ara. You have done some amazing things in the past week and special ability or not you can't deny that fact."

"But, Your Highness!" Ara said ignoring Vale's obnoxious twin, who was winking at him. "I feel that I am not completely qualified to assist you in his matter. However, I am not so ignorant to refuse a royal dictation. If it is your wish, than I shall oblige. Please know that I will do my very best to serve the Royal Committee and you, Your Highness, to the best of my abilities."

Vale beamed and Ara blushed. "I know that you will, my new friend. Then it is all settled. From this point on, Ara Tataman is Royal Protector to the Throne."

No sooner had the words come out and Ara felt a nauseous feeling of foreboding as he stared out the enormous windows at the thick snowflakes as they fell from the sky in droves. Awful things were on the horizon and he wasn't sure that he was ready for any of them by any means. Grim was just the beginning.

Chapter 5

As Grim raged on, Ara decided to make the best use of his time, trapped in the Ivory Towers, to educate both himself and Crown Prince Vale on the art of self-defense. It may have seemed pointless to some of the guards but if Vale was threatened again it would be better to have some knowledge and confidence than none at all. Much to Ara's chagrin, Vale's twin brother, Prode, the Ambassador of Tacia, was spending the month in the castle as well.

Being a drifter, Ara was well-versed in basic combat and self-defense techniques. However, he always tried to make peace. These times, however, may not be times of peace. It may have been an isolated attack on the Prince or it may have been a more sinister force at work. There was no way to know. And so for several days following the Regulation Committee meeting, Ara locked himself in the castle's armory, located in the east wing of the 7th floor training with other members of the Royal Guard.

The armory was one of the most impressive rooms in the Ivory Towers and that was saying something. It was an enormous square that was 40 yards long and 40 yards wide. The ceilings had the same ornate, arched ceilings that the other rooms had, but that was where the similarities ended. The floors were covered with a soft blue mat that was very plush for duels and training exercises. One wall consisted entirely of windows that allowed massive amounts of sunlight in and boasted glorious views of the fields and village. The opposite wall was completely covered in assorted weaponry and pieces of armor. Overall, in spite of his aversion to fighting, he found that he enjoyed spending time in the massive war room.

He honed his skill with members of the Royal Guard for days. He sparred with several of them both hand-to-hand and using a trelamna.

He had seen the weapons of the Royal Family before. There were two of them crossed in a large "X" on every royal crest across Eliantar. Still, he had never actually held one before, but he found them an easy-to-use and graceful weapon. Each one was basically a staff measuring in at five feet in length. Usually made of a dark, solid wood, the trelamna was exceptionally light, but strong. This made it easy, even for novices, to use. On either end of the staff were three spikes that jutted out like an enormous fork. When confronted, a guard could hold the staff with both hands and use it as a stick to beat away enemies.

It could be far more interesting than just that though. When holding the staff, with a turn of each wrist and a pull the rod came apart in the middle making two smaller weapons. This doubled its effectiveness since, if used correctly, it could completely catch an enemy off guard.

When Ara felt that he was competent enough with his trelamna, he summoned Vale and Prode to the large armory. He wiped the sweat, which was flowing profusely, from his bald head. He didn't know if he was perspiring because of his exercise or because of his lack of experience as a bodyguard and trainer. Maybe, he thought to himself, he might be nervous because he was starting to truly feel affection for another. This made him most uneasy, as it was not a feeling that he had any knowledge of how to deal with.

Ara wasn't sure why he felt so drawn to Vale. He was great looking, but hadn't he dismissed handsome men before? Certainly it wasn't the Prince's power or authority, for those were two qualities that never impressed him previously. He could only assume that it was the combination of his innocence and ambition. He was innocently thrown into a world that he clearly didn't know what to do with. Dealing with assassinations and political upheaval in the first day was not what he had signed on for. Nevertheless, he had accepted his destiny and showed the ambition to endure and make the necessary changes. Yes, those self-sacrifices made Vale highly likeable and charming to be around.

He was snapped back to attention as the heavy metal doors to the room creaked open slowly and the twins walked in. Both wore black athletic-style pants and sleeveless, tight shirts. Ara could immediately tell them apart because Prode's was a deep forest green and Vale wore a pale blue. It was a kind of requirement that Ambassadors wear their realms signature color and as Prode represented the forest realm, he wore green. It suited him, but Vale stood out as more handsome to Ara in his various shades of blue. They perfectly accented his bright blue eyes and dark as night hair.

Prode had personally requested to be trained along with Vale. Ara had originally said no for a multitude of reasons, the biggest being his immaturity. Eventually Prode had convinced him by pointing out that, as a twin, he could be used as a decoy if need be.

Ara was impressed to see that they were both well-muscled; especially considering they had lived rather pampered lives. Their long dark hair fell loosely onto their shoulders and they both smiled at Ara as they walked towards him. Prode gave a stupid grin and raised his eyebrows suggestively. His brother, who was embarrassed by Prode's obnoxiousness, merely blushed and looked away sheepishly after he had smiled at his new bodyguard.

"The purpose of today's exercise," began Ara trying not to stare at Vale, "is to learn how to use the trelamna. I realize that as members of royalty you've already had some basic training. We shall review only the basics. We're going to do this in three phases. After all, the last thing I want to do is overwhelm you. To start off, we will practice how best to handle the trelamna as a shaft."

Prode immediately burst into giggles. Running up alongside Ara he made a play grab at Ara's crotch before running away sniggering ridiculously. Vale looked away, aghast with embarrassment.

"You know every man's dream, Ara. I know the drill. You get some alone time with a set of twins and then 'handle the shaft.' Trust me Ara, we've heard it all before."

Ara rolled his eyes in disgust while Vale punched Prode in the arm and shushed him. It was becoming crystal clear that this was a common scenario for the two twin brothers.

"If I can continue," Ara said rudely. "The second phase of our exercise will be to separate the trelamna into two pieces, two separate weapons, and fight accordingly.

"In the final phase, we will discuss the ways to use our special abilities while battling with trelamnas. Now, if you're both ready, then let's begin. If you could please do some quick stretches and then bring out your trelamnas we can start the day's exercises immediately."

Prode continued to laugh like a fool. He clutched his stomach as tears welled in his eyes. Ara wondered what his problem was this time.

"Seriously? Everybody whip out your sticks so we can clash them together! Oh, that's just too rich!"

The rest of the day progressed in much the same way. The balance of the morning Ara taught the twins how to use the trelamna as a single weapon. They learned how to strike high, strike low, perform a sweep attack, and how to judge where their enemy would strike.

Ara was taken with how mature Vale was and what a quick learner he could be. At the same time, Ara found himself disgusted with how little Prode paid attention and how many immature jokes he would make, followed by the standard cackle. How two brothers could be so different, he wasn't sure. He tried his best to maintain his patience but it was becoming increasingly difficult.

"That's excellent Vale," encouraged Ara. "You're catching on so quickly. That's it! When your enemy strikes high, you must also strike high. As soon as you block the high attack perform a low attack and jab at the legs. If you're quick enough, they'll still be off balance from their high stab."

"You two are far too serious," scoffed Prode. "It doesn't always have to be life or death you know? I think the two of you could both use a good jab at the heads with those things to get you to relax."

After a quick lunch of some fruit and nuts, which of course Prode had to cackle about how much he loved eating nuts, Ara taught the twins how to separate the trelamna into two weapons and use them both. This proved to be more difficult and much more dangerous, even though he strongly emphasized only using the motions and not actually striking. In no time the twins both had cuts all over their arms.

This only proved to bring their defining characteristics out even more. Vale became even more serious and determined. Prode became even goofier and overdramatic, accusing Ara of intentionally trying to cut his arms off so he could take advantage of him. It didn't seem possible, but Ara was finding himself even more appalled by the crude twin.

"The trick with the trelamna, as two weapons, is defense. You're used to countering only one attack and in the back of your mind planning your own retaliation. With one weapon, the enemy can only strike in one direction at a time. However, when separated your mind is being split into two different directions. You must accept that there is too much going on to plan your own attack and you must focus on keeping your weapons where your enemies' weapons are headed. If you can do this properly and strongly, you will stun your opponent and then be able to strike your own attack. This will take more time and practice without a doubt, but I'm sure you'll learn. Now, let me show you some of the attacks you can use with the two weapons once your enemy is distracted."

With that he taught them how to twirl the mini-trelamnas to distract the opponent. He taught them how to perform an upper attack by holding both weapons over their head and bringing them down on their opponent's shoulders. They learned how to do the scissor and reverse scissor by spreading their arms out and swinging them in to a cross and then swinging back out. He reminded them to be careful as the trelamnas were highly dangerous and any of these attacks could behead, impale, or cause severe damage to each other.

After a great deal of practice, Vale and Prode were at least able to defend each other's assaults without receiving any damage of their own. This was a great accomplishment for two young men who had rarely been exposed to weaponry or battle before.

"Very good, I'm really impressed with both of you," Ara repeated, trying not to stare too hard at Vale's body as he wiped the sweat from his brow. "I haven't asked either of you about your powers. I certainly don't know if they will even be useful in battle but I have noticed that several Elite Guards have trained themselves to use trelamnas along with their power. And I have to say that some of their abilities are more powerful than the weapons they carry."

"Well I could show you my gift while I hold the trelamna, if that's what you want," began Prode. "My only fear is that the trelamna may look a lot less impressive next to my "gift."

"Don't you ever cease to talk?!" yelled Vale as his trelamna that had been lying on the ground, lifted up by itself and flew through the air at Prode. It looked as though it was going to take Prode's head off.

Prode stared at the flying weapon and waved his hand. The trelamna flew off to the far side of the room and clattered against the metal doors before falling to the ground, motionless once more.

Ara stood transfixed, "You're both telekinetic! That is such an amazing gift! And if I may say so, that's a very useful gift to have in battle."

"Not quite," Vale sighed. "Our powers are opposite in nature. I am able to move organic things with my mind such as the wood of the trelamna. Prode can move inorganic objects, such as the metal of the trelamna. We've played this game for years, throwing things at each other."

"I think you may both be ready. I'd like to have you both stand in the center of the room facing each other. We're going to have a little sparring battle to see what you've learned. Please be careful as you are not real enemies. Remember to use fake attacks. Use the motions that you would use, but use them slowly. It's not an active battle. You should use any skills you have learned to this point and incorporate your telekinesis at any point during the sparring."

The twins stood in the middle of the room facing each other. Vale had a serious, committed look on his face. Prode, to no one's shock, sported a silly grin. This wasn't going to go well.

"On your guard, Highnesses...get poised...and begin!" bellowed Ara and the twins attacked.

They were fast, faster than Ara wanted them to be for a sparring event, which immediately made him tense. Vale swung his staff high and Prode blocked it high. The two clashed over and over again from high to low. Ara was pleased to see that they had both mastered a good sense of defense.

"Do not assault each other!" Ara yelled over the clashing of metal. "There aren't enough healing ointments in the storage room if one of you gets injured."

They ignored him and continued. After what seemed like an hour of this, Prode blocked another high attack and fell to his knees swinging his staff low to the ground. He succeeded in sweeping Vale off of his feet. Prode leapt up and struck his staff down but Vale had already rolled aside and jumped into the air separating his trelamna before he had touched the ground. Ara was speechless thinking that Vale could have just been stabbed, had he not rolled away. This was getting dangerous.

"Maybe we should take a little break," Ara called out. "This is getting tense for an exercise."

Vale swung his weapons together in a scissor attack and Prode avoided this by bending so far back that he fell down in pain. Quickly as he could he separated his trelamna and crossed them into an X over his body as Vale brought his down to strike. Their sets of weaponry clashed between their bodies and stayed in place as both tried to overcome the other's strength. Strain and anger showed on both of their faces, surprisingly even Prode's.

"Cease now!" We've finished for the day!"

Prode smiled and pushed hard. Vale fell back onto the ground and laid there for a moment. Prode got up fast and stalked towards his brother with his weapons drawn.

Vale mentally lifted his own weapons and sent them hurling across the room at Prode, blades first. Prode swung both his weapons hard at the first trelamna that sailed in his direction and knocked it to the ground. He wasn't fast enough for the second one that sliced his arm as it sailed by and he howled out in pain and rage. It was obvious that Vale was trying to get his brother to stop, rather than actually hurt him but that made little difference.

There was a definite look of fury on Prode's face as he examined the trickle of blood from the flesh wound. Raising his hands he sent a tremor through the ground that shook the opposite wall that held the hundreds of different weapons. When the weapons began to loosen and fall, Vale raised his arms and used his power to slow them so they wouldn't crash to the ground.

Ara continued yelling for them to stop, but dared not step between them. He had only wanted this to be a friendly sparring contest and all of a sudden he felt that both brothers were dead serious about winning. Being an only child, Ara never did quite understand sibling rivalry. But, judging from this he could see that it definitely existed and it was ugly.

Standing up finally, Vale raised his hands and Prode's own weapons flew out of his hands, flew directly behind him, and cracked him hard in the back of his legs, with the wood and not the blades, thank goodness. He fell hard on his back and Vale, furrowing his eyebrows with his arms still outstretched, used his mental energies to keep Prode pinned down.

"Well done to both of you! End game! Vale wins!" Ara yelled before there was retaliation.

"Isn't this a surprise?" Prode said sarcastically. Vale wins again."

Vale released his brother and leant down to give him a hand. Prode took it and rose to his feet, brushing himself off and then smiling. The anger that had been all over his face washed away as quickly as a downpour might wash away a speck of dirt or dust.

"I mean I could've won but I know how sensitive you can be and I just didn't want to hurt you. I certainly don't want to embarrass the future King of Eliantar. And besides that, if I had won, wouldn't that be considered treason?"

They caught their breath for a few minutes and enjoyed a couple of laughs. Overall, it was a very successful training session and Ara was impressed. Even Prode, who Ara had been sure wasn't paying attention, had the potential to be a fierce warrior. Somewhere in the midst of all his silliness, Prode must've been making mental notes of Ara's lessons.

This moment of relaxation was only brief as the large metal doors swung open and Forr Suosor came in looking quite upset. Vale approached him quickly to see what was wrong.

"Forr, what in the world is the matter? What is it, my friend?"

Finally Forr focused his eyes on the Prince and a look of mixed pride and fear filled his old face as he whispered to Vale with a touch of glee in his voice, loud enough that Prode and Ara could hear him.

"I know who it is. It took me a while to figure it out, but I know who's trying to kill you."

"What?! Who is it?" Vale asked. "How in the gods' names did you find this information?"

"It's her. I don't know why I didn't assume it right away. It's that awful woman, the one we knew would come back and cause catastrophe."

"What are you talking about Forr? What woman?" Vale sounded just as nervous as Forr did, his eyes wide with worry. "I don't have any idea who you are talking about. Please speak clearly.

"The corpse woman had sworn her revenge, Vale." Forr looked up, tears in his eyes. "I've failed you, Your Highness. I couldn't foresee her evil. I couldn't foresee that the Lady of Death would return."

With that Forr collapsed on the ground. Ara picked him up and Vale asked him to carry him back to his quarters. Twilight had already fallen and Ara was terribly lost in the monstrous castle as he followed Vale through long, dark corridors and winding staircases. When at last they reached Forr's tower, Vale asked the guard standing there to unlock the door.

Ara had met this guard before. Kally was very young for a soldier in the Royal Guard but very eager to please and very polite. This young man was definitely going to go places, Ara thought as the teenager fumbled with his keys.

Upon entering, Vale directed Ara to place the old man on his bed. Ara did as he was told but felt very uncomfortable. Being in the old psychic's room gave him an eerie feeling. It was dark and all around the room were black curtains keeping any light out. Dozens of candles littered the room, hardened wax covering the floor. There were jars that lined the walls filled with assorted crystals, future cards, and anonymous liquids. The room gave off odd red and purple glows from the mixture of lights that hit the billowing smoke that poured profusely from a small cauldron in the corner. Why in all the gods' names would Forr have a cauldron in his chamber? What was he up to in here?

"Please leave me with him for a few minutes," Vale requested. "Wait for me outside. I won't be long. He'll calm down quickly if there aren't so many people surrounding him."

Stepping outside, Ara saw Prode had already sent Kally away for privacy. He closed the door and looked at Prode, who was staring back, and couldn't help but give a slight shudder.

"Oh you don't have to tell me," whispered Prode. "That guy has always given me chills. Mother always loved him and had him around her all of the time. She practically worshipped the ground he walked on and frankly I'm worried that Vale's starting to do the same thing. I, for one, have always thought he was nothing more than a crazy, old charlatan."

"Has he made mistakes before?" Ara questioned. "He claimed the Prince was in no danger before he was nearly killed."

"No, I don't think so," Prode responded, thoughtfully. "I'd never heard any of his prophecies before Mother died but she swore he was quite good. She would brag about his accuracy and say that he never led her astray. Ever since Vale has taken over though…"

"Who's the woman that he's talking about? He sounded all mystic and overdramatic about it."

"Oh I don't have a clue. I suspect he's making it up for dramatic effect. You were the one that told all of us that Scurus Subo said he

60

was working for a woman. Now, all of a sudden, Forr sees a dark lady behind the attack. Go figure.

"If you want my honest opinion, Forr's lost his visions of the future. Nothing wrong with that at all, don't get me wrong. Every Elite knows that when we get old, our powers sometimes fade or disappear completely. It's just a natural part of aging. A lot of Elites don't handle that very well if it happens to them. I'm guessing he's afraid that without his powers Vale will cast him out on the street with nowhere to go, hence these outrageous false visions. It's becoming a bit like one of those small town "psychics" with all the smoke and drama and no real answers. Do you know what I mean?"

Having been to several small towns, Ara knew exactly what he was talking about and was even inclined to agree. Still, he thought it may be unprofessional to voice his own opinions too readily since he was still new to his post.

"And that old cauldron," Prode went on. "He's in there acting like one of those old Skars Shadows that we learned about in our history classes that used all of that dark magic to terrorize the country. Mark my words, in the next week or two, he'll be in there charging money per visit."

Ara let out a little chuckle as the beaten door to Forr's room swung open. Vale gave a dirty look to Ara who lost his smile immediately. The look continued over to Prode who was already pretending to admire an old painting on the wall.

"I love the way they've blended the oils in this piece, Ara. It's a bit like looking at the clouds coming from a cauldron. You know, like the ones that those fake seers have in their chambers."

"I want to see you both in the Regulation Committee room in one hour. I think we've got some serious problems to start worrying about. I'll thank you both not to carry on like a couple of immature children during this time."

With that Vale began to walk off, but Prode and Ara hurried after him. Ara was worried and even Prode seemed a bit concerned as to what had upset Prince Vale so thoroughly.

"What is it? What's going on?" questioned Prode. "What did the old fraud tell you in there?"

"I know there have been questions and jokes at Forr's expense as to his ability to predict the future," Vale snapped, coldly. "Let me assure you both that if Forr's vision is correct, then all of us are already dead."

Chapter 6

The darkness outside poured into the Regulation Committee chambers. Torches on the columns in the room cast everything in an eerie glow. On the crystal throne, Vale sat in a blue robe looking a mess with his tousled hair. Prode sat in his usual seat, facing his brother, for the first time in silence. Ara abdicated his, now usual, seat next to Vale and instead took Plucid Duru's seat aside Prode. They sat in silence for several moments until Forr came in with swollen, red eyes and took his seat.

"The woman who tried to kill Vale is named Sorpa Veneficus. I have seen her in my visions. I've come to the conclusion that she is the one who hired Scurus Subo to kill him."

Prode spoke up immediately, "Who is this Sorpa Veneficus lady? You were acting like we should all know who this is. Why have I never heard this name before?"

"Probably because it was assumed that the threat was dealt with," Vale sighed. "We have never met her before, Prode, although we only just missed having the same encounter that Forr had with her. We suspect it's been about a year since anyone has seen her."

"What do you mean?" Prode sounded frustrated. "Has she been in the castle before?"

And so, Forr began to tell the story, as best as he could remember, of the time a year ago, when he, Opo, and Queen Jenneka had first met Sorpa Veneficus, in that very same room.

"The monthly meeting of the Regulation Committee had just ended. It had been quite the lively event. Prode had just been elected Ambassador of Tacia. Vale had been invited to watch the proceedings. Prode was thrilled. He had longed for months to be put in office, but he had never expected anything so prestigious. He had sat there in his new seat, beaming during the whole meeting, and kept interjecting with nonsensical ideas and suggestions, as was expected for someone new in a position of power."

"That is not true!" Prode interrupted.

"Let him go on," Vale said.

"At the end of the meeting, the Queen dismissed the Ambassadors, but asked her bodyguard, Opo Scoloos, and I to stay behind. Before

63

we could begin discussing anything else, there was a knock on the heavy doors to the chamber and Kally, who was a new guard at the time, came in and handed Opo a small bit of parchment.

"It said that there was a woman named Sorpa Veneficus outside who had absolutely insisted on meeting Queen Jenneka in person.

"It was certainly an odd request from a lady that she'd never heard of, but the Queen was kind and inquired what the woman's purpose was at Ivory Towers.

"Opo had scoffed and said, 'It says here that she is looking for a job in the castle and that she has talents that will prove greatly useful to both you and the Royal Army.' And he asked if he should turn her away.

"The Queen seemed not at ease with the request. It was rare indeed that an Elite would apply for a post within the castle by approaching the Queen in person. After a moment, however, she asked that the lady be shown in.

"Moments later a tall, horribly thin woman strode through the chamber. She wore a long, flowing black dress that looked as though it had been moth-eaten. Her skin, what little could be seen, was the color of snow, and her long black hair was scraggly and disheveled. She glided across the room, towards the throne and I shuddered looking at her.

"She wore a black funeral veil that covered her face but one could make out that her face was just as pale, bony, and cold as the rest of her body. The sight of her sent a shiver up my spine and, glancing around; I could see that she had the same effect on Opo. Queen Jenneka, on the other hand, seemed utterly terrified. She was beginning to sweat and her nails were gripping into the armrests of her throne.

"Sorpa walked with a man who was even more gauntly thin than her. The man was shrouded in a gray cloak and wore gray bandages that covered his entire face. I felt uneasy watching these two and was surprised at myself. I'd met many different kinds of people in my travels, some unpleasing to the eye, but I'd never been put off by them. This time, however, was very different.

"Your Highness, it is a gift to be able to see you again after so long,' the woman croaked with a half bow.

"Opo and I shuddered at the same time. The woman's voice was like death. She spoke as if she was breathing with the whisper of a breeze. The Queen had composed herself and remained completely detached from the woman's eeriness and, it seemed, from what she even had to say.

"The Queen responded sweetly that the woman was mistaken, that in fact they had never met. She then asked the woman how far she had traveled to get to Ivory Towers.

"'My name is Sorpa Veneficus,' she had said 'and I have traveled a long distance to pledge my services to you. It is my belief that we have the ability to greatly assist each other in future endeavors.'

"She continued proudly and without hesitation that she came from the realm of Tacia, deep within the forests and that she'd spent several days traveling in order to meet the Queen.

"I do not need to tell any of you that the forests are not the most hospitable place for an Elite to call home. I'd never heard of living so far from civilization. The Queen asked her what her offer was to Ivory Towers that had caused her to travel so far. Sorpa smiled through her veil and apologized for her rudeness. She started to introduce her assistant but confessed she didn't even know his name. Her behavior was getting more peculiar by the moment and I could sense Opo reaching for a dagger on his belt. Sorpa turned to the frightening man beside her and ordered him to take off his mask.

"The gaunt man reached up and slowly began to remove the thick, heavy bandages that shrouded his face. When at last they were all off, he turned and faced the Queen and we all gasped.

"The man's face was rotting. Pieces of his white skull were clearly exposed and the skin that was left was a foul color of green. His eyes were sunken so far back into his head, they almost couldn't be seen. His hair was mostly gone, save for a few long strands that hung over his disintegrated face. This man, by all accounts, had to have been dead for several weeks.

"Opo drew his dagger and cursed at Sorpa. I could not believe what I was seeing. It was unreal. Flakes of rotten skin on the man's face continually flaked off as he stood there.

"Without a word, Sorpa Veneficus pointed at the skeletal man and the most horrifying thing happened. The man's beady eyes rolled even further into the back of his head and his knees buckled. He crumpled to the floor like a child's doll and a great cloud of dust came up from his body as he fell.

"I stood there with my mouth agape and announced that the man was dead, though it probably did not come as a shock to anyone.

"The Queen was furious and demanded to know what was going on. She asked Sorpa why she'd just killed this man before her and couldn't believe how audacious she was for doing so in a palace filled with security. Sorpa Veneficus just smiled. She asked for our patience before we made any conclusions. She then looked back at the man's corpse and waved her hand at him once more.

"Remarkably, like a monster out of a nightmare, the man's bones linked back together and he began to scramble to rise. He slowly crawled onto his knees and then got to his feet and faced Sorpa with no words spoken and no expression on his face. Still dead and yet not.

"Necromancy is the dark art of conjuring dead spirits for one's own personal use or gain. It is a completely unethical practice and a vile disrespect.

"She defended herself by claiming that she could not help the special power that the gods selected for her. She ranted how the spirits were happier reunited with their bodies than they were floating through the astral plane for an eternity. She claimed she was gracious enough to grant the gift of life. I disagreed and told her that most people would tell her that it was not her place to decide such things. Who was she to say that it is not one's time to die after the gods have made it so?

"The Queen began to speak to the man. I suppose she wanted to see how genuine all of this was.

"Sorpa let out a laugh that sounded like the creak of an old door and apologized to the Queen saying that the man couldn't hear or respond to what was said to him.

"When the Queen asked why, Sorpa told her that he would only obey her. She said if a person was dead for a long time, it was terribly difficult to extract their soul from the netherworld. The result that we could see was along the lines of a mindless slave. She insisted that a remnant of a soul is better than no soul at all.

"The Queen had seen enough and was furious. She told her that Ivory Towers had no use for dark arts like this. How in the world could mindless slaves, rotting away help the kingdom?

"Sorpa was persistent and remained completely nonplussed by everyone's horror. She gestured at the corpse and said it was just a small bit of what she could do. She claimed to be able to resurrect masses of corpses at a time. She shared her vision of a massive, new and improved Royal Army that could not be defeated because as soon as one falls, he would get right back up again.

"She attempted to seduce Queen Jenneka with a vision of controlling an army that is completely unstoppable.

"Judging by what we had just seen, we gathered that it would hardly be the Queen controlling this unstoppable army and Her Highness insisted that she was fully content with the army that she had and saw no reason to 'improve' them. Even more so than that, what need would she have for an invincible army? Eliantar had not been at war in over 300 years.

"The woman maintained her confidence and spoke of an ancient evil that had reawakened. Skarsend, the fallen god of death and darkness had been freed from his confines and was once again planning to destroy Eliantar. It was up to Queen Jenneka to do whatever was necessary to stop this threat to her land.

"The Queen stared hard at Sorpa Veneficus for a minute before she told her that she wanted her to leave the castle immediately and never return. She further said that she never wanted to hear that Sorpa ever used those foul powers again. She told her that her power was evil and had no place in Eliantar.

"Sorpa looked as though she couldn't believe her ears. She was in complete shock that her grand idea to help the Queen was rejected. She stared at all of our faces but found only disapproving eyes staring back. Even my fear had been overcome by my repulsion of this woman.

"She threatened that we would all regret this day and would find the time comes when the power that we shunned is the same power that destroys everything we hold dear and then it will be too late.

"As she turned to leave she again waved her hand at the corpse who, for the last time, fell to the ground in a pile of bones and dust directly in front of the crystal throne. Her long black dress and wild hair billowed around her as she stormed out of the Regulation Committee chambers. She never looked back as the heavy doors slammed behind her.

"For a few minutes we all stared at each other not knowing what to say about what had just happened. It certainly wasn't every day that such a lunatic burst through the castle doors and threatened the Queen with dark powers like these.

"The Queen asked me if I had any hints of foreboding while the woman was there and I confessed that I had not then or leading up to it, but that I would retire to my quarters and give it more thought.

"She turned to Opo and told him he knew what he needed to do. Opo nodded and left."

When Forr had finished telling his tale, Ara found his mouth hanging open. This was the most abnormal thing that he'd ever heard.

Vale said, "Mother confided to Forr that she'd wisely sent Opo to follow Sorpa and find out as much as he could such as where she was from, who her friends were, or anything of importance and then…dispose of her."

"What did he find out?" Ara asked.

"Not much," Vale sighed. "He returned a few weeks later. He had followed her, as she had claimed, deep into Tacia, into the forest. He had removed her threat from this world, but didn't give any details. I doubt that he took much glory in it. To my knowledge my mother had never asked such a favor before. Forr and my mother put it out of their minds. The deed was done. To add to that, Forr had concluded that he sensed no danger from that woman.

"I suppose warning signs were there, however. Opo was never the same after that. Even after he'd returned from killing her, he just stayed very distant at times and then overly protective, after Mother's death especially. He wouldn't let anyone leave Ivory Towers without an escort. I suppose it's possible that perhaps he found more in that forest than he was willing to let us know. Maybe he never did kill her and was too ashamed to let us know. It's difficult to guess and impossible to know, especially now that he's dead."

"Well, I've got to tell you that I would have really appreciated a little warning on all of this since I am Ambassador to Tacia," barked Prode. "Why was I kept in the dark about this?"

"Your mother wanted to keep it quiet," Forr responded. "I don't think that she thought this woman was going to be any threat once Opo went after her. Why cause a panic when there's no cause for concern? I saw no danger, but..."

"But, you're losing your foresight. We know," Prode snapped.

"Where do we go from here?" Ara asked, quickly diffusing Prode. "Should we send troops to Tacia to hunt this woman? Since Prode knows Tacian geography so well, he can supply the men with maps for the deeper, wilder parts of the realm. They can have the entire area combed in a week or two if we send out half of the Royal Guard."

"No!" said Vale. "I think that would be a very dangerous idea. I agree with my mother's thinking on this matter. We can't overreact and cause hysteria until we have more proof than just an old threat from a potentially dead woman that we can't completely justify. Forr may have had a vision about her but, and forgive me my friend, by his own admission his powers are suspect as of late. I am going to seek her out myself and see if she even still lives. It's still highly likely that Opo did, in fact, kill her."

"You mustn't!" retorted Ara. "As your personal bodyguard I have to tell you how unwise it is to let you leave this castle. Royalty has no place going on secret missions looking for dangerous criminals."

Prode leaned over and whispered, "Don't forget that he's the Crown Prince of Eliantar. I don't think you can refuse any request that he makes. I'd start packing your bags...and watching your tone."

Ara squinted his eyes at Prode, "Packing my bags? Why would I be packing my bags?"

"I agree Prode," Vale smirked. "Ara, I wouldn't want to find myself in a position of danger so I am asking that you accompany me when this year's Grim has ceased. We will not tell anyone other than Prode and Forr what our plans are so we don't cause anyone to fret without reason. It is of utmost importance that no one knows what we're doing until we apprehend the necromancer, Sorpa Veneficus."

Chapter 7

A few days after Vale had told his brother and his bodyguard about Sorpa Veneficus, the suns came out once more and almost immediately all of the snow and ice that covered Eliantar began to melt. It was the day after the thaw that Vale and Ara decided it would be best to depart.

"I think you should both travel with me by carriage," Prode had suggested, eyeing Ara up and down. "After all, we're both traveling to Tacia. I could use the company and it will be safer to travel in a group."

"For the last time, we're going on foot, Prode," Vale had repeated. "It's important that we not make a spectacle of my absence from the castle. I don't need any citizens wondering where I am and I certainly don't want them to know the name Sorpa Veneficus until we have proven that she is responsible for all of this."

After Prode left, it was Forr's turn to be a distraction. He sorely wanted to go along with Vale, and begged until finally the Prince conceded. It was after all Forr's job to advise the Prince in all of his doings. Vale had relented out of pity more than Forr's usefulness. He didn't want to be cruel, but lately with the old man's powers slipping in and out, he hated to risk being slowed down.

And so early one morning the three travelers walked out of the castle and through Castle Village before the townspeople had risen. They had chuckled at themselves as they left, since their current dress didn't match their titles. Ara wore a long, dirty looking poncho along with a brown scarf that covered the lower part of his face. Vale, on the other hand, wore a blue scarf that covered his lower face. His shoulder-length hair was pulled back into a ponytail and tucked under his scarf, as it was only for the wealthy to have such long hair. He wore a dark blue cloak that covered him from neck to feet. Vale and Ara had truly succeeded in looking every bit the part of paupers.

Only Forr remained not amused with his current appearance. He prided himself on his golden robes and looked completely miserable in his tattered rags. This only served to make Ara and Vale laugh more.

They exited together through the large city gates and looked out at the endless fields of crops and flowers that lay before them. Without a pause they continued walking towards the South.

"We'll probably want to head west after a while," Ara suggested. "I've spent a lot of time in some of the villages outside of Tacia and there are more of them outside the northern borders rather than the southern ones. We'll be able to eat and rest there."

"That's exactly why we're heading south for right now," Vale insisted. "We want to avoid as many towns and people as possible. Ara, it's deadly important that we don't get recognized so I'd like to avoid stopping in any of the cities. And please don't be confused about my knowledge of Eliantar's geography. I've spent more time touring this country than I have living the royal life in Ivory Towers."

Ara dropped his head and felt a twinge of hurt. It seemed like all that he suggested to Prince Vale in the last week was either replied with a pretentious smile or a rude disagreement. It was a sharp contrast from the kind man the Prince was prior. He began to realize why he had never allowed himself to become attracted to another before, it was too much work. When Ara raised his head again, he saw that Vale was several paces ahead of him.

"Hey! Slow down!" he called out as he jogged to catch up to Prince Vale.

"This isn't a vacation or a casual nature walk, Ara," Vale snapped. "It's very important to me that we end this quickly. We must find Sorpa and get to the bottom of this before things get worse."

They walked in silence for several hours through the grassy fields. As the suns raised high in the sky, Vale suggested they stop at a nearby orchard for a little break and some lunch. Forr, who had been walking a distance behind them, sat and ate away from Ara and Vale. He claimed being isolated helped tune his powers and seemed to be deep in concentration.

Ara was thrilled to be eating, he'd become concerned that with all of Vale's determination, he wouldn't allow any stops for food or relaxing. As they sat and ate, Ara kept stealing glances at Vale and wondered why he was attracted to him. The young man sat eating a single pear with a look of misery on his face.

"I should apologize for my sour spirits as of late," Vale mumbled quietly. "I'm not usually this nasty or on edge. I realize that I haven't been making things easy."

71

Ara looked up a bit surprised at Vale being the first to start a conversation. He didn't know what to say since it was as though the Prince had read Ara's mind. The look on Vale's face was impossible to read. He looked as though he were about to break down but was determined to stay as stony as possible.

"I don't think you're acting so terribly," Ara began, thinking before he spoke. "I have to say that I don't think this cold persona that you've taken on is really you at all. I suppose that's the way you have to be if you want to be a king or queen."

"I don't want to be a king," Vale chuckled. "And my mother was never cold a day in her life. She was the kindest and wisest woman that most people could ever hope to meet. We only ever disagreed when it came to me being King one day."

"What do you mean? Of course you want to be a king. You can have whatever you want and respect from every Elite in the land."

"When you say respect, do you refer to the kind that gets arrows launched at you?"

They both had a light chuckle, but Ara stopped immediately. He could tell this was weighing heavily on Vale.

"When you're born into wealth in a fantastic home you...rebel against it in a way. Most people would love to be a prince, but not I. When I was old enough, I got away whenever I could, taking trips and sleeping underneath the stars. So many times I would fall asleep pretending that I was a nomad with nowhere to go."

"You can't run from responsibility, Your Highness."

"And what are you doing, Ara? We've heard so little about your past before Forr asked you to become a hunter for the castle. Are you not running yourself from responsibility?"

Ara said nothing in response. He had ended up here on a whim and accepted a post that he didn't particularly want. He certainly wasn't going to be forced to have a conversation that he didn't want to have.

"And I take some offense that anyone would assume that I run from responsibility," Vale went on. "It had nothing to do with responsibility or prestige. When a person becomes the King or Queen, they lose the life that is theirs. Outside the castle it's easy for a citizen to imagine a glamorous life, but it is the life of a slave with the rest of your moments planned out for you. It is not the life that I wanted. I want to live my own life and I feel guilty that my mother and I fought so often about that."

A single tear rolled down Vale's right cheek. Ara sat in complete silence. He didn't know if he should try and comfort the Crown Prince or if he should simply mind his own business.

"I suppose it's just been a very stressful couple of months," Vale continued. I just feel a little lost with Mother being dead and then being thrust into this position that I feel I am not cut out for. It's overwhelming, that's all."

They ate the rest of their lunch in silence. Neither knew what to say and the tension was obvious. When they had finished they rose and walked out of the orchard continuing south with Forr a distance behind them, rubbing his temples and muttering to himself.

"If we go the way that I have planned," Vale started. "We should only be traveling two and a half days. I hope you don't mind avoiding all roads and sleeping under the stars, since we won't be passing any towns."

"Not at all. I spent several nights sleeping under the stars while I was pursuing Scurus Subo and of course the ten years before that."

"Of course! Odd how quickly one forgets the kindness of strangers," Vale laughed.

"I hope you don't still see me as a stranger, at least not after the past month, Ara said."

"That's the problem with Eliantar, you know" Vale complained, ignoring Ara's comment. "Let's say you come into a person's life and you give them 100 rubies, but then the next day you steal 25 rubies worth of food from their cupboards, which do you think that person will remember most about you?"

"Well that's easy. They'd remember me stealing," Ara replied without a second thought.

"That's exactly my point. No matter all the positive things you do for another, if you do one bad thing, that will be what lives in memory. It's really pathetic and it's as though we have no recognition of good anymore."

"I think you're making it a bit worse than it is," encouraged Ara. "I mean there are still plenty of good people out there making the right choices."

Vale waved him away, "I'm just trying to say that I won't forget that you tracked the man that tried to kill me. It was a truly selfless act and when all of this is over, you shall be rewarded."

"That won't be necessary. I haven't had the desire to possess large amounts of money at all my whole life."

Vale smiled and nodded. It was clear to Ara that he appreciated being with someone else who did not worship riches.

"As I had said before I am no stranger to spending my nights under the stars. Ever since my mother died, I haven't felt at home anywhere, so I just travel the countryside and work where I can so I have enough money to eat. I'm not interested in more money than that. I've grown terribly accustomed to sleeping out in fields and forests, watching the stars."

"How did your mother die, if you don't mind my asking?" Vale inquired with some nervousness in his voice.

"She caught the Iniquitous Virus," Ara said looking down. "She never told any of her friends, just kept her distance so no one else would get sick. She hid the symptoms so one day she was fine and then she was dead. I had found a job and saved up enough money to buy a small cottage of my own just down the street from my mother. I was so excited to tell her," he began to trail off.

"That was when I found her. She was lying in bed, completely white and unmoving. I just couldn't stay there any longer. I've been on the road ever since. She was the only one that I ever had…I never knew my father."

"Who does? Almost no one knows both of their parents. Procreation is just a form of slavery to keep the Elite race going."

"That's not true!" Ara said in shock.

"Yes it is. We're homosexual by nature but of course we can't have children naturally. Paying a poor member of the opposite sex to provide us with a child and then to disappear forever is just a way to keep those with noble blood feeling like they'll live on forever. Our race goes on because of arrogance. The poor people make deals amongst themselves to have children only out of necessity, unless they're unlucky enough to be heterosexual. They reach out to their neighbor to help them bring a child into the world to run their farms when they're no longer able to while the wealthy have children to pass on their infinite wealth. It's all about money, while those without are left to do what is necessary to survive."

Vale had a point. In general, children were born either as symbols of wealth or as a necessary evil to keep up the hard work that kept their aging mother or father fed. It was a cynical approach, but it was truthful.

"My mother's name was Jenneka. She was a beautiful, petite woman with long black hair and a magnificent spirit. She had only lived 44 years before she got…sick."

"Got sick with what?" Ara asked quietly.

"She…um…" Vale choked. "Oddly enough, she also became infected with the Iniquitous Virus.

"What?!" gasped Ara. "That's not possible. They wiped out that out completely a few years ago. Even when my mother had it, they had a cure for those wealthy enough to afford it."

"It's more obvious than ever that you've never been to Castle Village before," Vale snapped. "We had a resurgence in our area recently. No one saw it coming. They had no cure ready for it."

The Prince dropped the heavy bag he was carrying and waved to Forr. He was apparently done walking for the day.

"It's nearly dark," he grumbled not looking up. We should make camp here, while we're completely surrounded by fields."

They didn't speak as they spent the next hour unpacking their bags and kindling a small fire. When they were both done, they lied on opposite sides of the fire staring at the sky. Forr had already gone to sleep away from the fire. Being so old, the day's journey had been hard on him. The stars had speckled the sky the moment both suns set. It was a perfectly clear night and both could see the millions of lights spread across the black sky. After what seemed like an eternity, Vale spoke.

"I miss my mother so much. Your mother sounded lovely and you must miss her terribly."

Ara was glad that the ice had broken once more. He always felt so torn with the Crown Prince. Deep down he knew that Vale was a kind, sensitive man, but the walls that he had built up made it near impossible to get to him.

"Apology accepted," Ara whispered back. "I know it must be very hard for you, with your mother passing so recently. I remember how hard it was for me. I still don't feel that I've completely accepted it and it happened ten years ago. I'm sorry that she became ill after the world assumed it was dead and gone."

Vale sat up and looked at Ara. I haven't been completely honest with you Ara and I really should be."

Ara sat up too, looking anxiously at the Prince. "I want you to be honest as well. My job is to protect you. Please don't keep secrets from me."

"My mother killed herself," Vale began. "She had been sick for a few months but always remained very optimistic. She was sure that they would find a cure and everything would be alright. Then one day, after being in the market, I'd come home and she was gone. Forr had a sense that all was not right and ran to the throne room to advise my mother and found that the large colored glass window behind the throne had been shattered."

Vale began weeping and Ara sat in silence, again unsure of what to say or do to improve the situation. After a moment and a drink of water Vale continued, though still unable to look Ara in the eye.

"I've never shown you the throne room or even been in there myself since then. I do all business in the Regulation Committee room. Even though they fixed the window all I can picture…"

"I don't understand. What happened?"

"It seems that Mother, for some reason that only she'll ever know, threw herself out of the window, onto the briar patch twelve stories down."

Ara got up from where he sat and sat next to Vale, wrapping a muscular arm around the Prince's shoulders. Vale turned and cried into his new friend's shoulder.

"No one outside the castle ever heard that story before," he continued to sob. "The official story is that she died unexpectedly and the gossip is that she succumbed to the Iniquitous Virus, but no one suspects what really happened. It's been killing me ever since it happened. My mother was never sad a day in her life. Then for some reason she kills herself. How do you ever explain or recover from an event like that?"

The two fell asleep just like that. Vale, with his head buried in Ara's shoulder sobbing himself to sleep and Ara consoling the handsome young man who had finally opened up to him. As Ara's eyes closed, all he could think of was how sad he felt for the Prince to have to carry such a burden.

Ara shut his eyes and took a few breaths preparing for slumber when he felt a hand move from his shoulder down to his chest. His whole body tensed as the hand slowly traced light circles all along his muscular torso. His eyes shot open as he realized Vale couldn't be doing this in his sleep.

In the dim light from the dying fire, Ara could see Vale still lying on his shoulder staring at him with a look in his eyes that Ara had never seen the young Prince have before.

Slowly Vale sat up and swung his right leg over Ara. He leaned down and exhaled his hot breath into Ara's ear, who remained unable to say or do a thing.

"I've been treating you poorly," Vale breathed still staring at his friend with a smolder. "I'm going to make up for that now as long as it's okay with you."

When Ara said nothing, Vale again placed his hand on Ara's chest and began caressing slowly downward. Ara gasped as Vale's hand found his throbbing warmth and grasped it with determination. With a smile of lust Vale bent slowly forward, closing his eyes and preparing to place his soft lips against Ara's.

Ara snapped upright with a start. He looked around and felt his hopes crash to the floor as he took in the daylight. It had only been a dream he realized when he saw Vale and Forr were already up and packing both of their bags. The first sun hung in the sky warming the rough ground that Ara lay upon.

"Are you alright?" Vale asked smiling briefly at Ara. "You look as though you were kicked in the chest just now. We need to move on. We're already behind schedule and need to catch up."

With a groan of disgust Ara rose to his feet and took his bag. He tried his best to smile back at Vale and not imagine what his lips felt like or what his body would've looked like as his clothes were ripped from his body.

Forr was reclusive again this morning. He was polite enough but wasn't anxious to stay too close to the men. Ara knew without asking that no further premonitions had come to Forr, even after a full day and night of concentrating.

A few minutes later they were walking again towards the South. Ara had noticed a slight change in Vale. Perhaps he had begun to crack through some of the thick mental barriers that the Prince had erected. In place of the short, stern demands that Prince Vale used to make, were kinder exchanges. The two were finally getting along and Ara was pleased. They had more in common than either of them originally believed.

After a few hours, they reached the end of the fields of crops and flowers and began to cross open plains. For as far as their eyes could see was nothing but emerald green grass. It wasn't long, however, before Ara noticed a man crossing the grasslands toward them.

"This is not good," Vale said. "We have worked so hard to avoid any other Elites. We should divert our path a bit. We don't want to enter into any unnecessary conversations."

It was a loss. No matter how they tried to veer away, the man was continuing to come toward them.

"Hello there," he called and the two stopped in their tracks with Forr still a ways back.

"Let me do the talking," Vale whispered. "Please don't say anything. I'll take care of this."

"I'm so sorry to bother you gentlemen," the man began. "But, I felt it would be important to warn you as one traveler to another."

Ara looked the man up and down. He looked utterly ridiculous. He wore billowing robes of a deep purple color and a veil that covered the lower portion of his face. He was dressed far too regally for a traveler. Perhaps he was a noble of some kind, judging by the elegant robes as well as the long, sleek, black hair that was tied back. He looked to be about forty years of age and seemed to be an attractive man, if not for the over-the-top way he presented himself.

"Please go on," Vale told the man, making an effort to disguise his voice.

"I must warn you about dangers present in Quale and urge you not to go there."

Vale breathed a sigh of relief, "Quale is not our destination, but if I may be so bold, what is going on in Quale?"

His eyes looked frantically around, "I've never before seen a place so beautiful, so filled with evil. There is dark magic there now and…something else. I know I must sound crazy, but I tell you swearing to the gods that the dead walk in Quale."

Ara and Vale exchanged a quick, worried glance before Vale looked back.

"Well, sir" Vale said with a slight chuckle. "Whether we believe that or not, Quale is not our destination, but we thank you for the warning."

The strange man nodded his head and walked on towards the North, his plum robes flowing behind him. Ara and Vale walked for several moments without speaking. Forr remained oblivious to what had transpired. There was almost no reason to speak, for they both knew that a change of plans had occurred and where they were headed.

"Why are we changing direction?" Forr asked.

"There's been a change of plans, Forr" Vale answered. "Sorpa Veneficus is in Quale."

"There was an odd vibe about that man," Forr mumbled. "I sensed something…"

But, Vale and Ara were already several paces ahead and Forr shook his head and began to follow.

Chapter 8

Quale was more beautiful than Ara had remembered and he was thrilled that they had not had to pass through his old hometown. Little by little grassy fields became damp and puddles began to form. Before long there was more water than ground. Thin strips of land connected the very few islands that existed in this water world.

"On the sixth day of creation Bydra, the water god, stepped foot on the new world," Forr began. Ara and Vale exchanged a quick glance and smirk.

"Legend says he is the most patient and thoughtful of all the gods. They say he made the choice appear as a wise old human man. Where the others had been young and attractive people or powerful elements when they appeared, this god most respected wisdom.

"He only briefly surveyed what the other gods had done because unlike the others who were so obsessed with competition, he had bided his time imagining what his vision of paradise on the new planet would be. He already knew that he wanted to name his realm Quale and that it would be filled with the most beautiful, cerulean waters.

"And so, in very little time, the area to the east of Tacia and south of Steedo was filled with water. Sapphire streams and rivers trickled gently into the most peaceful, massive lakes. All of this, he kept away from the furious oceans that surrounded the land they'd created. His water would be enjoyed by all that lived there and never feared. There was very little land to be found in all of Quale by the time the water god was done.

"He looked around; surveying the beauty that he had created and he immediately knew what was missing. There was no life present and even though he planned on filling the waters with fishes, he feared it may not be enough. The only sounds that could be heard were of the many waterfalls splashing in the distance. Most of the planets that the gods had created revolved around water, and usually needed it more than the other elements to stay alive. So, it didn't seem right to have so much space be surrounded by water and have no living beings. Sitting down, the god began to meditate on what would be the best possible organism to create for this kind of environment.

"They should be fish-like and scaled, the god thought to himself. They should also be transparent so as to avoid being hunted by another creature that may enter this part of the world. He knew also that he wanted them to be highly intelligent. They must be as smart if not smarter than any human that the gods had ever created before.

"The water god had long gone before the day was even half past and already the Fonnes were flourishing. They were the height, weight, and size of a human but had many attributes only common to fish. The Fonnes possessed scaled, transparent skin, with large bulbous eyes. They lived underwater only coming to the surface to jump through the air, make brief conversation, or sing, because if there was one thing that Fonnes above all others were known for, it was their singing. Seductive and haunting at the same time, Fonnes drew as many creatures to the water world as the lakes and streams themselves did.

"This pleased the water god and he knew at once that his days of carefully planning his world had paid off. Quale was a place of beauty that all would cherish above all other realms. He knew that thinking this way reduced him to the same level as his siblings; still he wasn't invincible in the face of vanity."

"Thank you, Forr. What a charming story to hear as we arrive in Quale," Vale smiled.

"I love Quale," Forr beamed. And I'm not alone. Look at all of those beautiful manors on the various islands. Everyone dreams of spending their final years here."

"A pity few are able to afford it," Ara responded with a hint of spite. "Most Elites who get to see it here only do so because they have to fish for a living."

"I hardly see how that can be helped," Forr scoffed. "There are few pieces of land in Quale. Naturally the cost to live here would be exorbitant."

Ara had been here often, when he was a fisherman in his small village. He enjoyed the clear waters but he loved the Fonnes. The Fonnes were very human-like in size and intelligence, but also closely resembled fish with their massive, unblinking eyes and scaled body. They were almost impossible to see when they were submerged as their bodies were a transparent color of blue. When he could make them out, Ara had loved to watch them swim. They were amazingly fast and swam through the water faster than a horse runs on land.

Whereas Eliantar's other creatures were nasty or timid, the Fonnes loved humans and due to their high intelligence loved to stop and talk when Elites were around.

Ara was counting on being able to talk with a few Fonnes about the "dark magic" that was present in Quale. He immediately walked up to the first large lake he saw and crouched at the edge, with Vale and Forr following in tow.

The water was beautiful. It was the lightest blue color and looked terribly inviting. Ara's favorite pastime was spending days swimming and sleeping on one of the lakes' beaches. It was always warm and relaxing and there was an intoxicating feel from the gentle waves that were produced that allowed Ara to feel calm.

He smiled now, watching the water. The suns reflection on the lake's surface made it sparkle like a billion sapphires. He was so lost in thought that he almost jumped when three very excited Fonnes burst their heads out of the water, only inches from his face.

"Oh…Hello," he chuckled. "I was wondering if you could help us. We've heard from a passerby that there may be invaders in Quale and that they may be using black magic on the land."

"We know nothing about any invaders," one of them answered. "You're the first Elites that we've seen since Grim. The rest have not made their way back since the thaw."

The three Fonnes reached up and began to pat Vale and Ara approvingly before sinking back into the lake and blasting back away from the edge.

"Where do we go from here?" Ara asked. Do you think the man in purple was telling us the truth?"

"I can't imagine what he would have to gain from getting us to Quale," said the Prince thoughtfully. "Quale is a massive place to search. We can't possible rely on what the first few Fonnes have seen. I think we should at least investigate a bit for ourselves before we move back towards Tacia."

Without another word, Ara jumped into the cerulean waters and began to backstroke towards the opposite end of the lake. Vale looked like he didn't know what to make of this.

"What are you doing?" Vale called out still aghast.

"Come on," smiled the bodyguard. "By the time we get to a land bridge and walk across, we'll have lost an hour."

"I do believe that I'll take my chances and walk," Forr said, shaking his head. "I fear that I am not much of a swimmer. I shall find you further on."

With that Vale dove in and the two raced each other to get to the other side of the lake. Ara was truly surprised at what a good swimmer Vale was. He'd lunge deep under the water, appearing again a minute later, many yards ahead. When they climbed out on the other side they took a moment to catch their breath.

"You seem surprised. I told you that I liked to escape the castle as much as possible. Can you think of a more magical place to be?"

Ara had felt a little uncomfortable around the Prince since his vivid dream the previous night. He wanted so much to pull Vale underwater and kiss his handsome face, but knew it was not his place. Also, he needed to keep his mind on why they were here, which was not to enjoy the water. Turning to face what lie before them, Ara groaned when he saw a river on the other side of this thin strip of land.

"What do you expect?" laughed Vale, seeing the look on his face. "We're in the water realm!"

They began to wade across the river. It may not have been as deep as the lake had been, but the current was very strong. This caused them to have to wade very slowly across the rocks, to avoid being pulled downstream. As they crossed, they realized they had company waiting for them on the grass.

Lenta Benigg was smiling as they stepped out onto land, "I was in the area and some Fonnes told me that you were here. I do like to greet the first Elites of the new year, but I'm quite surprised to see Your Highness. If I may ask though, why are you dressed like that?"

Vale shushed her, "We're in disguise and nobody's to know who we are. Ara and I are conducting an investigation of the most serious kind."

Lenta stared from Vale to Ara, who wouldn't move his eyes from the ground. Her young, usually radiant face was furrowed with suspicion. She picked up the ends of her electric blue dress and stepped closer to Vale, pushing a few stray curls from her face."

"I can see that you are serious," she whispered. "As Ambassador of Quale, I wish you'd share with me of what purpose your investigation is here."

"I'm afraid that's confidential even from you," Vale responded. "Please don't mistake me, Lenta. We should only be here a short time and then we will be on our way."

Lenta looked a bit hurt, "I care not if you are here an hour or a lifetime. As a member of the Royal Family, you're certainly always welcome here. My concern is that a wrong has occurred in my domain and you're keeping it hidden from me."

"It's a training exercise," Ara burst in. "As you know, I am training the Prince in self-defense and had thought a change of environment was needed."

Lenta eyed him suspiciously before bowing to Prince Vale and walking off.

"She didn't seem to believe us," Ara said a short while later as they swam across another lake.

"To be honest, I would've been disappointed if she hadn't been suspicious," Vale laughed. "At times I really think that Lenta is the only Ambassador with any sense."

"If you don't like the Ambassadors, why don't you appoint new ones?" Ara asked.

"Once an Ambassador is appointed by a ruler, they are in office until they either resign or pass on. The thing that's always annoyed me about it is that they aren't appointed based on any personal merit or experience with their realm at all."

"What?" Ara exclaimed. "Well how are they chosen?"

"Let me give you a hint," Vale riddled. "Lenta's unique ability is that she has control over water."

"You're kidding," Ara laughed. They're chosen only because their power reflects one of the elements?"

"That's right," Vale chuckled back. "It's been that way since the beginning and as outdated as it is, I couldn't get my mother to change it. She said it was tradition. I suppose that they all have qualities that are…beneficial for an Ambassador, but Lenta Benigg has always been, I think, a very wise choice."

"If you don't mind me asking," Ara began cautiously. "How did your brother get selected for Tacia's Ambassador? I don't mean it disrespectfully, I just mean that I have seen his power and he has no control over plants."

The two finally climbed ashore and took a few minutes catching their breath. They were both happy to be on land and drying under the hot suns. When they could breathe again, Vale responded.

"I take no disrespect to your question and I don't think that Prode would either. The former Ambassador died about two years ago. My mother had spent years attempting to groom me to be ruler of Eliantar but, as you know, I wanted no part of it. It was my foolish assumption at the time that if I bargained with her and made a smaller sacrifice, I could appease her. So, I volunteered to be Ambassador of Tacia and told her that I was so sure I would make a better Ambassador than King. I suggested that Prode be King in my place and asked if I could abdicate the throne to him."

"And was that what that he wanted to do?" Ara inquired knowing very well the answer.

"What 18-year-old doesn't want to be a king or queen? I could tell he was ready to jump at the chance. But, Mother wasn't convinced and nothing in my future changed. However, that did give her the idea to give Prode a position of power. She had said something about it being important that her two sons work together and influence our world. That was the one time that Mother was able to overlook the tradition of appointing Ambassadors."

"Is he any good?" Ara asked with a hint of doubt. "It's just that he doesn't seem to take much seriously."

"Surprisingly he is good," Vale laughed. "I had my reservations as well but when it was presented to him, he leapt at the chance. The Arbestees seem to like him very much and his reports on the forests are always positive. Don't ask me how he makes it work with that infantile sense of humor, but he does make it work."

They slowly rose from the ground, both knowing they had to keep moving along. When Ara turned he gasped aloud. Vale looked up to see what was so shocking. There, off in the distance, was a magnificent fortress, the color of cobalt. Though not as large or as breathtaking as Ivory Towers, this structure was truly breathtaking.

"Is that...?" Ara began overwhelmed with the building's beauty.

"It is," answered Vale. "The Water Citadel, like all of the other Citadels, has been around for nearly 1,300 years. King Rynell VII the Lucky had them constructed as a reminder of Elite influence after he'd grown tired of the bickering between Elites and the tribes. He personally invaded the lands and slaughtered the tribes' leaders. He forced those that were left to sign a new treaty. The Citadels were built so the Ambassadors could stay in their land permanently to uphold the peace. Thankfully, we have much newer treaties that were made out of peace rather than force."

"I had heard the stories," said Ara with his mouth still agape. "I never knew if they were true or not. Nobody I know has ever seen one of these temples before. I thought I'd heard once that they were invisible to the eye of an Elite."

"Stuff of legends," Vale mumbled. "People believe that rumor because very few Elites actually enter the elemental realms and when they do they don't venture very far. The Citadels were not made invisible, but they were created deep in their respected realm so that intruders wouldn't be able to access them easily.

"The bridge for the temple is hidden now, as it often is. It's the only means of access to the Water Citadel. Bydra Lake isn't like the other bodies of water in Quale. The water pulls you down so strongly that you wouldn't get more than a few strokes in before you'd be sucked to the bottom."

"Have you been to all of the Citadels?"

"No, not all of them," answered Vale with a small smile. "There are some that are situated in inhospitable environments. And then again maybe it's the Ambassador that makes it inhospitable."

They both laughed at this. Ara could imagine which temples he'd been to versus the ones he hadn't. His mind drifted back to his brief experience in Fornar. He wouldn't have wanted to travel any deeper through that world, especially with the fanged Lexerros stalking around.

"I believe I have had a change of heart," Vale said thoughtfully. "Since we are here, perhaps it would be wise to go into the Citadel and wait for Lenta to return. It's impossible to search this realm by ourselves and time is wasting by the moment. I do trust her and I think she may be able to help us."

Ara was looking forward to it. He had been fascinated at the sight of the Citadel and now he would have the opportunity to see it firsthand. He imagined the walls and floors made of sapphires and diamonds. He pictured swimming pools and glass roofs as far as the eye could see. He became a little concerned with himself as he realized he was thinking of material things, which he swore he would never do. It was becoming increasingly hard though when surrounded by so many palaces and paradise locales.

Vale turned towards the fortress and clapped his hands three times. With that a planked bridge rose from the depths of the Bydra Lake. Looking towards the Citadel, Ara surmised that the walk across the fragile-looking bridge was a little less than a mile. He doubted that they got many visitors here, but then again, they probably wanted it that way.

Vale began to cross first, walking quickly across the bridge. Ara followed in terror. He took the smallest baby steps and clung to the ropes for dear life. The planks were very feeble and the waters were dangerous, he'd been warned. More than once Vale had to stop and wait for Ara to catch up to him. Try as he might, he couldn't get his eyes off of the dark lake.

This liquid was nothing like the other bodies of water in Quale. It was terribly dark in color and looked more like oil than water. Trying not to focus on the lake, Ara looked straight ahead at the Citadel.

A sharp whistle from behind, made them both turn around. There, back on the thin strip of shore only 30 yards away, stood a man clad in purple robes with a purple veil.

"Your Highness, it's that man we met," exclaimed Ara.

"Sir," Vale called out. "I know that you had warned us to stay away from here, but my friend and I felt it may be important to come to the aid of any innocents."

"This is a trap," Ara muttered shaking his head.

The man said nothing but looked up to the sky. Immediately the puffy white clouds turned into black sheets and thunder rumbled in the distance. Winds began to pick up and pull at the shoddy bridge.

"I've come for the Prince and any of you who try to stop me had better not mind a burial at sea."

Chapter 9

"Now what shall we do?" asked Ara turning to the Prince. He didn't have time to get an answer as a barrage of lightning bolts flew down from the sky, striking the black lake.

"I apologize for my deception," the man yelled sarcastically over the howling winds. "My name is Destor Caelu and I only want Prince Vale. No one has to be hurt."

"We need to figure out how we're going to get out of this and fast," Vale screamed. "I don't think I need to tell you that we don't stand a chance against him on this bridge."

No sooner had he spoken as giant raindrops began to fall from the sky pounding the ground, lake, and the flimsy bridge. They held onto dear life as they swung from side to side.

"I'm open any to suggestions that Your Highness may have," Ara retorted.

"Well, there's no way we'll make it to the Citadel," he yelled back, trying to make himself heard over the gale force winds. "He obviously controls the weather so Lenta may be able to help with that."

Ara looked at Vale completely confused, but when he turned back he saw what Vale was talking about. Behind the man in purple, Lenta was running to get to the scene and she looked furious.

With her dress billowing around her, Lenta closed her eyes and outstretched her arms. Ara figured that trying to stay concentrated through the torrential downpour wasn't easy, but if she could succeed, they may have a few seconds to get off the bridge before it collapsed.

Moments later, all the raindrops stopped their descent in midair before swarming around Destor. He cried out in shock at the barrage of water pellets as Ara and Vale rushed across the bridge to shore. With a wave of her drenched arm, two giant waves leapt from the lake and crushed down on Destor bringing him to his knees.

An abrupt lightning bolt ripped through the sky, striking the bridge where it connected to the Citadel. Ara and Vale touched land just as what was left of the bridge met its watery grave.

Ara ran up to Destor, as he was slowly rising to his feet, and brought an elbow down hard onto his head. As the man in purple again stumbled back, Ara kicked him hard knocking him onto his back. Stalking towards him, he bent down and grabbed him by his violet robes, holding him up.

"Tell us what you're doing here," roared Ara with fire in his eyes. "Why are you trying to kill us?"

Ara could see the hatred in Destor's black eyes. He looked furious and not yet ready to concede defeat. His plum veil may have covered the lower part of his face, but Ara could tell from his eyes that the danger was not yet over.

"You have no idea the amount of evil that surrounds this land even now," hissed Destor. "Even if you would be able to stop me, you're too late. The wheels are in motion and everything you know about Eliantar is about to become ash. You foolishly stare at me as though I am your greatest enemy but I assure you there is a greater threat than myself right now."

"What plan? What wheels are in motion?" Ara barked. "Answer me this second."

Destor just cackled and grabbed onto Ara's wrists. Pure, white energy crackled from his hands into Ara's body. Ara screamed in pain as he let Destor go. Destor dropped to the ground but held firm to the bodyguard as he unloaded electricity into his enemy's body.

"Do something," screamed Vale to Lenta. "I'm trying to pull them apart with my mind, but the electricity has them fused together."

"There isn't a thing I can do," panicked Lenta. "If I get one of them wet, it'll electrify them both and Ara will die."

Before Vale could respond, the sky turned a hot white-blue and an energy bolt flew towards the ground striking Ara hard. Destor and Ara fell apart. Ara, who had stopped screaming, collapsed to the ground, unmoving. Smoke rose up from his burnt body, as Destor stepped over it, clearly pleased with himself.

"Prince Vale, you are coming with me. Ambassador Benigg, please stand down and Quale will be spared," Destor Caelu commanded.

Lenta pushed past Vale in a fury. Her normally beautiful curly, dark hair hung like a wet nest around her face. Her pristine dress was drenched and torn. The kindness and wisdom that usually showered her face was gone. She now appeared to Vale like a destitute person who was ready to kill for scraps of food.

"Quale will be spared?" she snarled. "Moments ago you threatened that the entire world would be burned to the ground and now you try to bribe me with sparing me? You'll have to forgive me if I don't believe you."

"So be it," sighed Destor blasting Lenta with sparks from his hands. Lenta flew back and hit the ground hard.

Destor didn't see the massive tidal wave rise that Lenta had conjured before, rising from his right until it was too late. It began to sweep him away until he got his footing back. When he rose, he was greeted by a fist to the face from Ara.

"If you're going to kill me," he said with a smile. "You should make sure that I'm really dead."

He began to pummel the villain into submission. Vale had rushed over to help Lenta to her feet and the two watched as the man with the tattered and torn clothes beat the man in purple regality.

"He heals even more quickly than he gave himself credit for," Lenta said with a weak smile. "That will certainly come in handy with this monster."

Ara Tataman wasn't happy to be fighting. He had always avoided conflict with others, but his job was to protect Prince Procer. What was clear was that there seemed to be more and more enemies making that task difficult. In his experience most Elites were gentle, tranquil beings but within the last month or two he felt like he'd been exposed to a pack of savages.

Destor's face was beginning to bleed. His once regal robes were becoming torn and dirty. Destor Caelu clearly had had enough as he blasted Ara with another bolt of energy from his hands, knocking him back a few steps. Thankfully, it wasn't as strong as some of the other blasts he'd thrown.

Before Ara could react, an immense wind ripped through Quale. Ara stepped back even more, rooting his feet as firmly into the ground as he could. In a matter of seconds he felt as though he were about to be lifted right off his feet. Glancing around, it appeared that Lenta and Vale were having the same problem.

"Everybody relax," Vale bellowed.

Ara could see that Vale was concentrating hard. He must actually be trying to use his powers to keep them rooted to the ground. Ara's heart went out to him, because it seemed that, try as he might he was fighting a losing battle.

Destor laughed as a miniature funnel surrounded him and then lifted him into the air. He hovered there several yards above the heroes, cackling manically in the midst of his minute whirlwind. All around the skies were pure black and there were no signs of life to be seen. The Fonnes were smart enough to know when it was best to stay underwater.

"You can't keep this up forever young Prince," Destor mocked from above. "Your powers aren't as strong as mine and as soon as they slip, all three of you will be sucked into oblivion."

"Gods help us but he's right," grunted Vale, with his eyes still closed. "We're going to have to come up with a plan. There's no way I can hold us down much longer and I can feel that his power is only getting stronger."

"I could get a wave up that high," Lenta suggested. "But, it would have to be very strong and it would just drown us all when it came back down."

They all glanced around at each other for a moment unsure of what to do before Ara Tataman made his suggestion. If there was one thing Ara avoided when possible it was confrontation. But, that being said, if there was one thing Ara respected, it was the promise of one friend to another friend.

"Vale," he called. "When he strikes me down, I want you to release me from your hold."

"No!" screamed the Prince. "I won't do that. You'll get yourself killed. You're not invincible, Ara."

"Please just do it," Ara pleaded. "That will give you the chance you need to knock him out of the sky."

Before Vale could respond, Ara called up to Destor, "You're not taking the Prince, Destor. You'll have to kill me first."

Destor Caelu snarled from high in the sky. His bruised face contorted into a fit of rage as his scrapped, purple robes blew around him. Lightning once again flickered through the sky.

"There is something so genuine and yet naïve about an Elite peasant who is so eager to die for their master," he mocked. "I've made it quite clear that all I want is to take Prince Vale with me and yet you still stand in my way. Give the gods my best!"

The lightning bolt raged through the sky, flying right in front of Destor. It struck Ara hard and the sky lit up a brilliant color of blue.

Vale closed his eyes tight as he allowed his power to let go of Ara's body and concentrate more on Lenta's and his own. Just before he had released his bodyguard, he'd felt it tighten tremendously, then go limp, before it started to collapse. Now he watched as it was whipped like a paper toy, high into Destor's funnel. He saw the cold man in purple watch the lifeless body revolve around him, up and up. When at last it reached the top of the cyclone, Destor raised his purple-clad arms towards the body and then snapped them down, forcing the wind to propel Ara down hard on terrain.

Without realizing what he was doing Crown Prince Vale thrust all of his powers on the floating Destor, who had not expected this. Completely caught off guard, he stumbled back into his own wind storm and was sent plummeting back to the ground as well, hitting it just as hard as Ara did. The tornado was gone in an instant just like that. Vale and Lenta hadn't even been pulled into it when he released them from his grip.

They rushed over to Ara's side and knelt near him. Vale grabbed the man's hand and held it tight, Lenta Benigg began examining him. She felt for a pulse and then began to hold her hand around his face, presumably for a sign of breathing.

"I'm fine," came a small choke from Ara. "I just want to lie here for a moment if that's alright with you two."

"What were you thinking?" Vale snapped. "We don't know what your threshold is. Either the lightning or the fall could have killed you."

"Well, I was obviously hoping it wouldn't," Ara was grunting still in pain. "I knew that if I could free up some of your energy that you were using on me, you could knock him out of the air. Of the three of us, you were our only chance."

"Well please don't do that again. I truly thought you were dead."

"And so he will be," roared a hate-filled voice from behind. "The water woman will be joining him as well, I can assure you of that."

They jumped up and spun around. They didn't have to guess who would be standing there. Destor Caelu couldn't have looked worse for the wear. He was now bleeding heavily from his head and his clothes were shreds now, only memories of what they once were.

"Since you've both been so insistent on not handing over the Prince to me, I'm afraid you'll all have to be executed," he shouted, sounding completely insane. I didn't want to so boldly commit an act of treason, but I feel like I don't have a choice any longer."

"Look at his eyes," Lenta whispered. "He's completely losing his mind right in front of us. It doesn't even look like he's talking to us."

Before she could say anymore, the heavens opened up once more and gigantic hail began to wail on the small island and the surrounding bodies of water. Vale, Ara, and Lenta dodged as much as they could, but knew it wouldn't do too much. Across Bydra Lake, they could hear the sounds of hail smashing through the windows and tearing apart the tin roof and eaves of the Citadel. They all cringed at the sharp sound of twisting metal and flinched in fear as they realized that the chunks of ice were falling more prevalently and in bigger sizes.

Ara felt himself launched back into the black water and knew that Vale had propelled all of them into the lake. He knew there weren't other options to avoid being crushed by hail, but this lake was death as well. All he saw was black as he felt himself being tugged down. He struggled in the vacuum of wetness and fought to stay on top of the water.

Ara used all of his energy to keep his head above water and could just see Destor Caelu standing at the edge of the black lake watching these three struggle to keep from drowning.

"You all fight in there as if you stand a chance," he began to mock. "I'm no expert in geography, but I do know that getting into Bydra's Lake is a death sentence. I think I'm going to give you a gift, because I hate to see suffering. Please consider it a parting gift. Don't worry, Prince Vale. I'll have you out in a moment."

With that he waved his hands and a powerful wind blew from the sky and slammed into the lake. Seconds later the water began to move in a spherical motion. A giant whirlpool had formed and pulled them each into the abyss, one after the other.

Ara was the last to go under. He struggled and pushed against the invisible forces, but the more he fought it, the deeper he sank. He looked up for a brief moment and saw nothing. There was no sign of sunlight. There was no sign of anything and so he closed his eyes and let the water bring him closer and closer to the bottom.

It was only a few seconds after he had accepted his fate that he felt himself being pulled in the opposite direction. He supposed he was becoming so delirious that he didn't know which direction was up anymore. Then, before he had time to think another thought, he felt the sun and air hit his face. He was out of the lake and then…slam!

He hit the sand with a hard crack and realized that he and his friends had been carried in on a large wave.

"How…" he sputtered, trying to get all of the water out of his lungs. It felt like he had drunk most of the lake.

"Well," began Lenta, trying to appear collected. "I do control water, after all."

Ara remembered Destor and jumped to his feet but, seeing no sign of him, he rushed over to Vale's side and helped him up.

"Where could he have gone so quickly?" Lenta asked.

"That's my doing," Forr Suosor answered. None of them had noticed the old man at first. "A group of Fonnes led me here. We saw from a distance what was transpiring and they swam here and launched an assault on the purple man. By the time I'd reached this island they had chased him off and you were coming ashore. What happened?"

Lenta began to explain as Ara brushed the damp hair from Vale's face, staring into his eyes. Vale stared back for a moment and gave a faint smile.

"Are you alright, Your Highness?" Ara asked filled with concern for the young man he clutched.

"I'm fine," Vale whispered back, before blushing and looking away. Feeling his protector's eyes still on him, he pulled out of his grip and stepped away. "Thank you Ara. I feel much better now."

The conversation between Lenta and Forr snapped Ara back to attention and he helped Vale to his feet. Another awkward conversation quickly ended!

"Lenta, that cannot be possible," Forr exclaimed. "The powers that you claim this man had are unheard of. We all have unique talents, but this is unprecedented. Are you quite sure Quale wasn't just having a storm at the same time?"

"I am quite sure. And you are correct. I have never before heard of powers as great as this. They were immense and he gave me the feeling that he may actually be holding back."

"Now he's gone and we don't know where he's going or why he wanted Vale," Ara jumped in.

"He's going to Steedo," Forr announced. "I know my visions have been intermittent, but I can sense him heading there as we speak."

Vale and Ara didn't need to say what they were both thinking. They had originally believed that Sorpa Veneficus was somewhere in the forest realm of Tacia and now Destor was headed to Steedo. It made little sense, but it seemed clear that the two were in league with each other.

"Without asking Vale, I can assume that we'll be heading to Steedo from here," sighed Ara.

"What?!" gasped Lenta. "You can't actually be serious about following him there. Send the Royal Guard. Send all of them. The Royal Family does not apprehend their own criminals, Vale!"

"As I told you when we first arrived," Vale said quietly, not meeting the Ambassador's eyes. "This is a matter that I do not want others aware of but us. Please understand that if I get the Royal Guard involved, all of Eliantar will begin wondering what is going on."

"Well, what is going on?" Lenta responded breathlessly. "You still haven't told me what you're doing."

"I believe now more than ever that some terrible thing is going on that has the potential to end all that we've built in the past 2,000 years," Vale said. "I fear this may be beyond an assassination attempt. I can't risk the entire world going into a tailspin of panic, until I have confirmed my beliefs. When the time is right, we will escalate our resources, but until then I ask that you please keep this between us and let Ara and I continue to investigate what exactly is going on in my kingdom."

They said their goodbyes a few minutes later and Vale and Ara, with Forr in tow, began walking north towards the wind realm of Steedo. Ara turned around after a short time and saw Lenta staring after them with a look of appalled confusion on her young, pretty face. Ara shrugged back at her. He meant no disrespect, but he was clearly just as confused about what he was about to face as Lenta was.

Chapter 10

After several days of walking and swimming with limited rest, both Ara and Vale finally noticed that the landscape was beginning to change. Lakes and streams began to give way to more mountainous terrain. A powerful wind had also picked up, which made both of them shutter.

Under normal circumstances, Ara wouldn't have minded visiting Steedo, the wind realm, but after their encounter with Destor, he wasn't thrilled to be surrounded by any type of breeze or weather-related occurrence. Come to think of it, the thought of any inclement weather made Ara's stomach turn. To lighten the mood a bit, Forr began his history lesson of Steedo, to which Ara and Vale only half listened.

"On the fifth day of creation, the suns rose as the goddess of wind, Zefra, appeared on the planet as a giant storm cloud. Much like the others before her had done, she surveyed the new terrain and the new creatures that surrounded. Flying on a powerful wind of her design, she looked down for a place to make her own mark. Landing in the northeastern area of the land, bordering Fornar, she fumed at the chunk of land that she wanted to make her own. The goddess of land and rock had already created ridges of mountains all along the space that the goddess wanted to claim for herself. And, what annoyed her more was that the previous goddess already had a realm of sand, caves, and sinkholes belonging to her. The goddess was infuriated and yelled loud enough so those in the heavens could know it. She shared a fierce rivalry with all of her brethren, but of all of them, her sister who commanded the ground, infuriated her the most.

"What the goddess didn't realize was that the angrier she got, the more the wind in the area was picking up. Before she knew it gale force winds were ripping through the land and loosening chunks of rocks from the mountains. The goddess smiled to herself. She named the realm that would be hers, Steedo. Surely this was a terribly inhospitable place that few would survive. However, she wasn't a heartless or cruel goddess. She loved humans and other creatures as much as the others. So she concocted an idea for a breed of creature that would fit right into this cruel world, which would respect and fear the powers of wind as much as she did.

"This was how the Vintens came to be in Steedo. Vintens were small, dark brown, mole-like creatures that inhabited the gray, windy mountains.

"Turning back to the rest of the new world, the goddess blew out a slow, gentle breath which became the light breeze throughout the whole world that people came to love. It caressed the grassy fields and rustled the trees. It scattered the flames and embers from Fornar, but also made it slightly more pleasant for the Lexerros. Even they were not immune to the overwhelming heat.

"And in no time at all, the two suns were setting and it was nearly time to ascend back to the heavens. This is when Zefra remembered the nerve of her sister to build giant mountainous landscapes in a part of the country that clearly was not hers. Losing her cloud form and taking on a human one, she raised her right arm in the sky and began to slowly make it rotate. Each time she spun it around, she sped it up just a notch. After several moments her arm was spinning madly and with one final grunt she stopped her arm and pointed in the direction of Errandomn. She couldn't help but smile at how childish she'd been.

"Zefra was gone before the massive sandstorm even started. It was a new phenomenon to the world that the citizens of Errandomn had no idea how to handle. Many ran to their caves as the enormous tornado pushed through spewing sand and rock in all directions. The sandstorms came much the same as this way, every day. It seemed that the goddess was so offended that another's mark was left in her realm that she would leave her own mark in theirs."

"Thank you, Forr. That was interesting."

Ara turned away from Forr and rolled his eyes. The old man kept his distance while they were traveling unless he had something to say and then when he had finished, he would fall behind again. It was beginning to wear on Ara's nerves.

"Have you been to Steedo before?" Vale asked Ara. "I realize it's not the most hospitable place, especially compared to Quale."

"No," replied Ara gruffly. He wasn't feeling himself at all. They had spent the last week doing nothing but walking, not to mention surviving near death experiences. Ara was used to the life of a nomad, but this was getting absurd. He wasn't used to fighting for his life as he traveled, let alone fighting to protect someone else's.

"You may notice there aren't many Elites living in this realm," Forr stated, still struggling to keep up with the younger men. "Not that there are many that live in any of the realms, of course. The gusts of wind are strong down here through the valleys, but they become increasingly worse the farther you go up the mountains."

Ara looked around and saw only mountains. He didn't like it here one bit. It had none of the charm and beauty that Quale had possessed. The sky was gray for as far as his eyes could see and the wind that blew through the valley was biting and cold. Everything looked dismal. He was not pleased.

"It doesn't even look like you could get up any of those mountains," he observed. "There isn't a single one that doesn't look completely jagged."

"From what I understand there are very few people who attempt climbing them," Vale said as he walked on. "Somewhere atop one of these mountains is the Wind Citadel, but I've never actually seen it. Of course it's easy for Volaticas. He just uses his wind powers to lift him to the top of the mountains. I think he's become accustomed to being secluded up there.

"You probably noticed that I wasn't impressed him with him during our meeting," Vale grinned. "He can be so smug and selfish. Frankly, a man that full of himself has no business in the political arena. He seems to only make decisions that benefit himself rather than his realm. But, he is what he is. Mother always seemed able to keep him under control and she had wisely pointed an interesting observation out to me once about him. I mean look around you. Volaticas Temed has obviously descended from a very wealthy, aristocratic family and is used to living in divine locales. Then he accepts a job as Ambassador of Steedo. You almost have to feel sorry for him. The only Elites who live here are those that run the storage houses creating weaponry and building materials. But, even they're isolated on the other side of the mountains. Growing up I doubt he ever envisioned this place being his home."

Ara looked around and shuddered. He hated to ever think of this place as home. No matter how far they walked, slate-colored mountains and dark skies were the only pieces of scenery around.

"Look, Ara!" exclaimed Vale pointing up at one the mountains. "See them scaling that mountain over there. Vintens! We'll have to be careful. They're not the friendliest of creatures."

Ara looked up and saw the dark-brown creatures scaling halfway up the mountain. He had never before laid eyes on one but had certainly read enough about them. They were small creatures, about four feet long and weighing under 80 pounds. They were also completely blind, having no eyes whatsoever. They made up for it though by being highly aggressive. They possessed tremendously large claws on their hands and feet that they used to scale the high mountains. With their extra-long, rock-hard snout they were able to sniff out food that other creatures might miss with the powerful winds blowing so strong. Even though they were incredibly slow, they were efficient hunters as they could move along without being heard over the roaring winds.

"Have you ever been here before?" Ara asked as they continued walking. "You seem to know an awful lot about this place."

Vale looked upset and Ara immediately wished he hadn't asked. He didn't want to overstep his bounds as bodyguard, even though the Prince had been opening up quite a bit lately.

"I was here once two years ago and I swore I'd never come back again," Vale replied mysteriously. "It's incredibly dangerous to be an Elite in Steedo. I lost my best friend out here."

"Lost him?" gasped Ara. "What do you mean? Did he wander off? Didn't they send a search party or rescue squadron?"

"I'm sorry, no," Vale smiled. "I meant to say that *she* disappeared out here. I can't help but think between losing her and nearly getting killed, the last two years have not been my best."

"Will you tell me what happened?" Ara asked quietly. "That is, you don't have to if you don't want to."

Vale began with a slight shudder, "We were best friends for as long as I can remember. Her parents were Elite nobles, so she was often in the castle and we'd play together as children. As she got older, she started to develop into a powerful young woman. She became interested in the Royal Guard and begged my mother to allow her to train with them."

"Did she end up joining then?" Ara asked. "Would she have even been old enough?"

"She wasn't allowed to but my mother did allow some of the guards to train her in basic self-defense and attack skills. She was only about sixteen-years-old at the time, but she picked up the skills very quickly.

"It was right around when we had both turned eighteen, that Mother suggested she be trained as my personal bodyguard. Mother thought that since I was older and spending so much time outside of the castle that I should have some kind of protection."

"So, what happened?" Ara inquired, unable to wait.

"Well, she took her new assignment much more seriously than I did. I mean, she was my best friend for eighteen years and now she was my bodyguard. It's hard to treat a person seriously when all you know of them is light-hearted jokes and fun times. In any case we had gone out touring the countryside as usual, when we saw the mountains of Steedo in the distance. It was my idea that I wanted to camp out in the wind world for at least one night, just to say I could. My friend was very much against it and kept saying how dangerous she thought it would be and that it was far too windy to set up camp. I thought this was kind of strange since she was often more adventurous than I was."

"Were you attacked out here? Was it the Vintens?"

"No, we weren't attacked. I woke up in the middle of the night because I heard the wind when she stepped out of our tent. I got up and grabbed the bow and arrow from underneath her pillow. I pulled back the canvas and through the dark I could see her standing there with her back to me. There was no one and nothing around. She was just standing there, staring straight ahead at the gray mountain so I was concerned, especially when I saw the trelamna staff in her hand."

Vale took a deep breath before continuing, "I was about to step out and ask what was going on when she suddenly turned around and stalked towards me with her staff aimed down. The look in her eyes was...fierce and angry. She yelled that she was sorry, but she didn't look it."

"What did you do?" Ara gasped.

"I didn't know what to do," Vale began to tear up. "Before I knew what I was doing I had pulled the bow back and fired an arrow at her.

The first one missed, she glared at me and pulled the trelamna apart. I fired again and it went right through her. Then she ran off."

"What do you mean it went right through her?" Ara looked confused.

"She had the ability to dissipate herself into particles so that she could pass through thin walls or objects would fly through her. She could never hold it for more than a few seconds, but it was enough time for her to avoid my attack. And she ran off before I could get her with a third arrow."

"And she said nothing when she took off?"

"She looked....furious. It was Opo's impression that she meant to kill me and may have stepped outside to make sure there were no Vintens or other Elites in the area. For the life of me, we couldn't figure out why she would do it."

"Why do you think she would do it?" asked Ara thoughtfully.

"I do not know. My mother was shocked but had Forr come to my room and tell me all of the stories throughout Eliantar history where kings and queens were betrayed. It didn't make me feel any better about the situation. But, at least I knew that I was not alone."

"Yes, the history of the Procers is stained with blood," Forr began, wisely. "In the year 189, all the townspeople of Castle Village stormed the castle and dismembered Laus the Greedy for his tax increases and in 427, Kleok the Enchanter was killed with poisoned food fed to him by his own daughter."

"Those were treacherous times though," Ara exclaimed. "Even during the Civil Conflict 300 years ago, no one attempted to murder the King."

"I think you'll find that murder doesn't go out of fashion young man, especially not when thousands and thousands of people are expected to obey the rule of one person."

"Did they ever catch her?" Ara asked incredulously, turning to Vale.

"No and that's the strange thing. She's been on the Most Desired List of Eliantar for two years and they never caught her. It's not like she doesn't have a unique look about her either. Trust me, a woman that goes translucent would stand out in a crowd. It made her whole body flicker in and out and she was tall and strong with dark skin and long, black hair. She was exceptionally beautiful and you'd think she would have been spotted by now."

"How is that possible? There aren't that many places in Eliantar for someone to hide."

Vale sighed, "Frankly I think she's probably dead. When she took off, she phased through one of the mountains and didn't come back out. Like I said, she couldn't stay that way for long. I think her power probably failed her as she was passing through the rock and was crushed."

"Well that was unsettling," said Ara quietly. "After hearing that, this place looks even darker and more treacherous."

Vale laughed, "I do apologize. Do not be concerned with it. Whether I'm right about that or not she must be dead by now. Hiding out in Steedo or one of the other realms for any length of time is incredibly dangerous. Vintens or a band of thieves would have killed her by now. Still, it's just that that was the first time that I was ever in danger before. Now, it's becoming much more common."

Ara could tell that this had not been any easy subject for Vale to discuss. He felt terrible for the Prince. It wasn't any wonder that Vale had no interest in being a king. Clearly, his experiences with power and privilege usually ended with enemies or regret. Still, it made him feel special that Vale could share this with him.

"What is that thing?" Vale asked, straining his eyes. "See it there, off in the distance?"

"I don't see a thing."

"Yes, just down at the bottom of this hill. There's something hanging from off the base of the mountain there. You can't miss it. It's the only bit of color anywhere in the vicinity."

Before Ara could respond, Vale had jogged ahead. Keeping up, Ara chased after him down the little hill between the walls of mountains and stopped right behind his friend. Forr, achingly, shuffled along behind them. Ara glanced over at Crown Prince Vale and saw that the color had drained from his face.

"What is it Vale?" Ara was concerned. "Are you alright?"

"The mountain..." Vale whispered. "What in the world could have happened here?"

Vale looked and sounded frantic. Ara was not used to seeing the handsome man look so appalled. It was as though he had seen a specter and would never be the same again. When Ara walked around Vale and looked at the base of the mountain he could see why the Prince was so upset.

Streaks of a dark liquid smeared a few large boulders at the foot. Ara bent down and touched the rock with his fingers. It was unmistakably blood. He wanted to pretend and rationalize what else it could possibly be, but the stench and deep claw marks into the rock were unmistakable.

"There was a struggle here very recently," Ara whispered. "Look at those claw marks in the stone. I'm guessing the Vintens got an animal here and it tried to put up a fight."

"I know what that animal was," Vale cringed, looking just a few feet down from where they stood.

Ara looked too and saw a large black root jutting out a few feet from the mountain of dark stone. It twisted and curled as if frantically trying to escape from its rocky prison. There, at the end of the root, caught on a snag, was a piece of purple cloth. The shredded piece of fabric jumped and swayed in the incessant breeze.

"Is that…" Ara trailed off. "I think that might be…"

"It's Destor's veil," gasped Vale. "It must be. We have not seen any other Elites through this pass and now we come across this."

No sooner had they made this revelation when they heard a sound from behind, like sharp metal against glass. They turned and saw five Vintens slowly crawling down the mountain towards them, their long snouts desperately sniffing their prey through the air. Ara shuddered at their razor claws as he looked into an eyeless face.

"They're so slow," Vale observed. "They're even slower than I had been told they would be. I can only assume that Destor must've been sleeping for them to attack him like this."

The Prince closed his eyes and thrust both arms in the direction of the Vintens. The creatures let out a howl as they were all thrust flying from their mountain and off several yards into the distance.

"We're not safe here," Vale shouted, over the wind. "We won't be able to sleep or rest here or we'll be attacked. Obviously, it's a miracle that I wasn't eaten alive the last time that I was here."

"So what do we do now?" Ara was filled with desperation. "Do we assume that Destor is alive and keep looking for him or do we go back to looking for Sorpa Veneficus?"

To Ara's surprise, Forr responded, "Neither, we're going back to the Ivory Towers. Destor is more than likely dead and anyway we never should have diverted from our hunting of Sorpa. I should've been wise enough to realize before we left that this is a deadly situation and the two of you can't be expected to stop it alone."

"Forr..." Vale began before sharply getting cut off.

"My foresight is all but gone, but you've still kept me on as your advisor and as your advisor I am telling you that confronting your enemies alone will only put you and your kingdom at risk."

"I did not want to cause a panic among the Elites, but I suppose you are right. We shall return to Ivory Towers."

"You're ready to get the Royal Guard involved?" Ara asked. "I think you're making a wise choice. Even if the Elites find out and panic, it will benefit them in the end."

"I suppose from time to time we need others to tell us what is the right path to follow," Vale looked to Forr. "Let's get out of this godforsaken realm and back to Ivory Towers while we still can."

Chapter 11

The next day Ara, Vale, and Forr were finally out of Steedo. The winds had died down, the mountains lie behind them, and once more the suns lit the sky. They were thoroughly exhausted, but simply with the change in atmosphere their moods were greatly improved.

"The moment that we stepped out of those mountain paths, the winds died down," Ara exclaimed. "How is that possible?"

"You may not believe in the gods and their powers," Forr smirked. "That does not mean they do not exist."

The situation with Destor and Sorpa had become even more mysterious over the past few days, but just knowing they were heading back to Castle Village seemed to put them at ease. Vale and Ara laughed and shared many an amusing story as they strolled through the flowery fields of Eliantar. Forr did not approve and though he continued to warn that he had an impending sense of dread, he could get no clear visions to prove it. With no solid reason to be fearful at this moment, Ara saw no reason not to maintain a positive attitude and it was clear to him that Crown Prince Vale felt the exact same way.

With that in mind they sauntered along at a quick pace, thrilled with the knowledge that they should be arriving back at the Ivory Towers tomorrow around midday. More than once Ara was sure he'd caught Vale looking at him with more than friendship in his eyes, but every time he'd glance over to confirm this, the Prince had looked away.

This bit of knowledge made Ara's heart soar with happiness. In spite of all the terrible things that were occurring, just being in Vale's presence gave him an intoxicating sense of peace.

"Do you suppose this will be over soon?" Vale asked after they had just finished a lunch of fruit that they had found on some wild trees. "That is, do you think the Royal Guard will find Sorpa Veneficus quickly so we can understand the attempt on my life? After all, I think we had both expected these problems to be resolved by now."

"I certainly hope so," Ara sighed.

"If I don't get a wash down soon and burn these filthy clothes, I think I'll have killed off the whole land myself before Sorpa gets the chance."

They both laughed for quite a while at this. It was true. When they had started their journey, they had looked like vagrants, but now they appeared like vagrants that hadn't seen any form of civilization in years. Forr came walking over, having finished his meal and obviously eager to get home.

"The Royal Guard has been trained for generations to deal with traitors and assassins like this. She may be good at hiding, but she won't be so good as to elude our security."

"I have to be honest," said Ara. "I truly believe that this Sorpa Veneficus is a maniac. While that's dangerous for us, it's more dangerous for her. I think she's been lucky enough to get a few other crazy allies to assist her, but that's it. Vale, she has no plan, other than to cause chaos. In my opinion, the army will find her and she will be arrested with no problems."

The Prince looked relieved. Ara stared at Vale's torn clothes and greasy, black hair peeking out from his scarf. Even in his disheveled state, he was beautiful to Ara.

"Even if she does succeed, you still have a chance," Ara went on. "You haven't looked like royalty in over a week. If we fail, you'll be able to look like a member of her undead army and she'll never find you. It definitely couldn't hurt that you must smell like death right now as well."

Vale punched Ara in the arm. It was hard, harder than Ara had expected the Prince to hit. Thank goodness he learned a few things from the self-defense classes.

"Would you two stop it?" snapped Forr. "We're wasting time and I would like to be in my chambers again by tomorrow. Honest to gods, you both act and look at each other as though you've never seen another man before."

The moment quickly became awkward and Vale hurriedly pulled himself to his feet. Ara, also feeling tense from the situation rose and brushed himself off. He cursed himself under his breath for once again lacking the confidence to express what he felt.

"We really should get going," Vale said quietly. "We also need to formulate a plan on how we're going to issue the alarm for the Royal Guard to find the necromancer."

"You keep talking about it like it's terribly complicated," Ara said, finally able to meet Vale's eyes again. "Don't we go into the castle and you announce that we're in danger and order the army to go find her?"

"Well, yes," laughed Vale. "But, the army is made up of hundreds of Elites. When they leave the castle, everyone will wonder what is going on. As far as I know whenever the Royal Guard has been sent out, the king or queen has always made some kind of declaration to the people. I would like to avoid that."

"I agree," Forr nodded. "My advice would be to say nothing at this time. It's for their own good."

"Say nothing?" Ara couldn't believe his ears. "Everyone will be talking. They'll wonder what is going on and if they're in danger."

"Let them talk. If there is no announcement, they will hopefully think it is a training exercise and that there is nothing to fear. If I'm right on this, we'll have captured Sorpa within a day, if they travel by stallop, and there will be no need for concern."

Ara was very concerned at the idea of sending the army out without alerting the public to a potential threat. But, they had very little to go by besides a few suspicions. Vale would look a fool if he alerted the public over nothing. There was no proof that Sorpa Veneficus was alive, much less behind the assassination attempt.

"I think that the best bet is to have the Royal Guard leave the castle in the middle of the night," Vale went on. "No one in the Castle Village will know that the Royal Guard has left if they do it in the dead of the night. We can order them to do as we did when we left the castle and simply avoid major cities and towns once they're away from Ivory Towers."

"I suppose that sounds reasonable," Ara said quietly. "I'm just hoping that this isn't worse than we are assuming and that you don't live to regret not issuing a formal warning. I know we think this will be simple now that the Royal Guard is to be involved. I just hope that remains true."

"If it comes to that then there will be time," Forr said reassuringly. "But, until that time comes, I think we should keep the Elites from panicking. It wouldn't benefit them anyway. No one has threatened Castle Village. We would only frighten them for nothing and I'm sure they're still a bit shaken from the assassination attempt as it is."

Ara bit his tongue and kept walking. Ara Tataman's job was to serve as bodyguard and General of the Royal Guard. He worked for the Prince and the Prince could certainly undermine him, but he couldn't help but worry about the possible outcome.

The next several hours seemed to drag on forever. If there was one thing that the men were getting tired of seeing, it was one field after another. As far as they could see, in every direction, there were only sunflower fields and crop patches. The occasional tree would break up the otherwise bland scenery. It had been their intention to avoid roads and towns, at the risk of Vale being recognized and they had been successful. The few times they'd see a cottage or the markings of a worn path, they had veered away. Now even Ara, who abhorred society, would have loved nothing more than to see something besides plant life.

When the suns had finally begun to set, Ara stopped and stared down a ravine at a structure that he had never seen before.

"What is that?!" he asked in awe. "It's beautiful. I've never seen a building like that before in my life."

"We need to settle down for the night anyway," Vale sighed, exhausted. "Let's head down the gorge and make camp there."

As they eased their way down the slope, Ara stared at the magnificent edifice. Though not as grandiose and elegant as the Ivory Towers, this structure had a raw beauty about it. It looked to be made entirely of a rich, black wood. The polished first level looked to be about sixty square feet and from there a thin spire rose from the center five hundred feet into the sky. The spire, like the base was a polished, black wood that came to a point where it touched the sky.

When they reached the bottom of the ravine, Ara followed Vale as he circled the perimeter of the building. He noticed for the first time that large oval shaped chunks of rock surrounded the entire structure. Each one was a few feet taller than Ara and there were several feet in between each one.

"This place is so amazing," Ara said. "What is it?"

"It's called the Chronometer Cathedral," Vale explained. And I can't believe you've never heard of it before. It was my favorite children's story when I was a young boy."

"Your Highness, he's been largely uneducated on so many aspects of this land," Forr sighed. "I'm not quite sure why you'd be surprised that he's not familiar with the Cathedral."

Now, facing the front of the large structure, Ara looked to the top and saw that it was actually a clock tower. An enormous triangle of green, cracked glass was at the top on this side and three giant silver hands adorned the face. They each looked to be about twenty feet long and extremely heavy. Both the face and the hands appeared as though they were made with precious gems and metals; a prime target for thieves, but alas there appeared no way to climb the smooth obelisk. He also noticed that the hands were not moving.

"I don't understand," he said. "This was part of a child's fable, but it's obviously real. I mean, I've never heard of legend before that was in a fairy tale and turned out to not be a farce."

"Go up the steps to the door and read what's on the podium," Vale suggested. "You'll see what I'm talking about."

Ara approached the building slowly. There were enormous black doors at the top of the few steps that looked as though they hadn't been opened in years. Large heavy locks adorned the entryways from bottom to top, making entry impossible.

As he made his way up the ebony steps, he noticed a dark grey podium a few feet before the doors. It was barely noticeable in the shadow of the dark spire. When he came to it, he glanced down and saw that words had been inscribed into the stone. Though the words appeared as though they'd been carved in ages ago, they were still clearly legible and he began to read it aloud.

> *When the people have lost all hope and the world turns to black,*
> *A hero will appear from out of the gloom to bring Eliantar back;*
> *He will travel across the land through desert, water, and fire*
> *And crush the Tyrant's plan; destroying his funeral pyre.*
> *He will unite the lords of realms, for only through them will there be*
> *A way to stop the coming doom and set their peoples free.*
> *When this hero is set to come, no one knows what the future brings.*
> *The spell is this: Eyes on the clock, for when the pendulum swings.*

"I don't understand. What does it mean?" Ara asked, walking back down to Vale and Forr.

Forr answered, "A long time ago, when the world was brand new there was a seer, just like me, who advised the very first King of Eliantar. Her name was Lileena.

"No one knows much about her, other than that she was highly respected in her position and took it upon herself to study all brands of magic. Near the end of her life she was regarded as a full-fledged witch and it is believed that she's the one who started the coven of witches, which many years later would become corrupt and call themselves Skars Shadows."

"I always thought that magic was illegal," Ara commented. We'd always learned through school that the gods didn't approve of us studying magic because they'd already given us special gifts to use. Prior to Scurus Subo, I'd assumed witches and the Skars Shadows were just an allegory for how magic corrupts people and makes them evil."

"Well," sighed Vale. "Forr probably should've started by saying that this is just a story and no one knows how much truth their actually is to it."

"In any case," Forr went on. "The story goes that at that time studying magic was highly common and this prophet was highly skilled at it.

"Towards the end of her life she went into hiding, probably because she was ill and about to die. But, before she ran away the King asked her for one final prophecy and she spoke the words that appear on that podium today. She asked the King, as her final request, to build the Chronometer Cathedral, and told him that when Eliantar was ready to fall into despair, a hero would appear from out of nowhere and burst out from those doors."

"What's in there?" Ara asked, still in amazement. "How does one get inside to look?"

"No one knows. No one has ever been in there. Every time an attempt was made to break the locks, they couldn't be destroyed. Lileena must have sealed it with her magic. Gods only know."

"The clock doesn't work," Ara pointed out. "It's a bit strange that it's so impressive looking and has this miraculous story about how it's the starting point for some great hero, but it doesn't even function."

"Historians and story tellers agree that it has never worked," Forr explained. "They believe that were it to work, it would move just as all other clocks do. If you look up there, you can see it has thirty hours marked and a hand for each sun, and of course the third hand for the season. Those that believe say that there is a gigantic pendulum that hangs down the spire and rests somewhere just above this large first floor. What's in the first floor, neither the historians or story tellers know. But, they both believe that when this tower was constructed, it was made not to work and that it would only come to life when Eliantar was at its darkest and the hero was about to arrive."

"So, you're saying that the clock counts down Eliantar's redemption and not Eliantar's destruction?"

"Ah that's the question, isn't it?" Forr said with a twinkle in his eye. I'm glad to see you're finally interested in one of my stories."

"Well is it just a story or do you think there may be truth to it?" Ara couldn't keep his eyes off the macabre-looking structure as he asked. "Do many people really believe the legend?"

"Surprisingly, there are many that do, including Forr," Vale answered before Forr could. "Every morning, there is a large group of Elites who gather right where we are on their knees and pray silently. They just sit here, staring up at the metal hands waiting for them to move. In my travels I've occasionally been by here, and I've seen more people kneeling here than in any of the gods' churches. I always thought it was a beautiful story and I think it's wonderful that there are some people who think it's real. Some people need stories like that, you know? More than likely though it is just an exaggerated tale passed down to give people hope and keep them positive when their times are rough."

"You don't believe it then?" Ara asked, noticing how disappointed Forr looked.

"No, I guess I don't. Vale said his eyes full of strain. "As I said it's a beautiful story, but I am sure there have been many hard times where people have surely felt that this tower must be ticking away. Obviously, it hasn't."

"Well, it seems as though it already works, even if it doesn't tick," Ara wisely observed.

"How do you mean?" Vale asked.

"Because it's brought the people hope. If there are crowds outside that are praying here every day, then obviously if nothing else, it is a monument of optimism for the people of Eliantar."

As Forr and Vale began preparing to camp for the night, Ara continued to observe the dark tower. It was completely eerie, yet beautiful. He imagined that it was quite a spectacle during the day, but at night it looked more like a mausoleum and a reminder of death rather than a symbol of the preservation of life. He assumed this was probably some kind of statement about the darkness that the witch saw to come. He imagined that whoever built this designed the outside to reflect the gloomy state of Eliantar from Lileena's visions, but the inside was probably brilliant shades of white and gold.

"You've been staring at that building for almost an hour," Vale called over to Ara. "You're becoming like everyone else who comes here. Just biding your time and waiting for a dead clock to come to life."

"I can't help but think," Ara ignored Vale's skepticism. "Maybe the time has come. Your mother has died a terrible death and then the Crown Prince was nearly murdered. Maybe this is the darkness that the witch foresaw and the Chronometer Cathedral is just seconds away from springing to life."

Vale walked over Forr's sleeping form to Ara and held his hand. He squeezed it gently. When Ara looked over at the Prince, he saw pity in his eyes. Prince Vale felt sorry for him which suddenly made him feel very small.

"Please don't take this the wrong way," Vale said with a hint of patronization. "There are Elites who spend their whole lives waiting for the world to change, staring at this building. They live their life, they die, and nothing has changed. I'm begging you Ara, I used to be very idealistic myself. I hated Opo for how blunt and uncaring he could be. He would come across so negative about the world and the people in it. But, I've realized over the past few weeks that in our professions we don't have the luxury to be idealistic. We have to be realistic and make changes ourselves rather than wait for heroes and gods to make fixes for us."

"It doesn't hurt to have faith in things outside of our control," Ara said quietly, eyes still on the Chronometer Cathedral. "Do you think it is so wrong to hope for change in a broken world?"

"Believe in yourself," Vale stated. "Change is possible and I truly believe that if you work at it, good can conquer evil. However, sitting around and waiting for some 2,000-year-old magic spell to revive itself is foolish. The world will rot and die before magic ever takes the place of direct action."

They laid down a few moments later. Vale was asleep in moments after the long day. Ara tossed and turned for hours before he was finally able to drift off. Symbols of grandeur rarely amused him, so why could he not stop staring the Cathedral? Why did he feel so drawn to it? He'd close his eyes and then quickly open them to stare at the clock face. No matter how many times he did this, the clock did not move. He stared up at the cracked, green glass that shone in the starlight and waited and waited until at last, like Vale, he could wait for hope no longer and drifted into a dreamless sleep.

There was no magic in Eliantar that night. Ara had begun to realize what Vale had been trying to tell him. There was no magic for the people, no matter how much they wished for it. There was no magic for Forr, no matter how much he believed in it. And there was no magic for Eliantar, even though, unbeknownst to the world, it was nearing its end.

Chapter 12

The next day they arrived back in the castle town right at midday. They'd never been happier to see Ivory Towers beaming in the suns as they approached. What Ara had once seen as a symbol of pretension, he now saw a place to finally enjoy a moment of respite. The towers touched the sky and exuded not affectation, but rather a sense of beauty and calm.

They had barely passed through the gates when Plucid Duru, Ambassador of Errandomn, came running, as fast as his old legs could, down the white marble path. His brown robes blew around him as he came down to meet them. Behind him, walking at a normal pace came Volaticas Temed, Ambassador of Steedo, with a scowl on his face. His long, blonde hair was pulled back as usual and he wore the same gaudy yellow and white robes that he had at the Regulation Committee meeting.

"Thank goodness you're back, Your Highness," Plucid gasped, completely out of breath. "We were just going down to the barracks to send the Royal Guard out to look for you when I saw you walk into the courtyard. I was so worried you wouldn't return in time."

"Oh be quiet," snapped Volaticas. "What are you going on about? All doom and gloom all of the time. Tell the Prince the good news."

The sneer that formed across Volaticas's face was obvious. He barely pretended to like Vale, that much was obvious to Ara. By the look of it, it made little difference to Vale. He didn't seem overly fond of Volaticas right now either.

"Of course," sighed Plucid, his wrinkled face furrowed. "Master, the Regulation Committee has met and we have named you King of Eliantar. The gala is tonight, which is why we're so glad you've come home. As I said we were about to send the Royal Guard to search for you and bring you back. We couldn't delay any longer."

"What?!" gasped Vale. "I've only been Crown Prince for less than two months. You can't become the King until you've been approved by the Committee after three months of service."

Plucid glanced around and spoke quietly, "Lenta sent messages to all of the Ambassadors about what happened in Quale. She's persuaded the Committee to vote in an early election. Congratulations, Your Highness."

"But, why would you do that?" Vale inquired. "There is no reason to speed up the process more than usual."

"I can assure you that I was against the majority in this vote," Volaticas snarled, his cold eyes staring through Vale. "It seems that with an assassin attempting to murder you and then another trying to kidnap you, mere weeks later, the Regulation Committee would prefer you stay…local."

"You're going to name me King so that I can't leave the castle again?"

"Do not think of it like that," Plucid smiled, warmly. "Sir, you do no one good dead or kidnapped. We've all known for years how you like your adventures and prefer not to be in the castle, but being King will keep you and Eliantar safer by keeping you here."

"Welcome home," Volaticas smiled. Ara took a step forward, but Vale stopped him with his arm.

"In any case," Forr went on, trying to avoid any confrontation between Volaticas and Ara, who was staring daggers at him. "We've got to get you both cleaned up for the party tonight. Come along."

He grabbed Vale and Ara by the arm and began pulling them up the path. Ara turned around and found Volaticas at the spot where they had left him, staring coldly at them as they left.

As they crossed through the foyer, the guards present saluted, save one. Kally, the young guard who had been standing outside Forr's chamber when Ara was first there, ran forward.

"My liege, I beg your forgiveness for this intrusion. You must wish to rest from your journey. But, you should know that some events have transpired in your absence."

"What is going on, Kally?" Vale asked him quietly, so as not to draw attention from the other guards. "What happened here?"

"I'm so sorry to make this day any more stressful for you, with your inauguration and all," Kally's voice was filled with fright. "I was cleaning out Opo's room as I was asked to, in order for Ara to settle in, and I found something. There's an item there that you should see."

"What is it?" Ara inquired, growing tired of the secrets. "What did you find that can't wait?"

"Just come along," snapped Forr. "If it wasn't important, he wouldn't be so persistent. Frankly I'd like him to tell you without inquisitive ears hearing everything," he gestured back towards the other guards who were clearly trying to eavesdrop.

Kally led them up several different staircases and through dark passages filled with portraits of people Ara didn't know. It occurred to Ara that they had tried to hide certain chambers in the castle. He remembered back to when Vale and he had gone to see Forr in his room and how hard it was to get to. And now Opo's room seemed to be at the end of a gigantic maze. Surely this castle had more secrets to it than he would ever imagine.

"I'd been staying in guest quarters out of respect for the deceased," Ara began. "I had assumed my official room, Opo's old room, would be in the barracks with the other guards."

"No, sir," Kally responded. "His room was directly next to the Queen's. As her protector, he needed to stay close by."

"What could he possibly have to show us that is such a secret," Ara whispered.

"Mysteries are becoming more and more prevalent around here," Forr responded gravely. "I sense that we all need to take great care from here on out. It's best that we've returned when we did. Whether you care to admit it or not, Ivory Towers is the safest place in the world for the Prince and the rest of us."

At last Forr stopped in front of a large candelabra, hanging against the wall. He fumbled around one of the candles and a portion of the wall pushed forward and flung to the side. There, Ara saw a room the same size as Forr's but much different. It was lit well with many windows allowing the suns' light to pour in. Various weaponry littered the walls of Opo's quarters and all of the furniture seemed to be in a state of disaster. Clothes littered the floor, sheets on the bed were a crumbled mess, and books on the shelves were scattered all across the room.

"What a mess," commented Ara.

"What did you find, Kally?" Forr asked the young guard. "You should know that whatever you did find is confidential and no business of the other guards in the castle."

Kally ran over to the bed and reached inside the crumbled sheets, pulling out a ratty leather-bound book. He beckoned Vale and Ara over and opened to the middle of the book, pointing out the spot to Vale.

"This is where I found it. It's Opo's journal."

"Forr, I can't read this," Vale exclaimed. "It's personal and I wouldn't feel right about it. It's disrespectful to pry into someone's thoughts and disgraceful to the deceased."

"It's important," said Kally, his eyes pleading. "Please read it. Read it aloud for Ara's sake too. This is information that we may all need."

Vale looked at Forr for a moment, who merely shrugged. He didn't want to disrespect the dead, but he could see the desperate look in Kally's eyes. He sighed and began to read.

The 14th Day of Seed in the Year One Thousand Nine Hundred and Ninety Nine

I've just arrived back to the castle after being ordered to follow the necromancer, Sorpa Veneficus. It was a stressful trip to say the least and I've arrived back home to find myself more confused than I was when I left. It took me several days to locate her. For someone so frail, she was a quick mover. I was able to track her to Tacia, but then I lost track of her in the dense forest. I attempted to ask several of the local Arbestees for help, but they offered none. They are a strangely timid creature. Night had fallen and I decided to make camp when I was attacked by what I can only describe as a group of corpses. They drug me deeper into the forest and threw me down in a massive graveyard. I had heard the stories about the largest cemetery in Eliantar being in Tacia but I had never seen it. Headstones appeared to go for miles. It was truly a disturbing scene. Sorpa was there and said she knew I'd been following her. I closed my eyes and didn't move as I waited for death.

Death never came. Instead she asked me for my assistance. Her voice gave me chills and her emaciated appearance made me shudder. She asked me if I knew a force was coming that could destroy Eliantar, wouldn't I want to side with it, rather than against it. She told me that Queen Jenneka was a fool to not heed her warnings and that even though she may appear dark and mysterious, her intentions were pure.

I was unsure so she invited me to a meeting of the Skars Shadows, the dark tribe that practices magic illegally. Gods help me, but I told her that I would go. As protector of my Queen and my land I cannot take the chance to turn my back on an impending danger. The part that makes me uneasy is that I had to lie to the Queen when I returned. When this is all over I am sure that Queen Jenneka will be thankful for my decision.

The 2nd Day of Reap in the Year One Thousand Nine Hundred and Ninety Nine

I had to lie to the Queen and say I was taking a few days to train new recruits in Errandomn, when in actuality I traveled there to attend the meeting Sorpa had told me about. I had rarely traveled to that area of the world before and I don't regret it.

Blinding sands are all that make up the realm making it impossible to move at a steady pace. There are several mountains but they do nothing to block the dangerous sandstorms. I spotted more than one cave but knew enough not to enter any of them as they are the homes of the Tamalus, whom I find to be disturbing.

They appear like men, albeit much taller. They walk and talk like men but their skin is the color of oil and they only come out at night, scavenging the desert. They each carry long staffs, which add to my fear. Who am I to say whether or not they will use their weapons aggressively? I know that they've seen me and it was much to my benefit that they appeared to be loners and kept to themselves.

I trudged through the golden sands for hours and hours. As I went further, sinkholes began to become a common obstacle. But, at last I reached the coordinates that Sorpa had provided. I wasn't thrilled to see that it was a cave.

When I entered there were several chairs around a long, black table. Sorpa Veneficus sat at the head of the table. This was getting worse and worse. Not only was I attending an illegal meeting, but the woman I claimed to have killed, was its leader. A frail, pale man stood behind her, who she immediately introduced as her assistant, Scurus. She gestured me to sit beside her. All of the others in the room wore black cloaks and masks to hide their identities. I took my seat and Sorpa did most of the talking.

Everything that she had to say made perfect sense. She spoke of the fallen god, Skarsend, and how the seal on his prison was growing weak. He was nearing escape and appeared to her in a dream, to ask for her assistance. As the leader of the Skars Shadows, she had to oblige. The reward would be significant for the danger. He promised that he would not attempt to destroy Eliantar as he had before, and that his war was one for the gods. He realized in his weakened state, from years of captivity, that he would be susceptible to attack and asked Sorpa to provide him with an army. The army need only protect him from those who would hunt him, until he regained his god-like powers. She would be granted anything that she wished in return. If she declined, he would eradicate every living thing on the planet as he waged war against the other gods.

I pointed out to her that she had propositioned the Queen to create the army in order to fend off Skarsend, to which she scoffed that we could never hope to fend off a god. Joining Skarsend was the only way to be on the winning side. She offered me the chance to lead this new and improved Royal Guard. I agreed to help her immediately. When I left, Sorpa promised me again that the only way to truly protect Queen Jenneka and the kingdom was to follow her plan. I pray she's right.

"I don't want to read anymore," Vale fumed, throwing the journal to the ground. "This is despicable!"

Ara sat with his mouth agape in complete shock. How cruel to make the Prince read about his mother being betrayed so shortly after her death.

"Please read the last section," Kally picked the diary from the floor. "I know it's difficult, but the last section is the most important of all."

"He betrayed my mother," yelled Vale. "I don't want to read any more about him. The one person my mother had to trust to protect her was conspiring against her."

"I understand but please," Kally begged. "If you have any interest in avenging your mother and stopping this awful woman, you have to read his last entry."

With a great deal of difficulty, Vale grabbed the book and fought back his tears. After a few moments, he began to read aloud once more.

The 86th Day of Reap in the Year One Thousand Nine Hundred and Ninety Nine

She's dead! She died this morning and it's all my fault. I had been wasting so much time meeting with Sorpa and neglecting my duties that I hadn't known she was sick. If there was one thing that I hadn't counted on, it was that Queen Jenneka would catch the Iniquitous Virus. She killed herself, rather than face the onslaught of illness that was coming. She was always so bold. She'd rather die on her own terms.

I knew Sorpa was staying right outside the city and I met with her. She had no sympathy and no respect for the amount of failure I was enduring. I pointed out to her that the only reason we were going to create an army of dead soldiers was to protect the kingdom, the Queen! It made sense at the beginning, but now...

Now that the Queen is dead, I don't know if it was ever worth all of that. I told her I wasn't interested in her plan any longer but she kept insisting that I was merely upset and that the time had come for her next move in the cemetery of Tacia. I walked out on her. She called me a coward and said she wasn't surprised that I would betray her as I betrayed the Royal House of Procer, the family I was to protect.

I feel like a fool. I've betrayed my Queen, my land, and that necromancer. I fear with all of this deception it's only a matter of time until I can no longer show my face so publicly. The Royal Guard will eventually find out what I've done or perhaps even Sorpa herself will come after me if her plan succeeds. I'm so sorry that I got myself into this. And I'm so sorry that Prince Vale is entering into a massacre. May the gods forgive me for all that I've done. If I stand any chance at redemption, I will get the Prince away from this before he too meets his demise, which will surely come soon if I do not intervene. The god of death rises and I fear we may all fall because of it...

Chapter 13

Ara had never been to such an elegant party in all of his life. The ballroom in Ivory Towers was exquisite. He was sure that it always looked beautiful, but the way it was decked out now was flawless with the dozens and dozens of Elites dancing in the midst of it and the minstrels filling it with the most beautiful music.

The room was massive and circular with a giant staircase going right from the dance floor up to the main hall. The staircase had a regal crimson carpet flowing down the center with polished silver rails.

The entire ballroom itself was the most pristine color of white. The floors were a polished ivory, as were the walls, columns and tables that bordered the room. Every table was covered with the rarest and most beautiful flowers from around the world as well as several small snow-white candles. On the walls as well were thousands of candles, high and low, keeping the entire room as luminous as daylight.

Looking up, Ara saw that the entire ceiling was made of glass. This would have been an excellent place to look up at the starry sky, had all the lights in the room not blotted them out. There wasn't a single trace of metal winding through the glass, but rather one magnificent chunk of glass shaped concavely over their heads.

It was still about fifteen minutes before Prince Vale was scheduled to enter and already the room was packed. All around him stood the wealthiest and most well-to-do Elites in the world decked out in their formal clothes. All of them wore gaudy, beaded robes and gowns with sparkled masks of all different colors over their faces.

"Maybe not the best idea at the moment," Ara had muttered to Forr, before the party.

"It's tradition," Forr had shrugged. "Hundreds of years ago, Elites hid their wealth for fear of being robbed or murdered for their money. They'd attend balls wearing masks so they could not be identified. It was a common occurrence that the King's Balls would be filled with masked guests. And now it's part of the custom."

Ara, himself, was not wearing a costume and he was thankful for it. As a member of the Regulation Committee, it was his job to stand out, not blend in with the other guests. He had been thrilled to get back and finally bathe and change his clothes, but he didn't feel much more comfortable now. Forr had forced him to wear a midnight blue tunic over tan pants. The only saving grace was that his bare, muscular arms were exposed. He'd always hated sleeves and uncomfortable clothes. He had to admit that he looked nice in the outfit, but that didn't change the fact that it simply didn't fit his personality. He felt overdressed and a bit ridiculous. He found himself becoming more and more grateful that at least Forr hadn't asked him to wear a little hat on top of his smooth head or the overbearing armor that Opo had worn.

No matter how much he tried, he just couldn't seem to fit the "royal mode" that Forr expected of him. The clothing was loathsome and even this magnificent party that was going on around him seemed a bit overdone. The only thing that got him through all of this splendor was knowing that Vale would be arriving shortly.

He anxiously stared at the timepiece that he wore on his wrist. It wouldn't be long now until Vale was here. This was the first time in the past week that he had been away from the Prince and he felt terribly lonely without him. For the first time in a long time, Ara realized, he had a friend. He began to chuckle to himself as he imagined what horror Forr was making him wear. He knew that Vale was sure to be just as miserable as he was.

One of the things that Ara found most appealing about Vale was how he too rebelled against this money-obsessed society that they lived in. He didn't enjoy attending galas in fancy dress any more than Ara did. He couldn't deny one thing, however. No matter his negative opinion on the nobles, Crown Prince Vale of the Royal House of Procer looked best when he was being just that. His authority and determination when he wore the crown were not at all judgmental or superior, but rather determined and gracious. Ara found this trait that Vale exuded to be more than a little appealing. It was nice to be wrong about assuming that all nobles were selfish and spoiled.

They had been through much together recently and this afternoon had certainly been no exception. Perhaps a fun evening was what they both needed. He had played and re-played the journal of Opo Scoloos in his head all day. It only served to further complicate matters.

He looked around at the various other members of the Regulation Committee and wondered if they should be made aware of all of the developments. Plucid Duru of Errandomn and Volaticas Temed of Steedo were probably best kept out of the loop. Plucid was afraid of his own shadow and it was probably best to not disturb him anymore with stories of secret meetings that took place right in his own realm. Volaticas was looking for any reason to point out that Vale was an unfit ruler so it would be unwise to alert him of security issues. Still, if nothing else, perhaps he should be told about Destor's apparent death in his realm of Steedo.

The two stood in a corner talking to each other. Then again it looked as though Volaticas was doing all of the talking, while flipping his flowing blonde hair. Plucid nodded every few moments, but otherwise seemed uninterested. They did indeed seem to be a peculiar duo. One stood exuding confidence and robes that only masses of money could buy while the other was petrified at his own speaking voice and looked as though he'd dressed in the dark. Then again maybe they weren't the worst pairing. Plucid was probably the only one in the whole world who would stand there and tolerate Volaticas's self-praise for an extended period of time.

Iradt Furich, Ambassador of Fornar and Prode Procer of Tacia stood against the opposite wall, also in conversation. This was also a strange twosome to see together. Prode was so silly and wound up and Iradt, as usual, looked terribly angry and stressed. Her gown was a deep burgundy, but had the telltale signs of Fornar all over it with the burn holes. As he watched Prode gabbed on and on, intermittently giggling at whatever he was saying, while Iradt paid him little mind.

Ara was probably right in not telling either of them as well. Iradt worked herself into a rage over anything that wasn't in order and Prode likely wouldn't take it seriously anyway. Perhaps that was for the best, Ara realized. Prode not being all doom and gloom all of the time probably made him a kind and warm Ambassador.

In contrast to his casual personality, Prode was dressed to the hilt in a long moss-green robe. He wore a necklace of green metal leaves. Ara watched as he whispered something to Iradt and then burst into uproarious giggles. This made Ara smile and shake his head. He was certainly as attractive as his brother, but clearly there was something to be said about the differences in their personalities.

Lenta Benigg stood in the middle of the room talking to a whole group of masked Elites. She looked radiant as always with her cerulean dress and long dark curls swept up on her head. Surely she could be trusted with the new information. She had been through a lot with Vale and Ara in Quale. In his brief experience with her, she certainly appeared to be the wisest and most clearheaded. He decided it would be best if she was alerted to the new developments that had occurred. Before Ara could cross the room to speak with her, Forr's voice echoed over the crowd.

"Welcome to all for this most joyous of occasions. The rulers of Eliantar are always beloved and respected and so it is a great tragedy when one of them leaves us for the heavens. However, every tragedy has a silver lining, for there is always another to take over in their parent's place. This occasion is no different. And so it is with great pleasure that I present to you the Crown Prince of Eliantar, Vale Procer."

You could hear a pin drop as Vale began to descend the wide staircase, followed by two members of the Royal Guard. Ara stared up at his friend in awe. He never looked more handsome. He wore a white body suit and white boots with a long blue robe over top, much like the one he wore when Ara had first seen him. His long, black hair hung down loosely and framed his handsome face well. Atop his head he wore a thin, silver crown.

There was no denying it or rationalizing it any longer. Ara's feelings for Vale were strong. He had never felt this way about any other Elite. Just watching Vale nervously glide down the stairs was enough to make Ara's heart flitter. How he wanted to rush over and offer his support to the Prince.

When he reached the bottom of the stairs, he crossed to the middle of the room and met Forr. Without a word, Forr reached up and removed the silver crown from Vale's head. He handed it off to Prode, who had walked over as well. Smiling at his brother broadly, Prode turned and strode away to place the crown on a side table. The two guards who had escorted Vale stood guard over the Prince's crown.

"Never before has there been such a demand for a crown prince to be made King," Forr beamed. "Clearly, this is a sign that your people need you more than you could've imagined and that is perhaps the greatest sign of success of all. Always remember that your duty is to protect the people of Eliantar. You must be strong, wise, kind, brave, and above all committed in order to achieve this goal. I have great faith and little doubt that you will exceed all of your peoples' expectations in your new role as King of Eliantar."

A third guard had descended the staircase and handed Lenta a much larger, gold crown. She walked over and handed it to Forr, with a bow. Unlike the thin, silver one that preceded it, this one was much thicker with at least ten points reaching up from the band. Small red and blue jewels adorned it. Forr accepted it from Lenta and reached up, placing it atop Vale's head.

"May I be the first to present," Forr grinned. "King Vale Procer, the newly crowned ruler of Eliantar and all who reside here."

The crowd burst into a volcanic applause. Vale looked over at Ara who smiled broadly. Vale turned a deep shade of crimson and smiled back.

"It is my hope and desire to be as much a success and beacon of hope as my mother was to you," Vale called out. "I promise that I will do my best to not let any of you down."

"Now let's all celebrate this joyous occasion," Lenta called out. "Minstrels, let the festivities begin."

A group of men in the corner began playing their instruments loudly with an addictive beat. Ara watched as all of the men and women around the room found partners and began to sway with each other hypnotically. The music, though beautiful, only added to the eeriness of all the nobles in their costumes. Several servants ran around the room, blowing out half of the candles, casting the room into a state of dimness.

"Might I have this dance?" King Vale asked, now standing directly beside Ara, who smiled and took his hand. "It's a bit eerie, isn't it? I don't think I like masks. It's as though everyone in the room is hiding something. I'm finding more and more that people with secrets to hide are dangerous."

"It's tradition, I've been told," Ara said, still scanning the room. "But, I know what you mean. We've been encountering some treacherous people lately and the least settling thing I can think of is to be surrounded by a group of masked strangers. Security has been checking them though, so I think we'll live through the night."

Vale stared into Ara's eyes, "Let's not focus on all of the things that are going wrong. Just for tonight, let's pretend everything is okay. I know that seems like denying the inevitable, but once in a while I just need to take a break from the madness and concentrate on the beauty of life. At times it's just nice to pretend that every story has a happy ending."

Ara pulled him slightly closer in response. It sounded like a supreme idea to him to just be and not focus on all of the things that had fallen apart. In fact it gave Ara, perhaps, the best feeling that he'd ever had.

Throughout the next hour several Elites came up to wish Vale their best. Masked stranger after masked stranger shook Vale's hand and patted him on the back as he continued to dance slowly with his bodyguard. Ara had to stay professional and try not to become annoyed at the constant interruptions and so politely smiled as Vale pulled away each time.

"Best wishes, Your Highness," Plucid Duru mumbled as he adjusted his baggy clothes. "It's so good to have you safely back in the castle."

"He really is a nervous one," Ara whispered after he had walked away. "Every time I've seen him or met him he seems as though he can't keep still."

"Which is why we shouldn't scare him more by telling him what we found out went on in Errandomn," Vale echoed Ara's earlier concern. "If he knew there was a meeting of witches in his realm, he'd relinquish his post. We can't afford to lose any political figures right now."

"I can't believe they still haven't found out who was behind Opo's death," whispered Iradt from behind, her short, dark curls bouncing on her head. "There was a time when the Royal Guard would leap on such an attack and they would have brought those responsible to justice."

"Please Iradt," Vale begged. "I assure you that it's being handled. Can't we just have fun tonight?"

Iradt stepped closer and arched her back making her enormous cleavage bounce against Ara and knock him back a step. She stared at both with annoyance in her eyes before turning and stomping away in her singed dress.

Vale and Ara chuckled a moment before falling back into their dance. In spite of the constant harassment from their guests and the seriousness of their state of affairs, they were happy. They'd finally found a moment when they were both truly at peace.

"I still say it should have been me that was made King," blurted out Prode, who had approached the dancing couple with Volaticas. "But, what can I say? Judging by the way the Elites are dressed tonight, it's obvious they have no sense of class."

His giddy laughter echoed through the chamber as he clutched his stomach to contain himself. It really never occurred to him that no one thought he was as funny as he did.

Volaticas Temed was trying his best not to look at Vale and when he did, his face was covered with disappointment and a hint of disgust. Now that it was official, he would have to show more respect. So he forced himself to give half of a bow before walking off with Prode, allowing King Vale to dance with Ara.

"You certainly are surrounded by a group of interesting people," Ara laughed as he continued to spin slowly around the floor. Vale said nothing, but smiled, resting his head on Ara's shoulder.

"I hate to intrude, Your Highness," Lenta said with a bow. "I was hoping that I could borrow you for just a moment."

"Of course," Vale replied. "Ara, would you join us?" he said to Ara as they followed Lenta Benigg across the tiled dance floor to the wall to an empty corner, where no one could overhear.

"Forgive me for being so bold and for saying this right in front of Ara, but I don't think you need me to tell you that your relationship with your bodyguard is becoming slightly inappropriate," she whispered with a concerned look about her face. "Have you given it any thought at all?"

"I know we're having a good time," Vale rebutted. "But, it's part of the ruse. We can't act like there is danger with all of these guests here or they'll panic. Let's face it. It wouldn't kill any of us to just have fun for one night."

"I wasn't referring to your carefree attitude tonight and you know it. You're not listening to me. I'm trying to tell you that it is not appropriate for you to carry on this way with your bodyguard, acting as if you're lovers. It just isn't acceptable for the King of Eliantar."

"What?!" gasped Vale. "That's not it at all. We're just friends who have become very close in the past few weeks. We've spent almost every second together. There's nothing more."

"Well I hope that's all," sighed Lenta. "I know it's only natural, but please remember that it's forbidden for a King or Queen of Eliantar to be in a relationship. Your spouse is Eliantar and, as you know, tradition allows you to have relationships for procreation only. I don't want to see you be the first one in 2,000 years to create such a scandal, especially with your bodyguard. I don't know why Forr wouldn't have said anything to you about this sooner."

Vale took a deep breath, "I understand your concern, but really there is nothing to worry about. Although, I do have to say that I think that 'rule' is outdated and I've never been sure what the purpose of it is. Why shouldn't the King or Queen have the same right to be happy that everyone else in Eliantar does? It makes it difficult to lead by example when there are such exceptions that do not allow that basic rule of thumb to be possible."

"It is outdated I suppose. I hypothesize that by disapproving of a marriage in the monarchy, but permitting procreation they can be sure that heirs are produced to keep the name going. It's ridiculous because almost every Elite in the world lives with a member of their own sex and families have children in spite of that. Who knows the reasons behind it. There are Elites that are heterosexual, though rare. Perhaps the first King of Eliantar, your ancestor, was one of them."

"It never seemed to bother Mother that she couldn't marry another woman," Vale stated bluntly. "She never mentioned women or men for that matter. You don't suppose she was heterosexual?"

"Your mother was guarded about her personal affairs," Lenta shrugged. "I do not know where her heart lied, but that's nothing unusual. Most of the kings and queens throughout history presented themselves as asexual but had children with outsiders, probably other nobles and such. Anyway, my point is that you don't have to be married or with a lover to be a good king. Also, I need to make it clear that your personal business is your personal business. Just please keep in mind that what it looks like is going on tonight, is frowned upon.

"Besides that, Forr showed me Opo's journal this evening. I think you've got bigger things to deal with than worrying about an illicit affair. We should start figuring out what we're going to do about this Sorpa Veneficus woman before more time is wasted."

"Leave that to me," Vale said, turning to leave. "I'm sending the Royal Guard after her tomorrow. According to Opo's journal, she's been in Tacia all along, which is where we were originally headed until Destor diverted us."

"Is it true that he's dead?" she asked. "You found bloody articles of clothing and that was it?"

"It appeared as though the Vintens got to him," Vale smirked. "Anyway, it'll take more than a couple of ruses to keep us from apprehending Sorpa this time. The secret will be out and I'll have the entire Royal Guard scouring the forest realm for her by the time the second sun rises."

"Was it difficult for you?" Lenta asked, a bit uncomfortable. "I mean being in Steedo after what happened two years ago with your friend? I can't imagine that was easy for you."

"It brought up a few bad memories," Vale admitted. "It felt good to be there with Ara, though. I trust him."

They both shared an uncomfortable smile before parting ways. Vale walked back to over to the dance floor with Ara who now looked a little depressed.

While they had been away, Ara had been practicing exactly what he wanted to say. He smoothed out his clothes and wiped the sweat from his bald head before Lenta had begun speaking. Now his hopes were dashed.

"There's something that I was going to say," Ara said. "I'd been thinking about it for a while, but after your conversation with Lenta, there doesn't seem to be a point."

Vale looked a bit confused at first. Then realization washed over his face as he realized what his dear friend was about to say. Ara watched his face turn a crimson red as the sweat began to dampen his brow. He looked at the ground and nodded his head.

"It's just that," Ara began nervously. "I know that we come from different worlds and that I'm just a bodyguard from a peasant's background. I know I'm sounding foolish right now."

"Not at all, but I wish you wouldn't continue," Vale whispered. "Please, Ara, before you say anything else..."

"Please let me finish," Ara interjected. "I've come to feel very close to you since the moment that we first met. I realize that I have nothing to offer you in a relationship. What could anyone offer the King? All I've ever had to offer any man since I left my hometown was my time and my heart. I think...you make me feel...that it would be enough to make you happy, if that makes sense. What I'm trying to say is when I think of my future and what's ahead...and all I want to see in it is you."

The King said nothing. He still had not looked up at Ara. He appeared, to Ara, uncomfortable and at a loss for words.

"Ara, I feel the same way, I really do. I wish it could be that simple. It's just that as King of Eliantar, I'm not permitted to settle down with just anyone of my liking."

He knew he'd hear no different but still felt as though he'd been stabbed with a trelamna. His eyes darted all across Vale's face trying to find an explanation beyond what tradition and law called for. But, the King's face only mimicked his own, confused and sad. He stared at Vale for a few moments longer before he could bring himself to speak. Even then, there was a tremble in his voice.

"I know that and I obviously always knew that, all Elites do. But, you are the King now. Can't you change the rules? I mean if you feel the same way as me, is there not anything that we can do to be together?"

"Lenta's right," Vale muttered, finally looking Ara in the eye. "Right now we need to focus on stopping Sorpa Veneficus before we become involved in any personal issues. We're in a complicated enough time without making things even worse. Please Ara, for the sake of Eliantar, can we discuss 'us' after we've made sure our land is secure."

"You're right, of course," he smiled weakly. "The Elites are lucky to have such a wise King. I wonder though if I might ask...Can we just have one last dance before you make your grand exit and we plan tomorrow's assault? It would absolutely honor me."

In response, Vale closed his eyes and leaned into Ara as once more they continued to slowly sway around the room, amongst all of the costumed Elites.

After a few moments they heard the drumming of rain from above them. It would have to be a downpour, Ara thought, to hear it over the crowd. Within seconds it became rampant and everyone was staring up.

"Rain!" a voice called out.

"There wasn't a cloud in the sky when we arrived," said another.

"It's coming down so hard," people remarked.

The entire sky lit up white for a second as streaks of blinding lightning ripped through the clouds followed by a thunderous bang. The party goers jumped, yet didn't take their eyes off the eccentric display.

"Oh dear gods," Vale and Ara said at the same time, looking at each other, realization sinking in.

Out of the corner of Ara's eye, he saw a man standing next to them and he turned. The man was tall and wore purple, regal robes and a veil over the lower portion of his face. His arms were crossed over his chest as he stared coldly at them. The age lines around his eyes temporarily faded away as he smiled broadly from beneath his purple mask.

"Your Highness," he sneered with a mocking bow. "Are you alright? You look as though you've seen a ghost."

Chapter 14

Ara dove in front of Vale and demanded, "What are you doing here? We had hoped you'd been killed."

"Sorry to disappoint," Destor responded snidely. "I've actually been here the whole night. I think it was a marvelous idea to have a masquerade party. Believe me, it made getting in here seem all too easy."

"So, now what? You're just going to kill us here with all of these people watching? That wouldn't be the wisest idea."

"Watching?" the masked man laughed. "I believe they're all too busy viewing my light show in the sky. And I know you won't be foolish enough to call the guards over. Can you imagine the chaos that would ensue? Can you imagine what I would do to this room if you were so bold?"

Ara and Vale glanced around the room and saw that Destor was right. They couldn't put these people at risk and to make matters worse, no one suspected the danger they were in. Every single person in the room had their eyes looking through the glass ceiling. And what a show it was. The lightning was constant, only allowing the sky to turn back to black for a split second. The thunder quickly followed each bolt and was completely deafening.

"How did you survive?" Ara went on, trying to buy them more time. "We saw the blood and the signs of a struggle."

"I departed Quale after I knew that I was outnumbered by all of the Fonnes. I realized that I would have to get the Prince at a later time. I sensed after a while that I was being followed. It didn't take long to figure out that you two were coming after me. I killed a Vinten and hid the body, leaving my veil behind so you'd think I was murdered. That gave me the advantage to follow you for a while. Now here we are and I can assure you, Your Highness, that this time I will get what I came for."

"Guards!" a voice from behind screamed as Lenta Benigg came running over. "Guards arrest this man. He's the one who attacked King Vale in Quale."

Iradt Furich overheard the ruckus and came bustling over herself, her cleavage bouncing with every step. Her ruby, singed dress trailed behind her as she pushed through the crowd to join Lenta next to Vale.

"What's the meaning of this," she barked, staring rudely at the purple-clad man. "Who are you? What are you doing here?"

"Enough!" screamed Destor, just as the guards were approaching. He looked up to the sky and an enormous bolt of lightning came shooting down. It shattered through the glass ceiling and hit the spot right in front of the weather master."

The party-goers in the vicinity were sent rebounding away from the spot where the blast hit. Shards of glass rained from the sky and Prode ran through the crowd, his arms extended. He formed a telekinetic shield that stopped the glass and slowed its descent to the ground so it couldn't injure anyone. Only Destor Caelu seemed indifferent to his own terrifying powers.

The force of the lightning had thrown Iradt and Lenta into opposing walls, knocking them unconscious. Similarly, Vale and Ara had been thrown apart from each other and landed hard against some tables. They rose slowly fearing what Destor would do next.

Ara looked over to see Forr gathering party guests together and ushering them up the stairs. The old man moved with remarkable speed helping fallen partygoers to their feet and gesturing them to the steps. Ara felt a wave of disgust as he saw Plucid Duru get to his feet and push past the guests as he, himself ran to the stairs and out through the archway.

After he helped King Vale to his feet, he took off to the other side of the room, charging at Destor. He could feel the look of rage contorting his face. Destor saw him coming and spun around, kicking the bodyguard squarely in the chest. Ara fell to his knees as the pain coursed through his body.

"You're so persistent and I don't know why," Destor said with contempt. "I don't know how many times I've had to tell you that this has nothing to do with you, but it seems like you're just insistent on getting in my way."

Ara could see that the guests had all gone and Prode had rallied from deflecting all of the glass. He raised his hands and conjured the two tables behind him to go soaring through the air at Destor, who turned to see them too late. One hit him hard and knocked him several feet onto his back.

King Vale made his way forward to check on Ara as another bolt of lightning came through the gigantic hole in the ceiling and narrowly missed the crown atop his head. Destor was already rising back to his feet, ignoring the thick blood that was oozing from his forehead.

"Your Highness, you and your friends are making this increasingly difficult," he roared. "I'm not leaving here without the King."

The skies opened up once more and enormous drops of rain fell from the clouded sky. Lightning crashed down on and around Ivory Towers. Wicked winds had picked up and blew through the open ceiling sending anything lightweight spinning around the room. All the while Destor's cold eyes stared into Vale's while Ara got to his feet.

Glancing around, Ara found Lenta and Iradt in heaps along the wall, still unconscious. Prode was bent in half, near them, exhausted at having used so much of his powers in a short span of time. And then he saw Volaticas gliding across the floor towards Destor and felt a rush of hope, realizing that they weren't alone.

"Who in the world do you think you are?" he yelled, planting a fist hard into the side of Destor's face.

With a wave of his hand the wind swirling through the room took a different turn and within seconds had lifted the purple villain several feet into the air. He dangled upside-down face to face with Volaticas Temed, Ambassador of Steedo. They glared at each other for a few moments as though trying to see who could make the most angered face. Volaticas's blonde hair swirled around him as he maintained the wind funnel that held Destor suspended.

"I apologize," he scowled. "I'm guessing that no one told you. I control the winds in this kingdom."

"Keep it," smiled Destor Caelu, from beneath his maroon mask. "I've got something much better."

He struck Volaticas back with a quick spark from his hands. This distraction freed Destor from his suspension and he quickly hurled jolt after jolt of energy at the man in the golden-yellow robes. They were low energy and it was clear to Ara that Destor was toying with him. But, Volaticas was powerless to stop the brunt of these attacks. Every time he would attempt to conjure a blast of wind, he was shocked. Finally he lay still on his chest with Destor standing over him.

"What do you want?" he managed to grumble.

"It's about time," laughed Destor. "Not once have any of you asked me what it is that I want. Maybe if you had asked, this wouldn't have had to be so difficult on you and the others. All I want is King Vale."

"Vale, Vale, Vale," Prode's voice rang out. "He's all anybody ever wants. But, he can't do this."

Ara turned to see Prode lift his hands and as if by magic every shard of glass from the ceiling rose from the floor and hovered in mid-air. They circled around Destor for a moment, who realized too late what was happening as every fragment raced towards him.

Destor's eyes became large as he jumped back trying to avoid all of the glass. He was too late. Bits of his robes pulled and frayed as they were shredded by the bits of glass. When he landed on his feet, Ara watched him realize that the glass had caught his skin in several places and that he was bleeding from his arms and face. He stomped towards the young King, electricity crackling at his fingertips.

"Do you know what's wrong with you?" Destor screamed as the blood poured from his half-covered face. "The problem is you're willing to be King of Eliantar, but you're not willing to take any of the responsibility that comes along with it. You'll let your brother and friends risk their lives for you, rather than just hand yourself over."

"Enough!" Ara bellowed as he slammed his fists down hard on Destor's shoulders causing him to crumble to his knees. He screamed out in pain as he collapsed, unconscious. Dozens of members of the Royal Guard burst in seconds later. They rushed down the steps grabbing Destor and dragged him to his feet.

"Take him to the dungeon," Vale yelled. "We can catch up with him in a moment. Thank you, Prode. We couldn't have done it without you.

"We need to check on Iradt, Lenta, and Volaticas and make sure they're okay," Vale glanced around.

Moments later the Ambassadors were coming to. Ara had called for more members of the Royal Guard to sit with them as they woke up from their unconsciousness. Prince Prode had been set out to retrieve Plucid from whichever hiding spot he was in.

"We're going to go pay Destor a little visit," Vale called out to the guards as he and Ara exited. "If they're able, make sure the Ambassadors meet me in the Regulation Committee chamber in thirty minutes."

As they passed back into the castle's foyer, Ara commented, "I never noticed a dungeon in my time here."

"It's not exactly on my house tour," Vale said blandly. "Follow me; it's at the very back of the entrance hall."

When they'd reached the end of the large vestibule, Ara and Vale stood face to face with a seven foot tall statue of Queen Jenneka. The statue was beautiful, carved from a rich white stone. The queen stood holding a trelamna in one hand and a book of Eliantar law in the other. Her face looked kind and sweet, with her long hair falling freely, framing her face and a magnificent crown atop her head.

Ara glanced at Vale, who stared at the statue for a moment, looking rather sad. Than he stepped up onto the large white stone block the statue was on. He grabbed a hold of the stone trelamna and jerked it upwards. The Queen's whole arm moved with it and with a deep rumble the statue began to move.

Ara noticed a seam that ran right down the middle of the statue. The seam grew as the statue split apart, sliding on their respective sides of the walls. Where the complete statue had once stood, was now a steep, dark staircase going down. Without a word Vale began to descend the cold steps and Ara followed.

They didn't speak as they walked for several minutes down the steps. It was impossible to see in front of them, save for the few torches that were sparsely placed along the black walls through their descent.

Ara felt the temperature get colder and colder as they went further down. He also became keenly aware of a rotten stench, like air that hadn't been breathed in a thousand years. He was beginning to see why this wasn't on Vale's house tour. He was certainly glad that this place existed for a place to put Destor, deep beneath the bowels of the beautiful castle, but also felt a bit concerned with its presence. The idea that this place had been here all along beneath Ivory Towers gave Ara chills.

At last they came out through an archway. Ara could see that he was at the top of a large round room, much like the ballroom, but more sinister. As he descended the last dozen steps, he looked around to see that in place of walls, there were large metal bars. The center of the room was simply a gravel pit with no distinct features. Unlike the staircase, the dungeon was lit with dozens of torches, making the eeriness only slightly better. When they stepped onto the stony floor, a guard ran over.

"King Vale, the man has been locked up," he announced as he kneeled.

"What have you done to prohibit his powers?" Vale asked. "He was capable of disabling many people upstairs with a mere thought. I want to make sure that he can be held down here."

"Sir, his powers are over the weather and there is no weather down here," the guard explained. "He isn't able to conjure winds or rains or the like without the sky. He is still able to produce electricity from his hands, but we are working on that.

"Your Majesty," he whispered now. "His powers are unlike anything we've seen. No Elite that we know of can do anything close to what this man has shown that he is capable of."

"Very good soldier," Vale said, ignoring the last comment and stepping over to a portion of the prison where a large number of soldiers stood.

Ara followed the King, trying to stay upright on the floor of pebbles. Walking seemed a bit difficult when the floor was so unsteady. He glanced around at the cells and noticed with curiosity that it was in fact only one large cell. It wrapped from one side of the staircase, all the way to the other. It was about fifteen feet deep, creating a great deal of space, especially for just one person.

As they approached where the guards stood, Ara saw Destor behind the thick bars glaring out at the guardsmen. They stood with their bows and arrows pointed directly at him. They looked fierce and angry, just begging for a reason to fire and put the man out of his misery.

"Your Highness," one of them called. "We have our arrows aimed for his skull and chest. If he tries anything while you interrogate him, we'll shoot to kill."

"Unacceptable," Vale said, adjusting his crown atop his head. "Should he try and assault me with his powers, I request you shoot at the limbs. That should be more painful than death, I think."

"I have nothing to say to you," Destor hissed as Vale stepped forward. "I know that you're not willing to kill me. You need me alive to find out why I've been trying to take you. So, let's just drop the charade. I won't speak, you won't act, and it'll only be a matter of time before I break out of these confines."

Ara glanced at Vale who didn't flinch. His stare was unwavering. He couldn't determine what the emotion was on Vale's face. It wasn't anger or fear, but looked to be more like pity. Not pity for himself, but rather his would be assassin. And then Ara saw the smile spread across Vale's face.

"As you wish," Vale casually said. "How's this for a charade? This prison has not been used in years and years. It is only maintained by my security staff once a year. For you to be down here behind these bars speaks more volumes about the crimes you've committed than you even realize. I may not be willing to see you murdered, but I assure you that I do not require your information. I may request it, but if not, I have no problem keeping security down here at all times so that you spend the rest of your days in this cell.

"I ask this once and only once before I leave you in this prison forever," Vale went on. "Why did Scurus Subo attempt to kill me and why do you follow in his footsteps?"

The look of confusion on Destor's face was so obvious that even his veil couldn't hide it. He thought over these words for a moment before he looked the King in the eye and slowly gave his answer.

"I do not know this Scurus Subo," he said quietly. "I have no associates. My reason for taking you is mine alone."

"What has Sorpa Veneficus offered you in exchange for killing me?" Vale demanded, ignoring Destor's excuses.

Destor cackled, "I do not answer to Sorpa Veneficus. I do not answer to anyone."

His cold voice sent a chill down Ara's spine. He could see that Vale felt the same and that the King was beginning to run out of questions. Things were only becoming more confusing. Ara stepped forward next to Vale to assist.

"When we first met you, you spoke of necromancy in Quale," he began. "You knew we were in search of Sorpa. Why would you misdirect us if you weren't working with her?"

"I shall not deny that I knew the purpose of your quest," Destor replied. "I had been tracking you for some time, and eavesdropping over your conversations at night, which is how I knew where you were going. However, I assure you that I was doing no favors for the corpse woman. I merely wanted to get you into the open so I could take the young Prince. It's amusing to me that you were so focused on where you were going, you didn't notice that I was following you the moment you left Castle Village."

"Why not just kill me and take Vale when you first met us?" Ara inquired. "Why drag this out?"

"I couldn't risk passersby seeing me," he replied. "You were doing a wonderful job of avoiding towns, but I knew if I could get you to Quale, which was still completely abandoned from Grim, I would have a better chance."

"Having no one see you has really worked out very well for you," Ara laughed. "By tomorrow morning all Elites will know your name and what you were trying to do."

When Destor did not respond, Vale grabbed Ara and began leading him toward the staircase. The guards didn't move from their positions as they held their weapons aimed directly at the man in purple.

"We don't have time for this right now," Vale whispered. "We need to get up and meet with the Regulation Committee right away."

Ara nodded and the two began ascending the stairs. When Destor called out they both turned around in surprise.

"Your Eminence," he yelled with a mocking tone. "I may not be working for Sorpa Veneficus, but having overheard your conversations, I hope you're prepared."

Vale stared at Destor for several seconds before turning and continuing to march up the steep, black stairs. Ara stayed rooted to the spot, unsure of what to say and confused about the sudden words of caution from Destor.

"Why would you help us now?" Ara asked.

"My goal was to capture King Procer," he responded quietly. "Be that as it may, I do not wish to see a world ruled by the undead. From

142

the sounds of it her power could destroy us all, whether she realizes it or not."

As Ara walked from the dungeon towards the Regulation Committee chambers, he thought over the evenings events. Destor Caelu had admitted that he was trying to kidnap Vale, but would not say why. And then he offers words of wisdom for confronting the corpse lady. It was all too bizarre. Ara couldn't wait to get back to the castle after they had captured Sorpa and find out more from Destor. He was fascinating to say the least.

He ran as quickly as he could up the dark stone staircase and through the castle's foyer. He made his way up the several flights of steps, covered in blue carpets to the fifth floor. The castle was dark, darker than he had ever seen it. He had to hold onto the golden handrail as he ascended. A couple of times he glanced at the walls along the staircase and could barely even make out the rich tapestries that adorned the castle.

It gave Ara a chill to see this place so cold and dark. It was as though Destor's mere presence created a cloud of darkness here.

When he reached the fifth floor, he found it just as depressing. Save for a few torches along the wall, the castle was dark. He supposed that the attendants had better things to do tonight with all of the chaos than keep the entire castle well lit.

The thick blue carpet felt soft beneath Ara's feet as he slowly made his way down the narrow hall, careful not to bump into any tables. In the darkness, he could see the silhouettes of many large busts and vases atop the elegant tables on either side of him. At last he could just make out the enormous wooden doors to the chamber. He pulled hard on the metal ring to pry one of the doors ajar.

His boots clicked loudly as he walked across the marble floors through the giant columns to reach the Committee. This room was as dark as the others with only a few torches lit to offer any light.

As he walked through the chamber he saw that all of the other members were already in their seats. He glanced at their faces, as he sat next to Vale. They all shared the same look of fear and concern. Volaticas and Iradt looked as though they wanted to speak up, but given the grave look on King Vale's face had thought better of it. Forr and Lenta looked utterly beaten as if they knew the situation was much worse than they had thought, and they were running out of hope. Plucid looked, as always, terrified as he sat in his chair with his eyes on the floor. Prode's face was unreadable. He sat there with a blank look on his face, staring at the floor as though trying to rationalize in his own mind what had just happened.

"After our last Regulation Committee meeting," Vale began, his voice filled with sadness. "We learned that Scurus Subo, my would-be assassin, was working for a woman named Sorpa Veneficus. Sorpa has the ability to raise the dead as slaves and threatened my mother shortly before her untimely death."

The officials in the room had their eyes and ears on King Vale. They listened with intent as he told the story of leaving the castle to search for Sorpa and being diverted by Destor. They sat aghast at the attack in Quale as well as the faked death of Destor in Steedo.

"Yet after all of that, you don't think he works for Sorpa Veneficus?" Volaticas asked when the story had ended. "What are his reasons for trying to kill you?"

"We…we don't know yet," Ara answered.

The small group burst into conversation, all speaking at once. Clearly they were not happy with the lack of information on a random lunatic trying to kill the King, especially one with such dangerous powers.

"So, who is the enemy then?" Iradt demanded as she adjusted her burnt dress on her corpulent body. "My problem with this whole story is how do we know that this Sorpa is the villain when all we've seen is this Destor Caelu trying to kill Vale?"

"Because one of the guards found the journal of Opo Scoloos," Forr burst out. "He was in league with Sorpa to raise an army of dead soldiers and overtake the world. What's worse is that Sorpa Veneficus is trying to free the dark god Skarsend from his prison."

The room was silent for a long moment. Plucid Duru put his head in his hands, clearly wishing he could be anywhere but here at this moment. The rest of the Regulation Committee sat deep in thought, surmising what they thought might be the best course of action.

"We will deal with Destor later," Vale announced. "Sorpa Veneficus must be dealt with immediately. Clearly she is more dangerous than we had originally perceived."

"When do you plan on going after her?" Lenta asked.

"Tonight," Vale said amidst the shocked gasps. "Ambassadors, please leave the Ivory Towers as soon as possible. Ara, be ready to depart in one hour. Assemble the Royal Guard. We will be riding out to the cemetery in Tacia."

"What do you hope to accomplish with all of this?" Iradt asked. "You're going out there on some witch hunt. Wouldn't it be wise to finish questioning tonight's attacker first?"

Vale thought for a moment and answered, "This woman, Sorpa Veneficus, she drove the one man my mother was supposed to trust against her. She has threatened to destroy the world that we know and love to build her army. We will do what must be done to see her stopped."

Chapter 15

As Ara got dressed, Forr nervously paced around the room talking about Tacia. He completely ignored Ara's comments about having been there many times before and told his mythologies anyway.

"On the second day of creation, the god of plant life and vegetation, Treak, appeared on our black mass of land in corporeal form. Like all gods and goddesses he assumed a form that pleased him most. He appeared as a young human and, at the same time, something very far from a young human.

"His skin was the color of ivy and his hair came off of his head resembling some kind of grass. His lips were the color of the reddest rose and to see him in this naked splendor, one would think he was as delicate as one. The other gods rolled their eyes at the fey form their brother had taken and scoffed to themselves as he skipped merrily along the black ground.

"He was terribly discouraged at being the first to arrive, since it was impossible to know where to start. But, as we all know, when you're not sure where to start, start at the beginning. So, with a deep breath and a stomp of his foot to the ground, all the land in his vicinity and for miles and miles all around became covered in thick green grass. The once completely flat, black slab of land in the middle of space was now a flat, green slab floating in the middle of space.

"Next with a mere thought he allowed trees and plants to burst forth from the fields he had created. The more life he brought to the fresh world, the happier he became.

"Setting his sights on completing what all the gods had previously talked about and making this world a paradise, the god chose a large section of land to the far southwest. He decided that this section of their new world be his vision of paradise that none of the other gods could interfere with.

"And so he set to work creating a dense, emerald forest that he called Tacia. He commanded hundreds of thousands of trees to spring from the ground, some that he had never even thought up before. The trees reached to the sky and completely covered the southwest corner of the new realm. The further into the forest the god walked the more power he used, so that eventually the forest gave way to boggy marshes which gave way to lush jungles. And when he had finished

146

his masterpiece and he knew that his day was coming to a close, he decided as one final act for a forest haven, he would give birth to a civilized species to rule over the forest and care for it. His hands swished back and forth as he departed for the heavens and thus the winged, arboreal Arbestees came to be the first creatures on the new world. They surveyed their forest home with their enormous bird eyes and they were pleased."

"Thank you, Forr. You know in some odd way, your stories have actually become rather soothing to me."

He patted the old man on the shoulder and received a weak smile. Then he turned and left to go meet with the others.

The sky still hadn't returned to normal since Destor's assault in the castle's ballroom. It was completely black without a single star to be seen as the Royal Guard filed out one by one through a small, hidden hatch on the side of the palace. Hundreds of azure-colored chariots had already been prepared and were strapped to regal horses. Unlike the chariot that Ara had ridden in to get to Castle Village, these were chariots of war, completely open up top.

Vale had decided early on that stragglers might still be loitering on the marble path in front of Ivory Towers. To counter this, he decided to make use of a secret passage that actually went through the ballroom, up ten steps, and out through the castle wall. From here the chariots could go along the castle wall. They'd still have to exit the courtyard and village the same way, but would draw a bit less attention than prepping right in front of the castle. Certainly the citizens would still see or hear a commotion, but this way would hopefully raise fewer questions.

The guards had finally all loaded into their respective chariots, clad in black shirts and pants with silver chest plates and helmets on. They were silent as the night as they waited patiently for their next order. As they had never found themselves in such a situation, it could safely be assumed that they were also quite nervous.

Ara Tataman came out last. He was still wearing the same blue tunic and tan pants that he had worn at the inauguration, except now he wore a silver chest plate over top. He carried a long trelamna like the other members of the Royal Guard and, like them, was very somber as he mounted the empty chariot before him.

The chariot was similar to the others, but grander. It was almost twice the size and was filled with emblems of the Royal Seal. Ara had seen the seal before, but now that he had 'traveled' more, it was more significant. It pictured a giant shield broken into five separate images: a flame, a tree, a mountain, a stream, and a gust of wind, all crossed with two trelamnas.

Ara turned to see Vale and Prode exiting the hatch, quickly followed by Forr. Prode was wearing a jade-colored shirt and black pants. Vale, on the other, had discarded his blue robe and was merely wearing a gray, sleeveless tunic with white piping. He also wore the large, gold crown. Vale turned back to face his advisor and Prode jumped on the chariot next to Ara.

"Hope you don't mind my joining you," Prode giggled. "I figure since apparently all of this trouble is going on in my backyard, I share some of the responsibility. I really do feel awful that I didn't know this was occurring under my nose," his look became serious.

"No one blames you Prode," Ara said without looking at him. "Sorpa deals with shadows and specters. It's not really her style to make her actions obvious to the observer."

Prode's eyes lit up as he realized that he wasn't being blamed. He began jabbing Ara in the ribs.

"Well I'll tell you this," Prode smiled. "If she's going to do business with ghosts and zombies, then she's *dead to me.*"

He immediately burst into raucous laughter. Ara rolled his eyes in disgust and tried to listen to Vale and Forr.

"I really hope that you aren't going to try and talk me out of going," Vale snapped. "It's my responsibility to go along and help in any way that I can. I need to lead by example."

Forr responded weakly, "On the contrary, I was going to tell you how very much you remind me of your mother. She also would never have thought of staying home if an event like this had occurred. I only want to tell you to please be careful and that I am so sorry."

Forr began to weep and quickly wiped his eyes with his gold sleeves. Ara looked on, confused.

"What could you possibly have to be sorry about?" Vale asked.

"My visions have failed you, Highness. I used to be able to clearly see the future when I meditated on it. Now, I only seem to be a hindrance to you and for that, I apologize."

"There is no need for blame tonight," Vale reassured. "Have you had any more visions of the future?"

"I see only blackness and nothingness. I don't know if it's to be an ominous sign or not. There is…nothing."

The awkward pause that followed seemed to last forever. Finally, Vale turned and pulled himself onto the chariot with Vale and Ara. He turned one last time to his old friend before they departed.

"Forr," he called. "The stallops are pulling our carriages so I will see you first thing in the morning. It will all be better by then."

Ara watched as he turned to address the hundreds of eyes that stared back at him. In them he saw anticipation, fear, and respect.

"We have an enemy not of the throne, but of all of Eliantar. She is a necromancer who means to destroy everything with an army of dead soldiers. We have learned that she is based in Tacia, in an old graveyard. I do not know where the location is, other than that it is at the border."

"Your Highness," a young soldier that Ara recognized to be Kally, the soldier who had stood guard outside Forr's chambers. "You're looking for the Woodland Tombs. I know this because I have been there."

"They have a name?" Prode asked. "Nothing in my jurisdiction has that name. I would know about it."

"With all due respect, I don't think most know it exists," Kally answered. "I grew up in a town a few miles from there and my mother told me stories about a cemetery that would only appear at night. It's existed for thousands of years and is protected by ancient magic to repel tomb thieves. That's what legend says anyway. I've seen it only once and promise you that it's very real."

"Forr," yelled Vale. "You once told me that the Royal Family was all buried in a secret graveyard that no one knew existed. Is that true?"

Forr went white, "Not just the Royal Family. Most nobles and members of the Royal Guard are buried there as well. Our tomb keepers are the only ones who know the location and they tell no one."

"Is my mother there?" Vale asked quietly.

Forr didn't need to answer. With a slight wave of his hand towards Kally, the young guard's chariot took off with all of the others in hot pursuit.

They rode hard through the night. They were out of Castle Village in a few minutes and flew through the fields of Eliantar. By stallop, the ride to Tacia would only take a couple of hours. After an hour Ara leaned towards Vale and yelled over the loud wheels.

"It might've made more sense to travel this way the first time around. It's certainly better than walking for days and days."

"I apologize again," Prode interjected. "Invisible or not, I feel like I should've known that this graveyard existed within my forest."

"What bothers me most about all of this is what part Destor plays," Vale said. "He claims he's not connected to Veneficus in any way, but then why keep trying to attack me?"

"He'll be interrogated by me personally when we return," Ara said bluntly. "His reasons at this point mean nothing. We've already got one lunatic one the loose. I don't see why you'd be so surprised that there might be two."

"Be quiet" shushed Prode. "It looks like we've arrived."

Sure enough Ara and Vale could see the other chariots had slowed to a halt just a few yards from the forest border. It looked identical to the rest of the border that stretched for miles and miles, so Vale was glad that they had a guide to help them find their way.

The young guard ran back quickly to King Vale's chariot and did a quick bow. He looked terrified.

"Your Highness, the Woodland Tombs are just beyond the first few layers of trees."

"Thank you Kally," Vale said full of genuine grace. "We could never have made it here without your help. You will not be forgotten in helping to aid us like this. Now let's get this over with."

"Wait Vale," Ara whispered before wrapping his strong arm around the King's waist and pulling him in close. "Tradition be damned. I won't hide my feelings any longer because an ancient king 2,000 years ago said that I should. I'm in love with the King of Eliantar and I don't care what anyone thinks about it."

With that he forced his lips against the King's and felt little resistance. For a few moments time stood still and it was just the two of them, hard bodies pressed against each other, tongues fighting for dominance as they wrestled in each other's mouths. Then as quickly as it started it ended. With a sly smile, Vale pulled away. There was work to be done at the moment.

Vale noticed as he jumped down that a thick layer of fog covered the ground. It looked as though the forest itself was secreting some peculiar smoke adding to the uncomfortable mood of the night.

"Tacia becomes a different place at night," Prode whispered. "Even as Ambassador, I feel a little uneasy wandering around once the suns have set. We will want to be cautious."

Vale and Ara slowly made their way to the arbor border. Ara waved his hand and the guards slowly descended and followed their King. Several carried crossbows while still more carried trelamnas. Prode stayed to the back of the group, eyeing his surroundings with caution. Ara glanced over and saw the bow attached to Vale's hip.

"I spent all of that time training you to use a trelamna and you walk around with a bow instead?" Ara quipped.

"I'm not expecting that this meeting will end in hand-to-hand combat," Vale replied quietly. "With any luck, she'll surrender herself immediately with no altercation."

Vale stopped dead in his tracks. Ara looked over and saw that the color had drained from his face as his eyes stared forward. Ara looked to see what he was staring at and there just a few yards away stood Sorpa Veneficus.

She was barely visible standing just in front of the line of trees. She wore the same worn, black dress that Forr had described. The same funeral veil flowed down over her face from her disheveled raven-colored hair. If not for her ghostly-white hands and neck, she would have been completely invisible in the darkness.

She stood completely still, facing the army with her arms at her side. Her expression was completely hidden beneath her shroud, but Vale was sure she could see the surprise and fear on all of their faces. They all remained still for several seconds, before she raised her thin bony arm and pointed at King Vale. When she began to speak her voice sounded like nails on a rotting piece of wood.

"So we finally meet, Vale," she croaked. "How far we've both come in just a year. When last I was in Ivory Towers, you were just a boy and now I stand before the King of Eliantar. I, on the other hand, was just a peasant in the eyes of your mother and now I'm...so much more."

Ara had shuddered when the woman had begun to speak. Her voice sounded as though it was carried on the wind. He imagined it was the same sound that was released when a coffin was opened after a hundred years.

"Sorpa, we have come here to take you back to Ivory Towers," Vale announced. "We have reason to believe that you have committed treason and will need to question you."

Veneficus scoffed, "I know why you've come. It hardly matters at this point though. I can assure you that you're too late. I've had a year to bring my plan to fruition."

Ara ignored her, "Why did you send Scurus Subo to kill Vale? What was in it for you?"

He could make out the confusion on Sorpa's face through her shroud as she brought her hands up to the sides of her head. She made a low guttural growl that Ara identified as a laugh.

"You're so like a member of royalty. You immediately assume that it must be about you. Surely if a dramatic event takes place in the kingdom, it must surround the King or Queen of Eliantar."

Her voice had become less arrogant and far more embittered over the course of her last statement. Her bony hands had begun to clench and ball up, making them appear even more skeletal.

"Scurus wasn't there to kill you," she snapped, her voice filled with venom. "He was there to kill the traitor, Opo Scoloos."

Realization washed over Ara. How had he been so stupid? No wonder Forr had detected no danger before Vale had stepped out to address his people that day. He never was in danger. There never was an assassination *attempt*, because in actuality it had been a success. Even after reading Opo's journal, Ara had not realized this and now felt dim-witted.

"We read Opo's journal," Ara bellowed. "We know that he was working with you and then abandoned you."

"He really was a dullard," hissed Sorpa. "How truly stupid to leave a journal outlining your betrayal in the very home of the one you're backstabbing. I don't know why I'm even surprised."

"Why kill him?" barked Ara. "You had to know that there was no way he would risk his own head and admit what he'd done to Vale. What could you have possibly obtained through his death? The Queen had already died!"

The silence that followed was endless. Vale and Ara waited for an answer while Sorpa stared at them, silent. When at last she spoke, there was a tone of sadness in her voice.

"If you truly read Opo's journal, I assume you read that it was not part of our plan for Queen Jenneka to die."

"Are you actually going to stand there and say you're sorry that my mother is dead?"

"You don't have to believe me, but it is the truth," Sorpa sighed. "I assure you that you're making me out to be far more sinister than I actually am. If you give me a chance, I can help you understand."

When Ara and Vale didn't give an answer, Veneficus took a breath and continued with her story.

"As you know, I had propositioned your mother to create an army of undead warriors to use. What you don't know is that I had very good reasons for wanting to do this."

"What reason could you have possibly had for wanting to kill all of those people?" Ara yelled.

"No one needed to die. I wanted to use only those members of the Royal Guard who had long been deceased. The unfortunate part of that is that the longer a person is dead, the less...durable they are."

"You forgot to mention that they'd be slaves," Vale snapped. "You weren't doing anyone favors by bringing them back if their mind stayed dead."

Sorpa chuckled, "Yes, an unfortunate side effect of my powers are that people lose their freewill once brought back. However, I see much potential in those who fall before their time. I've come to find that they still have so much left to offer the world."

"And so you wanted to raise an indestructible army for what purpose?" Vale asked. "To aid a demon?"

"To save us all," Sorpa replied. "Skarsend brings death with him. He offered the world salvation and I accepted his generous offer. You see raising an army of the dead as monstrous, but I'm saving all of our lives."

"That's when I had a purpose for Opo. He had been ordered to destroy me. All he need to do was lie and say that he'd carried out the deed and that would allow me to carry on with my plan without suspicion."

"And Opo actually went along with this?" Ara gasped. "He didn't have any problem betraying the one person he was assigned to protect."

"Opo loved the Queen and knew it was his duty to do whatever was necessary to promote peace."

"What in the world took a year?" Vale asked. "Opo lied to my mother like you asked and promised to lead your army. Shouldn't you have done what you set out to do then?"

"I may not have told Opo all that was occurring. First, I had to find Skarsend and set him free from his confines."

"What?!" snapped Ara. You're contradicting your so-called 'not sinister' intentions. You said he was freeing himself and that you had no choice but to join him for survivals sake."

"Be serious," barked Sorpa. "It's still for survivals sake. He's a god and I am a mortal. He would have eventually freed himself anyway. There's more to it than you know, but I won't deny that power and self-preservation have always proved irresistible to me. What more can I say?"

"Is he freed?" Ara asked. "Where is Skarsend now?"

"He's a god, you stupid man. He's everywhere."

"And now the Royal Guard is here," Sorpa laughed. "That was the real reason that I had Opo Scoloos assassinated. I assumed, incorrectly, that you would send all members out on a scouting mission to find me. You see I never had any intention of meeting Scurus Subo in Fornar. I told him that after Opo was killed, I would meet him there. I knew full well that he would be pursued, questioned and killed.

"I've been waiting here for many weeks for you to arrive and was beginning to think that you never would."

"You overestimated Scurus," Ara said. "He didn't reveal your identity. We had to figure it ourselves and even then, we felt pretty confident that you didn't require more than King Vale and me to take you in. But, now the Royal Guard is here. What purpose could you have with them?"

Sorpa Veneficus said nothing, but stood staring at Ara and Vale. Neither of them needed to see her face to know that she was brimming with confidence. The guards behind them were shifting nervously.

Prode slowly made his way to the front of the throng and stood beside his brother.

"Lady Veneficus," he began. "I am Prode Procer, Ambassador of Tacia. I insist you show us this hidden cemetery at once."

For the first time, Ara was truly impressed with the way Prode spoke. It seemed that, for once, he was taking his job seriously. Whether he was doing it wisely or not remained to be seen.

"As you wish," Sorpa bowed slightly. "I should warn you that seeing the Woodland Tombs won't facilitate anything. You may be Ambassador, but you have no power here."

"It may be a trap," hissed Vale. "We have Sorpa already. I think we should just take her back to the castle."

"We need to see exactly what she's been up to," Prode argued. "I don't want to assume that we're in the clear just because we've apprehended her."

Ara watched King Procer think this over for several moments. Either way possessed great danger. If they followed her into the forest, they could be walking into a trap. There could very well be an army of zombies waiting for them. However, if they captured her and simply took her to Ivory Towers, her army could cause massive amounts of damage before they became aware of it.

Vale sighed loudly, "Lead on Sorpa. Please be mindful that if this is a ploy, I will order my men to kill you."

"So be it," she replied.

She turned and began to walk through the trees. Vale and Ara stayed close behind as the combination of the dark foliage and heavy fog made it difficult to see. They hadn't gone more than a few yards before the ground dropped off steeply. Sorpa glided down with ease. Vale, however, caught his foot on a root and fell down the hill. He landed hard on the grass.

Within seconds, Ara ran down after him. He knelt down beside his friend and slowly helped him to his feet. As Vale gathered his bearings, he looked around and gasped.

There were thousands and thousands of tombstones in the clearing. All were different sizes and shapes that looked like ornate teeth rising from the dirt. They reflected the tiny bit of starlight and glowed eerily in the darkness of the forest. Most were faded and covered in overgrowth, but some stood out as being much newer and whiter.

"Oh dear gods," Vale exclaimed. "I would never have imagined that there would be this many. Ara, there's one hundred times more graves than there are soldiers here. It's a trap."

They hadn't noticed that Sorpa was now standing alongside of them, adjusting her long, moth-eaten dress and trying to maintain some kind of order to her mangled hair. She glanced around the clearing of tombs with a tinge of delight.

"Sooner or later you'd have to come to the Woodland Tombs," she cackled. "Just remember before you decide to judge me that it was your choice to make it sooner rather than later."

With that she raised her hands and looked to the sky. The ground rumbled furiously as mounds of it shifted. Vale didn't need to guess what the ghastly woman was doing.

"The dead will rise again," hissed Sorpa staring down at the King.

Chapter 16

Sorpa ran off into the darkness as Vale and Ara stood watching the scene in terror. Tombstones around them began to shift with the ground as mounds of dirt began erupting and bony hands clawed for the surface.

The Royal Guard had gathered around Vale and formed a barrier, though they looked just as petrified. They held their assorted weapons at the ready. Ara, too, stood with his trelamna staff gripped in his hands. Vale held his bow closely by his side.

As the dead began to rise to their feet, several of the guards gasped aloud. While a few of them looked intact, most were in various levels of decay. The zombie closest to them only had bits of skin left around his eyes and on his hand. What had once been regal clothes were now bits and pieces of molded rags that draped across the deceased. A few random strands of hair clung to the few bits of his head that were not skull and his eyes were long gone, but the empty sockets had a small glow, burning in the back.

The stench was becoming overwhelming as the long dead bodies were exposed to the open air for the first time. For many, the exposure to the air was too much and they began to crumble to dust before they had even gotten to their feet.

"She wants the Royal Guard here so that her army will be newly dead," Vale realized aloud. "Look at how the ones in the back dematerialize before they even have a chance to stand."

"That should make the fight easier, right?" Ara asked with a hint of doubt. "They're much more fragile than living soldiers so they won't be that much of a threat to us."

"You've forgotten a very important fact," whispered Prode, who had now come up to stand alongside Vale and Ara. "Sorpa can just keep resurrecting them as they fall, so even if they only kill one soldier in this first wave, they're winning. Every fallen soldier of ours will only come back as a stronger warrior that is a slave under Sorpa's power."

The fact that they were grossly outnumbered only added to the grimness of the situation. As the dead rose, it quickly became obvious that there were a hundred times more of Sorpa's warriors than there were living members of the Royal Guard.

Soon enough they saw that they were completely surrounded. It was the most frightening moment of Ara's life. He had never seen so many corpses as long as he'd lived.

Many could barely support themselves on their legs, as there was little more than a tendon or two, holding the bones together. The entire army of deaths skin and clothes were merely a memory of what they had once been.

"Some of them have weapons," Prode advised. "Apparently we bury the Royal Guard with their trelamnas."

The disgust in Prode's voice was mutual for Vale. One would think that burying a member of the Royal Guard with their weaponry, would be a symbol of respect. Clearly, no one had ever foreseen that the demonic necromancer, Sorpa Veneficus, would come to the Woodland Tombs to create an invincible army. But now it was too late.

"Why aren't they attacking us?" one of the nearby soldiers had whispered to his peer.

Ara looked around and noticed it as well. Sure enough the dead were maneuvering themselves around the Royal Guard, but once there, stood completely still. They had been so concerned with the frightening display, that they had just assumed they were about to be assaulted.

"What do you think they're doing?" Ara asked. "They're just standing there, staring at us."

"They don't know any better," Vale realized. "When Forr saw Sorpa in the Regulation Committee Chamber last year, he said that she had to give very direct and specific orders to the zombie that was with her. They will not attack us until she decides to order them to do so."

As he spoke, even more crypts became unearthed. The Woodland Tombs looked to encompass roughly a square mile and it was becoming obvious that Sorpa Veneficus could only use so much of her power at once, as evidenced by how slowly the resurrection process was taking.

More and more disintegrating skeletons hobbled over to the bottom of the precipice, where Vale, Prode, Ara, and the Royal Guard stood.

A few moments more and the ground had stopped shaking. The deceased rose no more.

Ara frantically scanned over the heads of the dead slaves, looking for Sorpa and knowing that she would soon shout her execution commands. Try as he might, he couldn't find her over the immense crowd until at last she spoke.

"The one thing in life that every living person fears is death," she shouted from a large crag, opposite them. "It's frightening to wonder how one will die and when. Therefore, I've never been able to figure out why so many are afraid of me. I offer liberation from the fear of death and even so I find myself condemned. You shall all find in your painful deaths that life will prevail in the end. Destroy the living!"

At once the army began to attack. The Royal Guard brandished their trelamnas and waved them malevolently at the zombies. An arrow shot from Vale's bow, striking a dead warrior square in the chest. The arrow ripped through its back and soared into the distance.

"Royal Guards!" he bellowed. "You are not as mindless as the soulless ones that the necromancer hides behind! Remember your training! Do what must be done and stop Sorpa Veneficus."

The Woodland Tombs erupted as every member of King Vale's army roared and charged at the wall of death. They swung their trelamnas at the deceased, who in turn tried to defend themselves with their own weapons and attacked as well. For the most part, however, the lifeless bunch was no match and fell quickly.

"I'm going after Sorpa," Prode yelled as he ran off into the fray, quickly disappearing in the combination of action and darkness.

"No, Prode!" Vale called. "We had a plan. We're doing this together."

"The plan is still on," Prode called back before disappearing in the crowd.

"He's going to get himself killed. Ara, we need to forge a path to Sorpa and put an end to this."

And so Ara rushed into the horde swinging his trelamna over and over at the slow-moving creatures. Vale ran behind, firing from his bow as quickly as he could reload it.

One that must've been newly dead came running at Ara, who held his staff low and swung it sharply upward, just in time to catch the corpse under the chin. He flew back, slamming into a tombstone and cracking it right down the middle. A silver arrow, fired from Vale, rocketed through the dead man's head and he rose no more.

Looking around them, Ara and Vale saw hundreds of corpses making their ways towards them. The Royal Guard were all involved in their own battles, but were trying to keep the zombies from getting too close to their King.

"Where are they all coming from?" gasped Ara. "There are more zombies than there are living people in Eliantar."

Ara Tataman continued to wield his trelamna with deadly ferocity. As the dead got closer, he separated it in the middle and swung both arms in opposite directions, sending enemies flying in all directions. With the sharp ends he tried to impale the ghouls, but there were far too many coming at them for him to do any more than simply swing with all of his might as King Vale looked around for a different course.

"I can't keep this up much longer," Ara called to Vale, clearly showing signs of strain. "More and more are coming and like you said, even if I do kill them, she can just keep bringing them back."

"There!" Vale yelled. "Look Ara, there is some type of mausoleum out in the fog. I can see dozens of them coming from there. If we can get over there and seal the doors, no more will get out and we may stand a chance here."

"There are too many around us right now."

"I can take care of that," Vale replied.

Ara looked around as Vale closed his eyes and seemed to concentrate hard. Seeing that no more undead could approach, Ara knew Vale was putting a mental barrier around them that the dead could not cross. He held it around them as tightly as he possibly could and then let it go with a snap. The hordes surrounding them flew out hundreds of feet in all directions.

"Guards!" screamed Vale. "Use your powers. Don't rely on fighting skills alone. If your power can be used in battle, please use it. We need to use all we have now."

The two immediately rushed off into the fog and darkness towards the gray catacombs that loomed in the distance. Ara could see through the mist that the monument was grand, yet simple. It was an immense cement block that was several feet taller than him with heavy, metal doors that hung open.

Masses of the cadavers lurched towards Vale and Ara from the opening. Vale fired from his bow at them and mentally sent the rest flying off to the sides until at last he reached one of the heavy doors to the mausoleum.

"I'm sorry that I'm not much help," Ara sighed. "The trelamna isn't exactly a projectile weapon and my power is useless in this environment. I'm not sure that I'm the one who should be protecting you."

"Don't be ridiculous," scolded Vale. "I've told you before that you're perfect for the job and besides that, your power may come in handy by the end. You can't die, remember?"

"I never said that," responded Ara. "All I've ever said is that I'm more resistant to physical attacks than the average person. I'd rather not test exactly how much it would take to kill me."

With that a corpse came around from the entryway of the mausoleum and wrapped a rotting arm around Ara's neck. Vale lifted his arm and the zombie, as if by his own will, released Ara, clutched his own throat and squeezed. Harder and harder he squeezed until at last there was a loud crack and the soldier fell to the ground, lifeless once more.

"A bit brutal," Ara chuckled.

"We need to get these doors closed before even more get out," Vale said, his voice filled with fear.

Before either could move they heard the scramble of a multitude of feet coming up the mausoleum steps. Looking at each other in terror, they nodded, both clearly aware of what they must do.

"We do have the high ground, after all," Vale attempted to be optimistic. "We can do this."

"Just stay behind me," Ara cautioned. "You're not supposed to be running headfirst into battle."

Vale merely shrugged as Ara ran around the door and swung his trelamna staff hard, knocking back half a dozen denizens of death. Vale leapt behind Ara and saw what looked like hundreds of armored zombies climbing the stairs.

Realizing that that many would merely knock the doors down, Ara called on Vale who began shooting at the coming army. He began to descend the steps, making sure to shoot at the enemies on the front line, obviously hoping they would knock down those behind them as well.

"Be careful with that thing," Ara warned, going several steps ahead and stabbing at as many of the cadavers as he could at one time.

It was dark and Ara began to wonder how deep these catacombs went since after twenty steps, they still could see no floor at the end of the staircase. The dead kept on coming which made it even more difficult to see any light at the end of this tunnel of death.

Hearing a noise behind him, he turned to see a dozen zombies entering the tomb from up top. It hadn't even occurred to him that the danger from above would keep coming even though they were in the mausoleum.

"Ara, they're coming from both sides!" yelled Vale.

"See what you can do with those new ones. I'm just a little busy here," he responded, as he slashed and stabbed endless amounts of the retched living dead combatants.

Vale fired his bow at the soulless warriors coming down the stairs while Ara continued to deflect the masses climbing them. When he shot one of them in the leg, it collapsed and began to tumble down the steps. Vale tried to move out of the way but was struck and began to fall as well. When Ara felt Vale slam into him, he knew they may be in trouble.

They slid backwards down the hard, stone steps taking down countless zombies with them. Ara felt an invisible force slowing him and knew Vale was saving them both. He had concentrated his energy and brought himself and Ara to a halt and lifted them both to their feet. Then with a concussive force, he sent the remaining enemies hurling down the steps at breakneck speed, literally. They could hear bones and necks snapping as they hit the hard ground far below.

"Good gods!" exclaimed Ara, turning to face Vale. "You can be really violent with those powers. Honestly, I don't know why you even bother carrying that bow along with you."

Before Vale could respond, a blanket of darkness covered the starlight that shone in through the entryway. Looking towards the doors they could see a large figure standing in the archway.

"Opo," Vale gasped.

Ara looked again and Vale was right. There standing just a few yards above them was Vale's former bodyguard, Opo Scoloos. He looked nearly the same as he had before he was shot down less than 40 days ago. He wore the same dramatic armor that he had that day.

In his hands he clutched a long trelamna menacingly. He stared with empty eyes at Ara and Vale and began to step very stiffly down the steps.

"Vale, if he gets down here we'll be cornered," Ara warned. "Use your power to knock him out of here. I will face him on ground level and you can seal off the mausoleum."

A second later, an invisible force picked Opo's corpse up and launched it clear out of the mausoleum. Ara chased after it, running hard up the stairs and into the open. Vale followed, but paused for a moment. The unmistakable sounds of moans could be heard from far below.

With that he jolted up the steps, two at a time, until he too was back on the grassy land. Turning back to the doors, he and Ara grabbed onto a metal door and pushed with all of their might. The heavy doors slammed shut and let out a groan. No one would be getting in or out of that mausoleum for a very long time.

Ara turned and looked around the war torn cemetery for Opo, but couldn't see him amongst the chaos. Vale must've thrown him much further than he intended. All around him there were members of the Royal Guard fighting the dead. By rough estimate it appeared as though for each Royal Guard, there were four zombies. However, seeing one of his soldiers engulf several enemies in a massive flame that rose from the ground, put Ara at ease. At least they were using their special abilities as well.

Distracted by this, Ara was suddenly knocked to the ground from behind. Spinning around quickly, he saw Kally, the soldier who had lead them to the Woodland Tombs, battling a horde of zombies. He had been knocked back by his attackers and stumbled right into Ara. He was easily outnumbered by eight or nine of the rotten corpses.

Vale ran up and aimed his bow and arrow at one of the closest creatures, but a sharp blow to Kally from another one caused him to misfire. In spite of having his trelamna, Kally was no match for the pack. Several of them carried trelamnas as well which was making it difficult for him to defend himself.

Regaining his footing, Kally swung hard in all directions. One zombie lost his head and collapsed as his cranium went flying off into the night. Another was cut neatly in half, right at the waist. The two halves fell to the ground in a pile. The torso immediately began to crawl at Kally while the legs kicked the air furiously.

Kally stared at the torso with his trelamna held high, ready to stab down. He didn't see another corpse coming at him with his own trelamna staff poised to strike and Ara hadn't gotten to his feet quickly enough to help.

The blade went into Kally's chest and he let out a slight gasp. Vale screamed as he watched the young man's eyes roll back in his head and he dropped his weapon, falling to the hard ground, lifeless.

Ara watched as Vale mentally grabbed onto the zombies' trelamnas and lifted them out of their owners' hands. Redirecting them, he lunged them at the remaining dead, impaling them through their chests. The trelamnas soared through the air, stabbing into several trees, pinning the zombies to the arbors.

Turning back around, Ara could see Sorpa in the distance, standing on top of her large stone wall. There crumbled in a heap at her feet, lay Prode. Vale let out a slight gasp, next to him, realizing that his brother had fallen.

Was he badly hurt? Was he even alive anymore or had she already taken the liberty of killing him? He didn't have much to ponder on this matter as Sorpa Veneficus, clearly thrilled with the slaughter she was witnessing, stepped over Prode and began to speak.

"Royal Guard, it certainly appears as though you're beating death itself," she announced with glee. "From where I stand, it looks like you've only lost a few of your men, which is to be commended based on how outnumbered you are. Let's even up the playing field."

She raised her hands and let out a deep, menacing growl. All across the Woodland Tombs, the fallen dead began to reanimate once more. They stirred slowly in their piles and then rigidly climbed to their feet again.

"I think you'll soon find that it may just be easier to give in to death," Sorpa's voice cracked with delight. "After all, you certainly can't keep this up forever. You must be getting tired by now, but my army never tires and will only grow in numbers. Feel free to surrender to your impending doom."

Ara's stomach turned as he listened. No one but Prode could even seem to get close to Sorpa to put an end to her, and he was down. How could they ever hope to defeat a force that was undefeatable?

"Ara!" Vale yelled and Ara turned, instinctively with his trelamna up high.

It clashed sharply against Opo Scoloos's. The man was strong, but so was Ara after years of hunting and every time Opo made an attack, Ara countered back as strongly as he could.

They had been at this for several minutes, with no sign of either being more superior. Ara fueled his energy by berating the dead Opo, even though he knew Opo couldn't hear it.

"It takes a lot of guts for you to even show your face to King Vale," he roared slashing at Opo's mid-section, who blocked the assault. "You betrayed Queen Jenneka and you failed to protect Vale. You're a traitor! You're better off dead than alive for the wrath you've incurred."

Ara was well aware that Opo was no longer himself, but rather a soulless slave to Sorpa. Still, it gave him peace of mind to finally say all of the things to his predecessor that he'd been dying to say.

He was realizing more and more why it was so important to Veneficus to control a "freshly dead army." Most of the other warriors from the Woodland Tombs were slow and collapsed after one solid strike. Opo, on the other hand who hadn't been dead for very long, still retained all of his strength, as well as his superior fighting skills.

A surprise kick to Ara's stomach knocked him back a few steps. He hunched over in pain as the dead Opo held his trelamna high. Ara quickly jumped to the side as the spear struck the ground. Opo tried in vain to pull his triple-bladed weapon from the ground, but could not.

Ara charged at Opo and leapt into the air. He landed a solid kick right in the small of Opo's back, which dislodged his trelamna and knocked him to the ground. The loud crack that rang through the night made Ara think that surely Opo was down for the count. He realized all too quickly that he was wrong when Opo rose to his feet once more.

"You're persistent! Why won't you stay dead?"

Ara became more and more frustrated knowing that no matter how infuriated he became, Opo remained completely emotionless and unaware. He didn't recognize that he was being attacked or ridiculed. All he knew was that his sole purpose was to kill Ara Tataman.

Ara stomped towards Opo, who slid his staff apart into two separate weapons. With one quick move he slashed the blades in an upward arc, nearly stabbing Ara in the chin. Ara jumped back and threw his staff at Opo, who moved to the side just a moment too late. The blade sliced up his arm as it sailed by. Opo, however, was unaware of the attack and clearly felt no pain. No blood even came from the fresh wound. And now Ara was left defenseless to the zombie warlord.

To members of the Royal Guard who caught a glimpse as they fought their own battles, the clash was brilliant. Two men, both holding the same titles that looked fairly matched, locked in a fight to the death. Both the same height and build with the same armor. They also seemed to share equal abilities when it came to wielding their weaponry. The irony was flawless. Unfortunately, most were too busy with their own duels to take notice to the battle of the bodyguards.

Ara was wary as he had now lost his trelamna and Opo was coming towards him. He made a quick dash to get around Opo, but was too slow. Opo swung one of his trelamna sticks at Ara and caught his side.

Ara fell to the ground and watched as the blood poured profusely onto the grass. He looked up at Opo who stared down for a moment, before turning to walk away. His eyes spotted up and everything turned to black as he waited for death.

He blinked and saw that the spots had gone as well as the pain. He sat up quickly and looked at his side, soaked in blood. His skin was already starting to repair itself. Never before had he ever imagined that he was this invulnerable. This was far beyond the advanced healing he thought he possessed. He should have bled out by now, but his wound had completely closed.

Jumping to his feet and grabbing his trelamna, he saw that Opo had realized his folly and was coming back. He swung his staff hard at the dead man, who easily blocked the strike. Rather than dwell on this, Ara repeatedly clashed his trelamna over and over again against Opo's weapon. Opo had not anticipated this fast, brutal attack and lost his balance, the trelamna flying from his hands.

He stopped and stared at Ara for a moment, face completely blank. For a split second Ara felt bad for the once noble warrior who had been so easily corrupted and now existed only as a servant. The sympathy was lost when Opo punched Ara square in the chest sending him back several yards, slamming him into a tree.

The force would've literally killed anyone, but Ara rose after a few seconds. Vale had been right; his invulnerability had come in handy. He had been under the impression that Sorpa's zombies no longer possessed their special abilities. Clearly that was relative to how long they'd been dead before they were brought back.

He rubbed his eyes in time to see Opo stalking towards him once more, fists clenched. Before he had time to deliver another crushing blow, Ara raised his trelamna and Opo walked right into it, the points sticking out through his back.

A soft sigh came from Opo's lips as his head slumped and he returned to death once more. Ara retracted his trelamna and ran back towards the Tombs to find that all of the soldiers were standing still with the respective zombies that they'd been fighting, standing nearby and watching them closely.

"Very impressive!" called Sorpa. "Not impressive enough to win the battle, however."

Ara looked up to her crag and gasped. Standing alongside Sorpa, next to Prode in a heap, stood King Vale held at knifepoint. But, who was that woman holding the knife to his throat? Why wasn't Vale fighting them? He should at least be defending himself.

And that's when he saw the elegant dress, the flowing, long hair, and the brilliant crown atop the woman's head. His heart broke for Vale as he realized what evil Sorpa had done. There, standing next to Sorpa Veneficus was Queen Jenneka with the glinting knife in her hand.

Chapter 17

Queen Jenneka had clearly been a beautiful woman in life. Ara could see that though she had lived forty years, she didn't look old enough to have Vale and Prode for children. Her skin was creamy white and smooth with small, delicate features and her raven-colored hair blew gently in the night air around her. She wore a sky blue, gauzy body suit and cape with a golden crown perched atop her head. Though he had seen many portraits and statues of the Queen in Ivory Towers, they hadn't captured just how stunning she was.

With the exception of some gashes on her Forehead and spots of blood on her suit, she looked intact. Ara guessed that the blood stains were from her fall into the thorns, when she killed herself. Other than that, he would've guessed that she was still alive, holding the dagger to her son's throat with no expression on her face.

Vale, on the other hand had a peculiar look on his face. He didn't look worried or upset, but rather disappointed. He stared at the ground unable to look at his mother, Sorpa, or even Ara. It seemed the other members of the Royal Guard were mimicking their King as they also wore a defeated look.

"Vale!" Ara called out. "Use your powers! Knock your mother back and get out of there!"

Vale responded, "I can't. I won't attack my mother. She doesn't know what she's doing."

"That's exactly the point. She isn't your mother anymore. She's just another one of Sorpa's zombies. Don't let her kill you."

"There's nothing I can do," the King sighed. "I'll die before I can assault her. What if there is some way that we could bring her back?"

"That's what she wants you to think, remember?" Ara pleaded. "Remember the first time that Forr met Sorpa? This is what she does. She wants you to believe that she can save the ones you love from death, but all she can do is puppeteer. Your mother is dead."

Before Ara could get another word out a sharp blow from behind brought him to his knees. His shoulder ached at the part where he'd been hit. He spun his head around and once more saw Opo Scoloos standing over him.

Though the stab wound still was present in his chest, he maneuvered as though he was ignorant to it. His dark, soulless eyes

168

bored through Ara's bright, blue eyes. Had he not known better, Ara would have assumed that he was thinking or feeling something. However, he knew at this point that there was no longer an Opo Scoloos, only a corpse that had superior strength and a tri-bladed weapon.

Opo raised his trelamna high, again ready to stab Ara, who quickly swung his leg around. It caught the back of Opo's ankles bringing him down hard onto his back. Ara rose to his feet and ran in the direction of the trees, knowing full well that Opo was stupid enough in his current state to follow him.

Sure enough, as Ara reached a row of trees, he turned to see Opo running at top speed towards him. His trelamna now separated, Opo was prepared to kill his enemy off this time. Ara separated his as well and looked ready to attack when all at once, he turned his head to the sky and made an abnormal sound.

Opo stopped in his tracks, which made Ara happy. He'd confused Sorpa. Looking back up at the treetops, he continued to make the low, guttural sound over and over.

"What in the world is he doing?" Sorpa hissed before calling out to him. "Whatever games you're playing are only delaying what you cannot escape. Distractions won't save you from death."

Just then a group of giant, feathered bird-men descended from the trees, letting out a howl similar to the one Ara had been using.

"Arbestees! Stop them!" screamed Sorpa. "Destroy them all if they try to interfere here."

But, it was too late. The massive bird-men, big as Elites, but far quicker, swooped down and clutched Opo with their golden talons and lifted him off the ground. Fast as a flash they flew back up to the top of the tallest tree and pinned the giant warrior between two massive branches.

Opo struggled and fought against the branches, but couldn't move his arms enough to break his confines. The whole time, he never took his eyes off of Ara, far below on the ground, who merely smiled back.

Ara again approached the necromancer, this time wearing a smug look upon his face. "Go ahead and send him after me a thousand more times. I won't kill him again. I'm done playing your sick games."

Sorpa stood staring at him blankly. Prode still lie motionless at her feet. What happened to him still remained unknown. The dagger in Queen Jenneka's hand glinted in the starlight as it pressed into Vale's neck. Seeing no change in this situation, Ara began to get nervous.

"Did you not hear me?" he roared. "I won't fight Opo Scoloos anymore, witch. No matter how much you want to see him kill me."

"You idiot!" she finally snapped. "Of course you won't kill him again. You can't kill him and I've just proved it. And you're a fool to think that those branches will keep him trapped forever. All you've succeeded in doing was sealing the Arbestees' fate by encouraging them to help you."

"It wouldn't have been long until they assisted anyway," he retorted. "I've spent years living in these forests and the Arbestees are the most benevolent, noble creatures that I've ever met. They would never have stood by and watched you take over Eliantar with your evil powers."

"I had hoped that they would come to realize that, like you, they had no hope. You see I gave them more credit than I gave the majority of Elites, who I knew would try in vain to put this to an end. Clearly they've proven me wrong."

"So why prolong this?" Ara asked, beginning to sense defeat.

"Why whatever do you mean?" Sorpa smiled. "Prolong this? I was the one who wanted to make this quick and painless a year ago. This one...," she glared pointing at Vale, "was the one who brought me to this point. I didn't want to stage a dramatic coup in this depressing place. He led you all here, not me."

"Then just do it," he screamed, not taking his eyes from the necromancer. "Kill us all if you've already won like you say you have."

"So be it," she whispered once again allowing her eyes to gaze up to the heavens and her arms rose.

Ara looked around and watched as all of the members of the Royal Guard who had fallen slowly rose to their feet. The open wounds that had killed each of them stopped flowing with blood as their bodies reanimated.

Ara frantically looked from one to the next, hoping to see some sign of intelligence or knowing in their eyes. He wasn't surprised when he saw none. He became very worried, but sadder than

170

anything. So many young warriors, who only a few hours ago believed they had their whole life to live, were suddenly lifeless, forced to watch from the afterlife as their bodies performed the duties of a madwoman.

Each warrior bent down to grab onto their trelamna and poise at the ready for Sorpa Veneficus's next mental command. Their red eyes stared holes through Ara, as if waiting for him to strike first.

A loud grunt behind him forced Ara to turn around. He saw Sorpa straining, still with her hands and face to the black skies. Turning back around, he watched as the re-slaughtered corpse army rose yet again. As they came to attention, they slowly made their way to join the Royal Guard. Together their numbers were massive.

Ara's stomach turned as he sized up Sorpa's army. The entire Woodland Tombs were completely surrounded. There was no way that he could take on this many warriors. Even if the few remaining members of the Royal Guard were to help him, he couldn't save the King and hope to get out of this alive.

Maybe Sorpa was right, he thought to himself. Maybe it was time to concede defeat and allow the unspeakable to happen to him, before the situation became any worse.

"I surrender, Sorpa!" he called out to the necromancer, who smiled with the delight of victory. "I have only one last request. If you're truly as honorable as you pretend to be, I pray that you hear it."

She stood there, pondering over what Ara had asked for several seconds before responding. "Go on with it then."

"What you're doing to Vale is cruel and unfair. I beg that you let him go. His regime has had nothing to do with forcing your hand at anything, as you claim. He is heartbroken over the untimely loss of his mother and to have her attack him is simply malicious."

Sorpa looked staggered at this request. She paused for a moment, staring hard at Vale through her black veil. Slowly she turned to Queen Jenneka who still stood with a dagger to her son's throat. She eyed the pair up for a bit before slowly turning back to Ara. Even through the black, tangled hair and long funeral veil, he could see that she was both saddened and surprised by what Ara had asked.

"Malicious you say?" she said with a tinge of bitterness. "You have no idea what malicious is until you've lived the life that I've lived. Malicious is being treated like a slave by the Queen.

"Oh yes," she laughed, seeing the surprised reaction on Vale and Ara's faces. "Yes, I knew Jenneka for years before that time I burst in on the Regulation Committee meeting. You see, I wasn't always like this," she gestured at her dark garb, hiding her emaciated form.

"I used to be quite a beautiful woman. We met each other when we were both young girls taking an Eliantar cultures class. I was just a commoner and I had no idea who she was. All I knew at the time was that she was the most beautiful girl that I'd ever seen.

"We took to each other quickly and she was so kind to me. We'd spend hours out in the field talking and gossiping while we were supposed to be studying. She eventually worked up the nerve to tell me that she was a princess. But, that didn't matter to me because I knew that I loved her no matter what.

"I discovered later that it was so difficult for Jenneka to tell me that she was a princess, not because she was embarrassed by her fortune or power, but because as a ruler of Eliantar, she was not permitted to take a lover.

"Both of our hearts were broken, but we decided to make the best of the time that we had together. We became secret lovers. I had all but moved into the castle under the guise of Princess Jenneka's best friend and confidante. No one in the castle need know that we were sharing the same bed and promising each other our hearts until the end of time.

"Alas, nothing lasts forever. A couple of years into my life of paradise, Jenneka's father died and she was thrust into the spotlight of being the Queen of Eliantar. I did not know what was to become of me. I thought I would be shown the door."

Sorpa paused for a moment to compose herself. Ara and Vale both stared, openmouthed at her. Ara could tell Vale was feeling the same emotions that he was, the urge to call Sorpa a liar, but deep down knowing that all they had heard was the truth. And so, it spite of the shock, they allowed her to continue.

"I was wrong about being forced out, however," she continued. "Your mother allowed me to continue living in Ivory Towers as her friend and friend only. As she took on more and more of her responsibilities, I saw her less and less.

"I still continued to keep her secret. I assume Forr always knew, but who knows what the old troll knew. He never even took an interest in learning my name while I was there. He didn't even remember me when I strolled through the castle last year.

"The few moments that I did have with Jenneka, I'd beg and beg her to be honest and let the rest of the world know about us, but she'd always refuse and beg me to keep my silence. Like a good lover, like a fool, I did just that. I lived bored as could be in my cell in the castle.

"It wasn't very much later than that when the good Queen gave birth to twin sons. I begged to the gods to give me patience and understanding but they failed me. Why would your mother take on a male lover? Just for heirs? How could she betray me like that after all that I had done for her? How could she be so cold when still at this point all I wanted in the world was to run to the tallest tower and scream how much I loved her? But, it didn't matter. Now that she had her full time job, as well as two adorable children, she had no time for me. It was days and days before I would finally get to see her. Even then it would only be for a few moments. Needless to say, we hadn't slept in the same bed in years. I felt betrayed.

"Suddenly it occurred to me that maybe this was all my fault! Maybe I wasn't doing enough to keep our love fresh and new. I had started under the guise of her advisor, but obviously never was. Perhaps if I became more political, I would be able to spend more time with my sweet Jenneka."

"What did you do?" Ara asked quietly, when Sorpa paused for almost a minute. "What did you ask her for?"

"The offensiveness at having to ask at all!" she ranted back. "Imagine having to ask the love of your life for some attention. Every time that I looked in the mirror, I could see my beauty fading. I could see lines from stress erupting across my face. And as for the will to eat, that's never quite returned.

"Since you asked...I begged for a job as one of the Ambassadors. It didn't even matter which realm. I told her that I would come to feel at home in the forests, the lakes, the mountains, even the fire. She, of course, asked if I was aware that I would have to live there and I told her that in spite of that I would still see her more than my current situation."

"Did you get the job?" Ara asked, already knowing the answer.

"No!" she hissed. "She told me some drivel about only hiring those whose power reflects that of the realm they rule. He proved that she was a liar!" she pointed at Prode's unconscious body and kicked it.

"I suppose it wasn't a total loss. After all, she did offer me a wonderful job as an alternative."

Her voice was filled with spite and venom as she directed her hatred at Jenneka's zombie, who of course, was none the wiser. Ara and Vale stood watching Sorpa's anger consume her. Hoping to buy a bit more time, Ara attempted to keep the conversation going.

"What did she have you do in place of being an Ambassador?"

"I was a tomb keeper!" she roared. "I was never so insulted in my life. My job was to work with a few other hooded Elites and come to the Woodland Tombs to bury all of the deceased nobles, guards, and such. That's how I came to discover this place. That's how I came to know so much about my control over the dead."

"Maybe that's why she had you work as a tomb keeper," Vale offered in a whisper. "She probably thought that with your knowledge of the dead, it would be a job well suited for you."

"Yes, you're right my dear," Sorpa mocked. "That would make perfect sense if not for the fact that she had no idea what my power was! I didn't even know what my power was until I began working there. I'd never seen a corpse before so how would I know I could raise the dead? And your mother was so arrogant, she never even cared that I didn't know what my gift was. But, she would fly around the fields and castle, looking down her nose on all of us."

"My mother didn't look down her nose!" snapped Vale. "Plenty of Elites never know what their powers are because they may only apply in certain circumstances, just like yours. You can't blame my mother because she didn't know you had to be surrounded by death to be of any use."

Sorpa ignored him and continued, "And so I continued biting my tongue and worked hard as one of her tomb keepers. I worked so hard, hoping to be recognized by Jenneka. I kept thinking that one day if she heard how well I was doing she might remember me and how much she loved me. That day never came."

"Had it ever occurred to you that maybe my mother wasn't in love with you anymore?" Vale asked, his voice filled with hatred. "Have you ever once thought that you were just a teenage fancy for her and that she just didn't know how to dismiss you with tact? Or maybe she did love you still but was overwhelmed with her responsibilities so she kept you as close as she could. If she truly felt nothing for you anymore she would've thrown you out of the castle."

"No!" roared Sorpa. "You're not listening to what I've told you. Yes, deep down Jenneka must have still loved me. Her selfish responsibilities to her country and her children overwhelmed her so much that she couldn't even follow her heart anymore. But that should not have driven her to push me away! She was being brainwashed by the very life that she was forced into."

Vale and Ara didn't need to say aloud what they were both thinking. Jenneka's seeming rejection had clearly driven Sorpa insane. Her fists were clenched and in spite of the number of years old her story was, she was still filled with obsession that crossed the border to rage.

Vale could see from where he was standing that the veins in Sorpa's neck were protruding, a hideous purple color. She frantically ran her fingers through her frazzled hair. Vale realized that they were running out of time before she finally broke down and went completely mad.

"So what happened next?" he asked. "Obviously you didn't work as a tomb keeper for long."

"Certainly not!" she barked. "That job was beneath me. I'd worked so hard and wasn't being recognized for it."

"Did you ever try telling Queen Jenneka how rejected you felt?" asked Ara. "She seemed to be a reasonable woman. Maybe if you had spoken with her directly, she would have realized she was hurting you."

"I never had the chance! She was always too busy to see me. Finally I worked up the nerve to storm into her chambers and demanded to know why she was treating me this way. She of course pretended to be upset and swore that her obligations kept her too busy but that she still cherished me. I demanded to be treated with more respect than I'd received and be given duties befitting of a Queen's partner in life."

"That couldn't have gone well," Vale said snidely. "Members of royalty don't usually like being given direct orders."

"That's an understatement young King," she replied with sadness. "That was the day she sent me away from the castle. She broke down right in front of me, but wouldn't say another word. I begged and pleaded to at least be able to stay in the place that I'd come to consider my home, but she wouldn't hear of it. She threatened to call the Royal Guard if I protested at all.

"I left Ivory Towers heartbroken that night with the few possessions that I actually owned. I lost the love of my life as well as my residence. I didn't have a friend in the world outside of that castle. I hadn't spoken to my family in years and your mother had been my only friend. I was officially homeless and didn't know what to do. But, then Skarsend, the fallen god of darkness, began coming to me in my dreams. He understood the pain that I'd been through. I spent years trying to locate him so that we could help each other.

"Once that was done, I knew that Jenneka would finally come to appreciate me. We would finally get the chance to be together because I would be the one to unify Eliantar and protect it from Skarsend's destruction."

She strode over to Jenneka Procer and began running her fingers through the Queen's flowing hair. She let out little coos and whispers as she did so.

"You hadn't counted on her death," Ara stated. "Is this really how you envisioned your future with her? She's a zombie."

"Better than nothing," she responded coldly. "At least in this function, I have no fear of rejection from her anymore."

"You must only be a shadow of what you were then," Ara said. "Did Jenneka even recognize you last year?"

Sorpa laughed evilly, "Well she of course knew my name. I daresay she couldn't hide the look of shock on her face at seeing how I'd changed. Her rejection ravaged my appearance and it felt satisfying to let her see what she'd done.

"I apologize for your mother's deception," she turned to Vale. "And I am so sorry that I'm forcing her to kill you. It's the only way that I can think of to punish her for her coldness to me. Wherever her soul truly is, I pray that she can see that it is by her hand that her son will die."

"So be it," announced Vale, who quickly turned to Ara and gave a panicked wink and began nudging Prode with his foot. He had a plan! Ara knew that he had to distract Sorpa for just a few seconds more.

"Where is the shadow god that you've planned all of this with?" Ara called out. "One would think that if he's been helping you mastermind this whole nightmare, he'd be here to assist you. That is unless he's so much of a coward that he's let you do all of his dirty work."

With Sorpa's attention now back on Ara, Prode opened his eyes, looked up at Vale's head, and concentrated. He hadn't been unconscious. He and Vale must have worked out this plan from the beginning. Ara watched as the large, golden crown atop Vale's head slowly rose into the air and high into the trees. Ara smiled and prayed that the twins' plan would work.

"He will be along shortly," she smiled. "This was to be my big scene. I had no interest in ruling Eliantar, but it seems that's the only way I can be with my love. I only want to live with my sweet Jenneka without the burden of her responsibilities or her children."

Ara looked at Vale and saw he was looking back with a small reassuring smile. Whatever, he was hoping to achieve, Ara could only implore to the gods that it succeeded.

"Go on then," Ara mumbled, filling his voice with defeat. "You win."

"Well thank you," she cackled. "Do you know that's the first time that any person has ever said that to me before?"

She turned towards the King and his mother and called out in a booming voice, "Jenneka!"

Immediately, the Queen turned to look at her former lover with the same blank look that she'd had throughout the whole night. Vale on the other hand, had a look of determination mixed with hope.

Sorpa pulled back her veil and smiled broadly. Her face was the color of snow and her cheekbones poked at her skin as if ready to burst through. She appeared as though at one time she could have indeed been beautiful. Now, she looked like she could pass for one of her corpses.

"Jenneka, dear," she beamed. "It's time to end this long life of misery. It's time for you and I to rule as queens! It's time for the ruler of Eliantar to die."

Vale smiled and breathed a huge sigh of relief as Prode, still lying down, mentally allowed the crown to fall. It landed hard on Sorpa Veneficus's head. She let out a sharp yelp at the surprise and pain of the golden metal cracking against her skull. Jenneka began to press the dagger against her son's throat.

"Sorpa Veneficus," Vale shouted. "I dub thee Queen of Eliantar and all who reside there!"

A look of horror spread across Sorpa's face as she realized what the young King had done. Before she could react, she looked up to see Jenneka leaping at her, dagger in hand.

Ara watched as the body of Vale's mother tackled the necromancer to the ground. She'd hit the rock hard on her back with the Queen straddled on top. Jenneka raised the knife high. Veneficus let out one last yelp as the knife plunged down.

An overwhelming feeling of relief swept over Ara as he rushed forward to embrace Vale, but the feeling quickly dissipated as his surroundings turned to black. He frantically looked from side to side but the void was all around him. He couldn't see Vale, Jenneka, or any of the Woodland Tombs.

Chapter 18

The world had gone black as pitch. Ara couldn't figure out what in the world had happened. One moment he was consumed with the thrill of victory. The next moment he couldn't see or feel a thing.

The closest he could come to describing how he was feeling was light and weightless. Was he dead? He wasn't sure. All he knew was that he was no longer standing, but rather floating through the blackness.

It was as though he was in a dream that he couldn't wake up from. He reached over with an arm he couldn't see and attempted to pinch himself. Nothing. He didn't feel a thing. He knew at a moment like this that he should be extremely panicked and yet he was not.

"I am dead!" he said aloud but could not hear the words or for that matter feel his face moving. Indeed it was as though his physical body was gone and he existed now only as a mist that swirled through the black void.

What had killed him? Surely there were hundreds of zombies in the Woodland Tombs, but they had all been motionless while Sorpa threatened to kill Vale, using her former lover as the weapon. He certainly hadn't felt any pain when he'd died. He began to wonder if the others there had been killed as well.

"You're not dead," a kind voice whispered through the mist. Whether he had heard this or imagined it he could not be sure. He wasn't certain what was real any more.

"I promise you are still very much alive," the voice spoke again. It was definitely a man's voice. One that he'd never heard before. "I saved you from death so you could stop the darkness that's coming. A chain of events has been started that will destroy all of Eliantar. You couldn't fall with the others. I couldn't allow it."

What was the voice trying to tell him? Fall with the others? Where were they? Was Vale alright?

"Look and see what's happened while you've been gone," the voice responded to the unspoken question.

"While I've been gone?" thought Ara. But, he didn't have time to question that statement as the darkness melted away and he saw a scene that was all too familiar to him.

He hovered several yards above the Woodland Tombs. He could see Vale staring frantically at the empty spot where Ara had just been standing. He was yelling towards him but Ara could not make it out. The zombies scattered across the clearing stayed motionless, unaware of what to do without their master.

He felt himself being forced to gaze to his far right and he saw a black, gnarled tree. He watched the tree began to twitch and writhe as it slowly changed shape. It was a man, a man garbed in black metal with razored edges on his arms, legs, and neck.

Skarsend was enormous, standing roughly nine feet tall and was as broad as four men. His eyes were the color of fire. His sharp, white teeth glinted with delight as he stalked towards Vale.

"Kill whoever is still alive!" he roared with a voice that sounded like that of a wild animal.

Ara watched in horror, unable to help, as the few soldiers who were left were slaughtered brutally. Though the zombies only obeyed Sorpa, it seemed they also responded to the power of a god. When the zombies that had been led by Sorpa Veneficus approached Vale and his brother, Skarsend ordered them to stop.

"Leave them for me!" he cackled with a laugh that would've chilled Ara's spine, if he still felt like he had one.

The scene melted away and he felt himself somewhere in the fields in the midst of the countryside. He looked around, but could not be sure exactly where he was. There were fields as far as the eye could see, but little else to separate this part of the country from the others.

Looking up he wanted to gasp, but of course could not. Thick, black clouds poured across the skies, blocking out the suns from view. The breeze that surrounded him became a deep chill and even though he could not feel it, he was extremely aware of it.

He could barely see a few feet in front of him anymore. The clouds, that looked more like smoke, had completely dominated the skies and it appeared to Ara that they were not going to dissipate anytime soon.

The fields melted away and he found himself in a room that he'd been in before. He couldn't forget the gauzy drapes that covered all of the windows. Then there were the hundreds of lit candles scattered around the tower chamber and the numerous smoking pots. He was in Forr Suosor's sanctuary.

Looking around, he saw Forr in a heap on his bed, weeping openly. He seemed lost and frantic. The tears flowed down his streaked cheeks and every few moments he would pound the bed with abandon, as hard as an old man could.

Stopping suddenly, he jumped up from his bed and ran over to a large cauldron in the corner. Grabbing several vials from a nearby cabinet, he frantically uncorked them and dumped their contents into the cauldron. The black pot hissed and smoked furiously.

"Where is he?!" yelled Forr. "Where has he gone?" He stuck his head over the cauldron and took a deep breath of the vapors that were rising from it. He immediately began gasping loudly and convulsing, his white eyes bulging out of his head.

He stepped back and collapsed once more onto the bed. "Where is he? Where has he gone?"

Glancing at the broken vials on the floor, Ara read a few of the labels. It seemed Forr had been concerned about his ability to read the future correctly any longer. The potions he was making were no doubt to put him a spiritual trance of some kind. He couldn't help but feel sorry for the old man, as he, himself, had recently come to realize that the old man's powers weren't completely diminished.

Hearing Forr mumble something else, Ara glided over to the side of the bed and looked down at the old man convulsing and writhing.

"No hope. There's no hope."

Forr was gone in an instant and Ara found himself back in the Woodland Tombs. Glancing around he could see the thousands of tomb stones and unearthed graves begin to fade from sight.

Obviously the first sun had risen so the Tombs would cease to exist for another day. If not for this, however, Ara would never have guessed that the day had come as the black clouds still littered the sky.

He hovered over the clearing looking for any sign of life, but there was none. The fallen soldiers were gone as were the zombies. Any sign of a scuffle had faded away with the graves. Hearing a grunt across the forest, Ara glided over to the sound's origin.

If he were able to gasp he surely would have. Prode marched along with two undead warriors escorting him in shackles. His moss-colored robes and handsome face were stained with dark mud. The look on his face was one of defeat and hopelessness. He trudged through the thick forest with great difficulty, occasionally stumbling, only to be punched from behind by one of his escorts.

He looked less like a prince and more like a pauper as the tears began to flow down his dirty face. Ara could see that he was trying in vain to compose himself, but was failing.

A few times Ara tried to swoop and attack the zombies, but to no avail. They remained completely unaware of his presence.

"It's no use trying to change what you see," the kind voice appeared again. "You are simply watching scenes from the past. You cannot interact with the visions presented to you."

"How far in the past is this? Where am I now?" Ara thought as loud as he could.

Rather than hear an answer, Ara watched as his surroundings faded into a greenish cloud, which slowly became a brownish cloud. A moment later he was in the midst of a vast desert.

Before him was a giant mountain with heavy metal doors. Besides that, all he could make out around him was an endless yellow desert with gaping sinkholes. Though he had never been this deep into the realm, he knew he must be in Errandomn, the land of the Tamalus.

Hearing one of the heavy doors open, Ara turned to face Plucid Duru wiping his fat, sweaty face with a handkerchief. His bulgy eyes looked from left to right, over and over again. Ara glided through the opening just before Plucid slammed the door shut.

"Oh, my gods. Oh, my gods," he whimpered to no one in particular.

Ara knew this must be the Errandomn Citadel, the capital of this realm. And no wonder Plucid was always so anxious. The entire structure was built out of a hollow mountain. There was no furniture or decoration as far as he could see in the massive entryway. He couldn't even make out where the ceiling or back wall were. All that he could see were large stalagmites far above his head and several stone staircases leading to who knows what.

Turning back to Plucid, he saw that the Ambassador had collapsed onto the hard ground and was sobbing loudly.

"Help me!" he roared. "Please someone for the love of the gods, help me!

The heavy doors burst open and Ara could just make out the outline of several figures standing there.

182

"Oh no!" screamed Plucid. And just like that he was gone along with his surroundings.

Before he saw the lava, he could sense the heat around him. The environment was filled with fire, both natural and emotional. As Iradt Furich came into view, Ara attempted to cringe before realizing that he could not.

She stormed through the red chamber in a fury. Her heels clicked angrily on the cracked, black floors as she twisted her tight curls atop her head. This went on and on for several minutes before Ara finally looked away and took in his surroundings.

The room looked to be Iradt's throne room, though quite small. There was a black door on the opposite side of the wall that led through the narrow room to a gigantic red throne, the only piece of decoration in the room. He looked at the walls and realized the room gave off a red glow because of the magma that flowed down through holes in the floor. Overall, Ara though that the red-hot room perfectly mirrored Iradt's incessant rage.

"Why was Vale there alone?!" roared the robust woman in her blood-red dress. "He had his bodyguard with him. What happened to *him*?"

Ara knew without having to wonder that Iradt was asking about him. He realized that his sudden disappearance from the Woodland Tombs made him look like a failure to everyone.

"...should never have even been appointed!" Iradt raged on. "Vale picks him on some whim or childish infatuation and we're all just supposed to believe and trust that this man is as wonderful as all his predecessors who had years of training. And now look what's happened to us."

He couldn't help but feel the pangs of guilt. As much as he disliked Iradt, he didn't want to disappoint anyone, especially Vale. As everything began to fade away, he wondered just how badly he had failed and what had become of the beautiful man that he had fallen in love with.

"Damn you Ara Tataman!" he heard her yell as she faded from view. "Damn you the way you've damned the rest of us!"

He saw a mane of blonde hair whip by him and knew immediately that he was in Volaticas Temed's Citadel in Steedo. Glancing around he wasn't sure how any of the Ambassadors could live in these unfeeling dwellings. Then he remembered the outside of the Water Citadel and how beautiful it was. Clearly it was a matter of personal preference and suddenly it didn't surprise him that Volaticas's home would give off a chill as he was Ara's least favorite Ambassador.

The room was a massive square and the walls were composed entirely of windows and glass doors that led to massive balconies. Even so the gray floors and ceilings made it clear that this was not a room where the self-centered Director would come to appreciate the sunshine.

There was a loud slam and Ara watched as Volaticas used his wind powers to angrily slam all of the windows and doors shut. One at a time the heavy glass swung shut making loud pops and Ara was entirely surprised that none of them cracked from the strength of it.

Turning on his heel, Volaticas strode to the middle of the room; bitterness covered his handsome face. He said nothing as he knelt in the middle of the room, on the hard floor. He cursed no one and didn't allow the hatred to leave his face.

It gave Ara an eerie feeling. It looked as though Temed knew something awful was coming and all he could do was wait for it. Wait with a bitter hatred for all to see through his glass palace.

The vision of Volaticas was gone and try as Ara did, he could not bring himself to feel sympathy for the man. Plucid and Iradt had never been his favorite people but they had a level of respect for King Vale, something that Volaticas Temed had never managed to muster.

The lake that appeared before Ara was beautiful. It was as azure and serene as one would appear in a storybook. Looking across the lake, Ara could see a figure kneeling at the water's edge and so he glided over.

It was Lenta staring into the peaceful waters, her long brown curls covering her face. Ara could see from the reflection in the water that she was sad and fraught with worry, though she was trying to disguise it.

When three Fonnes burst their heads through the water, Ara would have jumped if he could. Lenta on the other hand had clearly been expecting them. They seemed thrilled to see their Ambassador, gurgling and talking loudly at her with their bulgy eyes blinking rapidly.

"I am so sorry to tell you..." she whispered softly, just loud enough for Ara to hear. She took a deep breath and was clearly too broken up to continue.

The Fonnes stopped their gurgles and looked at each other, concerned. At least as concerned as they could look considering they had giant fish heads. They waited for her to continue as their transparent bodies bobbed up and down in the sparkling lake, which had lost much of its sparkle since the suns were covered.

"I've come to tell you goodbye my friends," she continued quietly, unable to make eye contact with any of them. "I sense...I don't think that I'll be around much anymore." Seeing their eyes bulge even more she quickly went on. "I don't want any of you to worry. I will be fine and so will all of you. I'm sorry, I have to go now. Good bye."

The Fonnes called after her as she walked away, probably asking her to explain further, but Lenta quickly rushed away in a swirl of blue gauze. Ara could hear her sobs as she disappeared.

Ara turned back to look at the Fonnes and it broke his heart. They made low cooing sounds as though they were at a funeral. They stared after Lenta for several moments before finally accepting that she was not coming back and diving back under the water.

The scene began to fade and all Ara wanted to do in the world was to appear in corporeal form in Quale and comfort the gentle Fonnes and go reassure Lenta Benigg that he would make everything okay. He wouldn't give up until he'd fixed the things that his absence had wronged. Unfortunately as Quale flew further and further away from him, he knew he wouldn't be able to make this possible.

When Ara was able to see around him again, he realized that he was in a place that he had never cared to return to: the Ivory Towers dungeon. Though the thousands of torches still burned, the circular room was still cast in an eerie shadow.

Ara swooped around and noticed immediately why the dungeon seemed so different than the last time he was here. There were no guards to be found. The room was completely empty. Somehow, judging from the other things he had seen, he knew the Ivory Towers were in the presence of something sinister as well.

He decided to ascend the stone staircase and see what was going on in the castle when a weak cough made him turn around. There, behind the bars, sitting cross-legged against the wall was Destor Caelu.

Caelu stared straight ahead completely unwavering. His purple cloth veil still concealed the lower portion of his face, but Ara could see from his eyes a look that he couldn't altogether describe.

Slowly he stirred and climbed to his feet. He shed his purple cloak and Ara saw he was wearing black pants and a maroon vest, leaving his bare arms exposed. Ara was surprised at how muscular the villain was. His veil and cloak had disguised his age, so Ara had merely assumed he was an older man, but his body gave him away as being much younger.

An explosion from above caused Ara to turn back towards the stairs as heavy footfalls approached coming quickly down the stone steps. The entire dungeon rattled. Dirt and dust showered from the ceiling, but Destor remained oblivious to it as a young soldier arrived on the pebbled floor.

"I tried to warn them that this was coming," Destor called knowingly. "I told King Vale that he and his friends had to be stopped and now look at what has happened."

The soldier ran to the barred door, bloodied and bruised. His armor was hanging around him in torn shards of metal and he looked as though he couldn't move his left arm. He looked in pleadingly at Destor, as a man with no hope.

"What can we do? How can we stop this?"

Destor's eyes flickered with that same hard to describe look that they had earlier. He just stood there knowingly, not arrogant about his knowledge, but completely aware.

The soldier yelled more forcefully, "If you are in possession of any knowledge that can help, than you are bound legally to help me or be tried for treason."

Destor didn't falter as he responded, "Once again, like your King before you, you foolishly assume that I'm in league with these people. I know nothing more about Skarsend than I did about the necromancer's master plan. What I can tell you is that he is not alone."

"What do you mean?"

"I assume you remember Culpata, the beautiful young friend of Vale's who tried to kill him in Steedo?   She escaped but was presumed dead."

"Yes."

"She's not."

"Go on with it!"

"As I said, I don't know what he and his allies have planned. I am not a part of their alliance."

"So, you're just another monster who was trying to cause your own chaos on the world before the other ones could?" the guard screamed, to which Destor just smiled under his mask.

"As I've already been jailed without any chance to defend myself, I see no reason to start doing so now. What I will tell you is that this is not the harshest of it. Things are going to get far worse and you should consider it a blessing from the gods that you will not live to see it. Eliantar is entering its final days and there's nothing anyone can do to stop it now."

The guard and Destor both dissolved into the nether and the metal bars that went around the circular room melted into the floor and yet Ara remained in the dim dungeon. He looked around wondering why he would still be here and what had become of the other two, as the torches also ceased to be present.

At once, out of the darkness a dozen beams of red light shot down from the ceiling making a complicated web in the center of the room. He stared at the net of light and realized there was someone standing in the middle.

Vale, King of Eliantar, stood on the pebbled floor, his wrists shackled with chains digging into the hard floor. Though he was looking down, Ara could see that his face was much thinner than before and covered in dirt. His long, black hair had been chopped and was a shaggy mess on his head. He was clothed in a large piece of black cloth that looked like a poncho, the color of midnight.

Ara swooped all around the man that he loved trying to get his attention, trying in vain to help release him, but knew before he had started that it was no use. Vale had obviously been here some time and looked near to death. Ara could see that much in his defeated look.

Looking back around, Ara realized that the red beams of light that created a netting around Vale must be forming a cell of sorts. Even if Vale could escape from his shackles, how could he escape the cage that had been created around him?

Ara glided towards Vale again, but the scene had already begun to fade. Ara cursed loudly in his mind as he tried frantically to stay with his beloved but it was not to be.

"I am sorry to show you such despair" the sweet voice returned. "You needed to see what's transpired while you were gone so that you can make things right. You were about to be killed by Skarsend, the Tyrant King. He can never be stopped if you are not alive. In order to protect you from death I had to hide you in a place that the Tyrant King would never look."

"Where is that?" Ara thought.

"Five years in the future," the voice responded, as if able to hear him. "Skarsend has scoured the land looking for you and after five years I believe he has lowered his guard for your return."

"But who are you?" Ara concentrated. "How were we able to travel through time?"

"It's time to wake up," the voice boomed. "Open your eyes and all will be answered. Fulfill your destiny and bring peace to this dying world."

There was nothing left to lose.

Everything was gone.

Ara opened his eyes.

Epilogue

Kaxon Plottus draped the dark robe over his short, thin frame and pulled the hood over his head. He surveyed the blackness of the landscape before him and the sky above him. Given the time of day and the fact that he was standing in the shadow of the Chronometer Cathedral, it should've been no surprise that it was completely dark. However, in the past five years, it no longer mattered what time of day it was. The world was always dark.

It had been five long years since anyone had seen the suns' light. The world had been drained of all color that day when Skarsend, the god of death and darkness, had declared himself ruler of Eliantar.

Whether or not it was the real Skarsend from the old legends, no one knew. The whispers were that he was indeed the god of death and that the gods had shielded themselves from his assault on the heavens. Therefore, he was forced to remain on Eliantar. Whether this was true, no one could say for sure.

All the people knew was that one day Eliantar was a beautiful world and the next day, Skarsend's dark arts had transformed their pristine planet into a place of nightmares and blackness. No one had heard from King Vale or any of his Ambassadors since that day, and the foolhardy ones that tried to seek their help, were punished with death.

Skarsend ruled with an iron fist and demanded that all who resided in Eliantar follow his rule. Business was to be followed as usual during the day, but at night it was commanded that all should be indoors and locked in until the morning. For it was at night, when Skarsend's army of undead marched the fields of Eliantar with absolutely no direction, other than kill whatever they encountered.

No one would have wanted to venture out into the night anyway. That being said, there were few who were willing to travel from their homes during the day. Skarsend's magic had disfigured the elemental realms, from what many had heard. He turned the fields and crops of Eliantar to black dust and transformed Ivory Towers into a dark fortress.

The people had to live on what they had stored, prior to the god's conquest, which for many wasn't very much. Skarsend rewarded those who were loyal to him with vast amounts of food. Those that he suspected of treachery were cut off from food supplies. As an example to thwart betrayal, Skarsend would cut off supplies, not just to the individual, but to the entire village where they resided. Needless to say, after a few towns were decimated with starvation and disease, all others were loyal to the Tyrant King.

Kaxon remembered that day clearly. He had just become a priest and had only been preaching at the Chronometer Cathedral for a few weeks, when one morning he had woken up to see the ground and sky were black as night.

He smiled to himself, remembering what a positive and idealistic young man he had been then. The world was beautiful and everyone was so much happier. How happy he had been, to preach every day to a multitude of people in front of the clock tower, about how one day the world would get even better as soon as the clock started ticking.

That seemed like decades ago now. He felt as though he had matured and aged forty years since that fateful day. Though he had never been handsome with his short stature and bony frame, he knew his eyes and smile were full of youth and hope. Now when he passed a reflective surface, he saw only loss. It was the face of a man who had become a hypocrite to all morals that he had once stood for.

He still came to this same spot every day to preach about the wonder of the grand clock and how one day it would start and save the soul of every citizen of Eliantar. The tragedy of that was that he no longer believed a word that he spoke. No one was coming to save them. Their fate was already decided and he could no longer accept the fairy tale that all of the insignificant dullards still believed.

They actually still came every day, maybe even more than had originally come in the beginning. It said a lot, considering that so many were terrified to go out even during the day. He stood up at the podium and secretly resented them all for their foolish hopes that they clung to.

So, why did he still come here? He'd pondered it more than once and he supposed the only reason for enduring his own lies was because it gave him the only sense of humanity that he had left. After all, he had done some pretty terrible things himself in the past five years. One had to be ruthless and give in to their dark side in order to survive, he had rationalized.

He no longer pitied the people he robbed in the middle of the night or the animals that he had butchered just so he could get something into his stomach. He barely even grimaced anymore when he thought back to the prostitutes that he had literally mutilated with his own bare hands, just for the fun of it.

One night, two years prior, was the night that Kaxon realized he was losing his compassion. His sense of reality was fading away and he couldn't have cared less. The new world that Skarsend had created had no use for people. Only animals could survive in the blackness that was once Eliantar.

And so, with no thought to the atrocities that he had committed since the previous day's sermon, Kaxon Plottus would don his grim robe and strike a friendly smile. No one ever suspected that the friendly, little man with the worn face and graying hair had become as twisted and cruel as the world itself. This fact made the priest more deadly than any of Skarsend's evil spells, and he loved it.

He took one last moment to look up at the Chronometer Cathedral, before he went to his mound. It hadn't changed any more in the past five years than it had in the past 2,000 but still it looked different to him.

It was a four-sided spire of polished, black wood that came to a point high above his head. Near the top was a large triangle of green, cracked glass with three silver arms, designed to tell time. Sets of stairs went up from the ground a few feet to the large base that the spire rested on. The heavy, ebony doors at the top of the stairs had never been opened since the Chronometer Cathedral's creation.

It was full of eerie mystery. No wonder it inspired so much hope, Kaxon thought to himself as he grimaced.

Hearing the sound of approaching voices, he quickly moved across the lifeless grass, to his mound of dirt facing the Cathedral, just inside the ring of enormous white stones that encircled the area around the Cathedral.

As they all began to take seats in the shadow of the epic Chronometer Cathedral, the priest raked his fingers through his graying hair and thought about what to say today. He felt, for lack of better word, stupid for insisting his listeners have faith, even as times continued to get worse.

Most of them looked even more pathetic than him, Kaxon thought. Their bodies were ravaged with starvation and exhaustion. Their clothes looked more like torn rags than garments. Their eyes were the only part of them that still held a flicker of life.

In spite of how dangerous it was for them to be here and how it was time away from finding food, here were dozens and dozens of people greeting each other with weary smiles and exchanges.

As the crowd quieted down, found their seats on the hard ground, and directed their attention towards their preacher, Kaxon Plottus drew a breath to begin his day's speech. And that was when he saw him.

The man was slowly making his way to join the congregation. His obvious limp caused many to turn and stare, but they quickly forgot about that when they saw the rest of him.

The man had long, black hair and wore a deep purple robe. The lower portion of his face was hidden behind a veil, the same color as his robe. The priest grimaced at the man, as he sat in the far back, on one of the Cathedral's steps. It was unsafe and foolish to be seen in this time wearing such elegant material. At the very least, it was disrespectful to show off one's wealth in front of the poor. Even more dangerous, was to appear so eccentric and stand out to the Tyrant King's soldiers and spies.

Feeling the priest's eyes on him, the man looked up and stared back. Kaxon immediately felt uneasy. What had originally started out as him staring down his nose was now in reversal. As the man in purple stared back with rays of contempt and ferocity, Kaxon Plottus felt as though he were on trial. He stood here and judged this man for his appearance, but felt sure that the man was judging him for his soul.

A ridiculous notion, he knew, but at the same time, he felt a little more human again having that old guilty feeling back again, even if just for a moment. It had quickly passed, as he finally regained his composure and shifted his eyes around to other members of the congregation.

And now that everyone was seated, quiet, and had their attention focused entirely on him, just the way he liked it, Kaxon Plottus took a deep breath. He was ready to begin, yet again.

"I'm sure by now that you must all be tired of hearing the same old legends," he smiled with a bow. "There's no doubt that you all know the stories of why we gather at the Chronometer Cathedral every day.

And yet, we never really tell it. Certainly, you go home and tell your children as they prepare for bed, but perhaps that is why the world is the way it is, because we treat our beliefs like fairy tales.

"I stand here every day and preach about how we must have steadfast faith and to always keep our eyes to The Great Clock for hope, but rarely do I ever refresh our memories about the stories that bring us our faith system.

"Surely this is foolish because how can we tell a story to our children that we don't fully understand ourselves. The adult version of the story, the true version, may be a different version of Lileena's Legend than you're used to, but I know you'll enjoy it just the same.

Kaxon paused and surveyed his audience. He was thrilled to see that all eyes were on him. It always gave him a jolt of superiority to know that in spite of the atrocities he'd done in his life, he still held the weak-minded in the palm of his hands.

He was just about to start up again when he saw in the back of the crowd, the man in purple, still giving Kaxon the same glare that he had walked in with. This silently enraged Kaxon, but he resigned himself to the idea that he would simply ignore the man until his sermon was over, and then confront him for his bold rudeness and lack of respect. With peace of mind, he was able to flash a smile, take another deep breath, and continue on with his story.

"The story, of course, begins over 2,000 years ago after the gods created Eliantar and all the beings that live here. At that time, King Arktur, took on an advisor named Lileena. They had been friends as youngsters and it was said that Arktur had always trusted her above all others, even before he became King.

"As with all Elites, Lileena had a special power that also made her a tremendous asset to the throne. Lileena had the gift of precognition. She could see things happen before they did, whether they were monumental or insignificant.

"In a way, we owe the way we live to Lileena. Seeing into the future, she knew where to build towns that would prosper rather than fail. She knew who would be most effective as Ambassadors of the various realms. Her power was so advanced that she could actually foresee many possible futures by changing various details. In this way, she was able to lead Eliantar towards a bright future of prosperity.

"Indeed all through King Arktur's years and for the next 2,000 years, Eliantar would exist in a golden age filled with art, architecture, wisdom, and beauty, all things that were passions of Lileena's.

"As all the stories agree, Lileena was filled with passion for the betterment of Eliantar and supposedly filled with great beauty as well. She was tall and thin with long, strawberry-blonde hair and blue eyes like the water of Quale. She was always dressed in the finest dresses and traveled in the finest coaches. The men respected and feared her knowledge and wisdom while the women envied her beauty and lusted for her. Yet, none should have her or even be closer to her than King Arktur, and in this way as well as so many others, she was the greatest Royal Advisor throughout Eliantar's history.

"Lileena was so much more than just a wise woman with precognitive powers though. She was also the most talented sorceress throughout the land. You will, of course, all understand that this was many years before sorcery was considered evil and illegal. Years later, as you know, it was decided that magic attracts far too many who would use the power for evil."

The priest paused and looked up at the black sky. He then stared thoughtfully at the dead grass beneath his feet and finally at the poor, worn faces of his audience.

"As you can see, that theory about magic attracting dark sorcerers proved to be true, but let's not dwell on the present during this tale. Lileena was a master sorceress and never used her powers for personal gain. She would bring rain to end a drought, she would heal the sick and injured, and she would conjure food from nothing to feed the hungry.

"Everywhere Lileena went, the citizens of Eliantar would come flocking to tell her of their problems. When her wisdom and foresight were not enough, she would pull out her wand and use her book of spells to right the wrongs.

"You've probably read in the children's version of this tale that the wand and the spell book were gifts from the gods themselves to Lileena. Unfortunately we cannot say whether this is true or not since there have been 2,000 years of descendants to muddle the stories and re-write them. Most scholars believe that the gods have not been on

Eliantar in corporeal form since creation, though then again how Lileena could've crafted such tools of sorcery and been so skilled in her lifetime remains a mystery. Suffice it to say, she was a benevolent witch who was most skilled at her craft."

Glancing up he saw the man in purple glaring at him ominously. Finding that the distraction had caused him to lose his thought, Kaxon became overcome with rage at the man and could contain it no longer.

"Sir, I can see the contempt on your face even with that silly mask covering it! Would you care to join me up in front of my followers and explain to them why you mock their very beliefs?"

"Why don't you explain first?" Destor spat as he rose to his feet and glided towards Kaxon. "It's true I may not believe that the gods are going to help us, but at least I do not pretend such things while secretly deriding them."

Kaxon sputtered, "Sir…I've never met you in my life. You don't know me. How dare you challenge me in front of my congregation?"

Kaxon Plottus had never been so humiliated in his life. This arrogant man was standing inches from his face and making direct accusations in front of his followers. He had never guessed something like this would happen and didn't know how to react.

"Tell them!" Destor roared. "Tell them how you don't believe in the Cathedral or in the gods!"

Tick Tock. The crowd began to whisper amongst themselves.

"Tell these people that while they say their prayers and sleep at night, you break into their homes and steal from them."

Tick Tock. Tick Tock. The crowd had risen and began to yell to each other in a mixture of excitement and panic. Kaxon Plottus was appalled at the accusations and even more so at the loud reactions of his followers, whom he was sure were now furious at the revelations.

"Kaxon Plottus, tell these people that you murder prostitutes and vagabonds that cross your path in the middle of the night."

Tick Tock. Tick Tock. Tick Tock. By now the crowd was screaming and going wild. Kaxon and Destor, now realizing this couldn't be for their argument, both turned their heads in time for the first strike that shook the ground.

Seeing the green clock face glow a deep emerald and the frightened look on the people's faces, Destor stepped back. Not

Kaxon Plottus, though. He needed these people. They were the only thing that allowed him to hold onto any shred of power in this chaotic world.

"People, please be seated. All is well."

They didn't hear him though as the clock rang a second time and the crowd erupted. They charged, running at full force away from the Chronometer Cathedral and directly into Kaxon. He fell to the ground hard and felt himself being repeated kicked in the face and chest as the congregation hurdled away. He choked on the taste of blood that now flooded his mouth and watched as everything faded to black as a heavy boot came crushing down on his skull.

It may have been moments or months later for all Kaxon knew. He couldn't move as his body was overwhelmed with pain. Hearing a loud creaking in the distance he opened his eyes to see the unthinkable. The heavy black doors to the Cathedral were opening and a strong looking man stepped out, scanning his surroundings.

As Kaxon Plottus began to choke on the blood that filled his lungs, his very last thought crept into his brain. And as he recited the words in his head, for the first time in five years he knew he was wrong and felt guilt.

"The spell is this: Eyes on the clock for when the pendulum swings."

Gary Gaugler Jr. was born and raised in the Lehigh Valley in Pennsylvania. He graduated from Penn State University with a degree in Psychology. This is his premier novel and he looks forward to sharing his expanded universe throughout the rest of the fantastical series. In his spare time, Gary enjoys reading fiction, going to see Summer blockbusters, and spending weekends with friends and family. He currently resides in Allentown, Pennsylvania with his partner, Stephen, and his two wonderful cats.

Visit the World of Eliantar at: http://eliantarbooks.wix.com/eliantar

Like us on Facebook: facebook.com/Eliantar

Coming Soon: The Emerald Gates of Eliantar

Five years after the events of The Woodland Tombs, Eliantar has fallen and become a place of nightmares and monsters. With the help of his love, the former Prince Vale, Ara must realize his destiny and fight to bring Eliantar back from ruin. However, the two young men quickly discover that Skarsend, the god of destruction and current ruler of Eliantar, is not the only form of evil to have flourished.

On a mission deep into the woods of Tacia to rescue Vale's brother, Prode, the heroes encounter an ancient estate filled with secrets and death traps. It also houses Vale's former friend and betrayer, long presumed dead, as well as a devious plot that will change everything you knew about the world of Eliantar. How can Ara and Vale ever be together and save the world when what lies behind the Emerald Gates may be worse than Skarsend himself.

22284744R00120

Made in the USA
Middletown, DE
25 July 2015